Praise for
The Visitor by Barbara Raffin

"Intriguing, surprising, amazing. I really enjoyed this story. An alien entity of pure energy sent across the galaxy to retrieve something needed by his people, clones a dead man to give him form and function on Earth. Then he meets the widow of the dead man. Mystery, plot twists, and a warm, almost impossible relationship. I couldn't ask for more from a novel. Well worth the read."

—S. C. Mitchell, Author of ***The Blarmling Dilemma***

***

"I read Barbara Raffin's alien clone novel, ***The Visitor,*** within a matter of hours. I couldn't put it down! It has an unusual plotline that's fresh and intriguing with three-dimensional characters so compelling I was drawn hook, line, and sinker into their quests. Barbara has a gorgeous way of writing that allows her readers to feel every nuance her characters feel. ***The Visitor*** is a book you'll want to tell all your friends about."

—Karen Wiesner, Award-winning author of romantic psychological thrillers and ***First Draft in 30 Days***

***

"A remarkable, memorable and extremely well-written story with essence of Sci-fi, fantasy, mystery and romance weaved together to create its own unique tapestry. It is sure to please many tastes. Read it and see where it takes you."

—Bill Koehne, Web Developer and Author of ***Reflections on the Camino De Santiago***

The VISITOR

BARBARA RAFFIN

PUBLISHING

Green Bay, WI 54311

Editor: Brittiany Koren
Copy-editor: Jessie Harrison
Cover Art Designer: Barbra Sprangers
Interior Layout Designer: Amanda Dix

Category: Romance/Supernatural
Description: *After her husband's death, a widow has an unusual visitor that teaches her more about life than she ever expected.*
Hard Cover ISBN: 978-0-9991870-7-4
Paperback ISBN: 978-0-9991870-8-1
Ebook ISBN: 978-0-9991870-9-8
LOCN: Catalog info applied for.
First Edition published by Written Dreams Publishing in August, 2017.

Green Bay, WI 54311

To the believers.

Chapter One

Light burned blood red through Rebecca Tierney's eyelids, as though a thousand-watt, bare bulb had been switched on inches in front of her face. Jolted awake, she forgot for a moment where she was. Forgot that she was in the Upper Michigan house built on a bluff overlooking the great Lake Superior, cloistered away from the main road by towering white pine. There were no street lights here to shine into her windows, and only one car at a time could thread its way up the drive on the far side of the house.

In that first stark second, she'd also forgotten she should have been alone. There *shouldn't be* someone else in the house turning on lights.

Rebecca sat up and blinked into the brightness blazing through her open bedroom door and across the foot of her bed. As a child lost in the foster care system, she'd learned an open door in the night invited terrors worse than any fear of the dark. Now twenty-eight, she slept with the bedroom door left open for a husband who could never return.

She pushed her snarled curls off her face and swung her legs over the edge of the bed. Air cooled by the fathomless Lake Superior sliced through the house, up her bare legs, and under the bottom hem of the over-sized tee she'd slipped over her underwear to sleep in. Eric's t-shirt. Its thin fabric clung to her sweat dampened spine, as did her memories of him to her soul.

Memory was all she had left of him now. The reality tore at her soul and squeezed the life from her heart.

She fled the room where they'd slept and loved. Fled into the hall where that blinding light allowed no shadows, and exposed a memory sharper even than those haunting the bedroom. She and Eric had made ravenous love on the top landing of the stairs, a pair of honeymooners too hungry to travel the final half dozen steps to their bedroom.

Memories too painful for a fragile soul to survive.

Yet, she had survived. She'd come back to the old Victorian house Eric's great-grandfather had built—where Eric had grown up. The same house where he'd brought her when they'd first married so he could teach her about his past.

The house to which she'd returned when there was no more future.

No future. That's what an urn full of ashes reminded her of every time she looked at it. Maybe that's why she'd avoided the front parlor since bringing the urn there a week ago.

Maybe that's why she didn't hide from the light. Why she didn't fear that someone might be turning on lights in an old house that should be empty, save for her shell of a soul.

Rebecca slid her foot over the hallowed patch of ancient carpeting onto the stairway. One step at a time, she sank into the brightness blazing up the stairwell, blinding her. She sank into an illumination brighter than any lamp or fixture in an old house could've produced. The scent of sulfur pinched at her nostrils. Fire?

But there was no heat, no crackling of burning timber, nor licking flames.

Then, just as Rebecca's foot touched down on the hardwood floor of the first-floor hall, the light flickered and went out.

She stood a moment, one foot on the hall floor, one yet on the bottom step, the banister post cool and smooth beneath her fingers. She listened for any sound beyond the tick of the hall grandfather clock, the howl of the wind buffeting the house, and the dull thud of her pulse in her ears. She listened as she stared into the blackness of the entry hall, waiting as her eyes adjusted.

The entrance to the parlor across from the base of the stairs came into focus, a yawing black rectangle. That's where the light had vanished into, whispered some remnant of memory burned onto her corneas. The parlor...where her husband's ashes waited for her to find the courage to let him go.

She pushed off from the banister and caught herself against the parlor doorframe. Her fingers scrabbled across the bumpy layers of wallpaper for the light switch that would feed electricity into the parlor's electrical outlets. No overhead lights for this old house...except for the dining room chandelier. As Eric had explained, his grandmother had grown tired of candle wax dripping onto her prized mahogany table. The concession led to a full conversion of gas lamps to electrical. Otherwise, the woman had wanted everything to remain as it had been when the house had been built.

Rebecca flicked the light switch, and a single table lamp popped on. It couldn't have sported more than a sixty-watt bulb, so soft, so low was its illumination.

But it lit the man standing between the camelback couch and the cold fireplace hearth, the soft yellow-gold glow of incandescent light shading his skin a deep, warm hue. He was splendid in his naked glory.

Splendid and…alive.

Alive!

"Eric!" She cried out, bolting across the room and throwing herself at him. She wrapped her body around his and covered his mouth with hers.

But no lips parted to the urging of hers. No strong arms came up to catch her, support her—hold her. Not one muscle on the man flinched.

Her legs slid from his hips, the cold, hard floor once again a reality beneath her bare feet. A materialization of a desperate imagination, that's all this bronze-hued form before her could be.

Because Eric was dead.

And she wasn't.

Rebecca crumpled to her knees, her shoulders shaking with her dry sobs. She was still in her living hell.

Rebecca woke to daylight with her cheek pressed into the threadbare oriental area rug that covered the center of the parlor floor. Her mouth felt like cotton, her eyes itched, and her hair was plastered to her cheek. She'd been crying again.

Or was it still?

People who called themselves friends would've told her to stop. As if commanding it was all it took to end grief and quell pain.

Then there was that bizarre dream she'd had during the night. Eric back from the dead and…

The sensation of his hard body against hers, of his lack of response telegraphed itself across her nerve endings. She winced. Another rejection. Damn. She couldn't even find solace in sleep.

Rebecca lifted her head a few inches off the floor and groaned with the promise of a stiff neck. Not good, falling asleep in a heap, face down on the floor.

She elbowed herself up onto her hip, and finger-combed her unruly curls back from her face. She sat between the couch and coffee table where she had seen the naked incarnation of Eric last night.

The threadbare cords of the carpet scratched at her bare legs. This was reality. An old carpet and the ashes of a dead husband. Eric in the flesh, nothing more than another dream.

Yet this one had been more real than any other. She swore she'd felt the solidness of his flesh. And if he'd been real, what would she have done?

She'd have locked the doors against the world and clung to him. She'd have never again let him out of her sight.

Provided he didn't reject her as the figment of her imagination had done last night. It had been a cruel nightmare.

Or payback.

She had clung to him in life. Depended on him more than a wife should have. They had fought about that very thing the last time she'd seen him. *The very last time.*

She closed her eyes against the guilt…and the truth. Her love had been smothering.

Wearily, she climbed to her feet, swayed, and sagged down onto the arm of the couch. Too little sleep. Too little food.

Too much grief.

The reason for it littered the table at the end of the couch. Ashes from Eric's urn…which lay on its side…as she'd left it the last time she'd tried to will her husband back from the dead, as if he were a Phoenix that could rise from its own ashes.

She pressed her hand into the powdery ash, letting it squeeze between her fingers and fill her pores. It was all she had left of him. This ash…which Eric's grandmother had commanded her to deliver to the place Eric had most loved, deigning to allow her—*the wife*—this one last farewell.

That's why she'd returned to The Bluffs, as the house built high on a bluff overlooking the largest of The Great Lakes, Superior, was called by the locals… the place where they'd been the happiest, her and Eric. She'd returned to The Bluffs not just to dispose of his ashes, but as Eric always had when he needed to lick his wounds.

She curled her fingers into the grit and dust. A bone fragment cut into her palm, but she wouldn't let go. Eric had once told her the house spoke to him. Now she waited for the house to tell her how to deal with the pain of losing the only love she had ever known.

Movement whispered from somewhere in the house. The wind? The settling of ancient timbers?

The answer she awaited?

She listened above the measured beat of the grandfather clock in the entry hall. The clock ticked away the seconds, a solid, measured beat. *Tick, tock, tick, tock, didn't you lock the door last night?*

What good did it do to lock a door against a nightmare?

The man in the parlor last night had been an illusion, hadn't he?

She rose to her feet and strode out into the hall. The front door stood wide open, the tile floor littered with torn leaves and puddles of rainwater…and one oddity. It had rained last night…stormed. Lightning could account for the bright light that had burned through her eyelids. But no storm, wind, nor rainfall could explain the dried footprints marking the entry hall floor, prints from a bare, man-sized foot.

Nightmares didn't leave footprints.

Unless she was still asleep…and dreaming.

Still in her nightmare.

She lifted her hand, the one that clutched the tiny bone fragment. She unfolded her fingers from the sharp shard that lay in her palm beside a dot of blood. Her blood. Real blood. She wasn't dreaming.

The footprints came into focus beyond her hand. The breath gasped out of Rebecca as though she'd been plunged into Lake Superior's frigid waters. She *hadn't* imagined the naked man in the parlor last night—hadn't dreamed him.

Shoosh came the whisper of a sound from behind her. Reflexively, protectively, her fingers curled around the bone fragment as she spun toward the grand staircase, at the top of which she and Eric had made love that first night of their honeymoon. But the sound hadn't come from upstairs. It came from the end of the hall beneath the stairs, from beyond the partially open door there. It had come from Eric's grandfather's library.

Had she valued life, she'd have turned and run. Instead, she moved toward the door at the end of the hall. She barely noticed the chill of the wood plank floor beneath her bare feet, so fixated she was on that slightly ajar door…and on the sound coming from beyond it.

Whish, thump.

Why did it draw her?

Thump, ump, ump.

Why couldn't she turn and run?

Whiiish, snap.

What about that whispering scrape compelled her to seek it out?

She pressed the fist holding the fragment of her husband to her breastbone and flattened her free hand against the raised panel of the library door. The door opened a few more inches, exposing the shelves on the far wall of the room— revealing a hand cradling a book.

Whish, snap, thump, ump. The pages of the book flipped front to back beneath the command of long, blunt-tipped fingers. A man's fingers with knuckles lightly furred attached to a square, sturdy hand. She knew that hand.

She pushed the door wide.

He stood on the far side of the narrow room in front of the shelf-lined wall of books, as naked as he'd been in her nightmare. Eric.

Profiled before her with his tight stomach and muscled thigh, she wanted to run to him and scrub her hands across the hard flesh of the man she had loved… still loved. She wanted to throw herself at his feet and hug her cheek to the muscles bunching in his runner's legs. She wanted the sprigs of hair covering that strong thigh to tickle her nostrils as she inhaled his musky scent mingled with the talcum powder he always used.

She wanted to beg his forgiveness for the fight they'd had the night he'd died—for being the kind of wife whose suffocating love had chased him away.

But, last night, when she'd touched Eric, he'd rejected her…as he had the night he'd walked away from her and never returned…until now.

But how? His private plane had gone down. He'd been the pilot. The flight plan said so. The witnesses who'd seen him fly away that day had said so.

The DNA had said so.

DNA taken from a body charred beyond recognition. A mistake could've been made. Her fingers flexed around the bone fragment.

"Eric?" She spoke his name barely louder than a whisper.

He didn't so much as flick an eyelash in her direction.

Maybe this was all in her imagination, the footprints, him standing just beyond her reach…naked. Why would he have come back to her naked? That didn't make sense.

Unless he'd returned in spirit form to punish her.

But punishing had never been Eric's way…at least not when he was alive.

Rebecca staggered into the room and caught herself against the edge of the massive, wooden desk that dominated the room…if she didn't count the naked replica of a dead man.

Dead? Or alive?

Eric. Figment of her imagination or ghost?

She reached out with trembling fingers and touched him.

Solid flesh. Cool, but not cold.

And just as unresponsive to her touch as he'd been to her speaking his name.

Just as unresponsive as he'd been last night in her embrace.

Eric…alive…here.

But, she'd thought that last night, too. Maybe he was nothing more than wild hope.

He flipped the last of the pages, closed the book, and slid it back into its slot on the shelf. Hooking the spine of the next volume with a long, thick index finger, he tipped it forward, its cloth cover scraping out from between those on either side of it. An old book, a musty odor stirred from it.

She would never have expected a hallucination to bear such detail. But then, she'd *felt* the unforgiving flesh of that mirage last night, felt it within the loop of her arms and against her bare legs.

Forgive me, she wanted to cry out.

He cradled the book in one hand and knuckled it open with the other. *Whish, snap, thump, ump* went the rhythm of pages flipping under strumming fingers, fingers that had once played unerringly across her flesh.

Forgive me, she silently wept, swaying there against the edge of the desk, suddenly unable to catch her breath. She drew a deep, shuddering breath, followed by another and another. She couldn't seem to get enough air into her lungs, couldn't seem to be quiet about it.

Still, he didn't look up from the pages flicking at measured intervals before his eyes. He must be deaf not to hear someone nearly hyperventilating within arm's reach of him.

And she must be insane to expect a naked, dead man to notice a tormented woman.

A dead man.

A ghost.

"Eric?" she ventured yet again. "Please. Speak to me. Look at me. Anything. Just let me know you're real."

He didn't respond. Not to his name. Not to her pleas.

Of course he wouldn't. Eric was dead. This man was an illusion of shadow. Wasn't he?

Rebecca flung herself at the room's single window. She tore open the drapes. Sunlight poured over her, stirring through the dust shaken loose from the heavy brocade fabric and circling *Eric's* legs, *Eric's* torso, *Eric's* head.

Eric is dead, screamed reality through Rebecca's mind while illogical hope thundered in her chest from the fist holding a piece of his bone.

He looked directly into the light, an index finger holding his place in the book. His Icelandic hued eyes were striking against Eric's dark skin, piercing from the frame of Eric's jet-black hair, and cold...dangerously, dispassionately cold.

She exhaled through her parched lips. "You are Eric, aren't you?"

He didn't answer. He simply returned his attention to the book in his hand. Focused, like Eric could be when a task demanded his attention.

Like he'd been when they'd made love.

But he wasn't loving her now. He wasn't even seeing her.

Rebecca edged around the perimeter of the room. The tender flesh at the backs of her knees bumped the corner of the chair behind the desk. She sank onto its seat and dropped the bone fragment onto the desktop. For a solid hour, she didn't look away from the man she wanted to believe was the husband she'd thought she'd never see again. For an hour, she feasted on his physical presence and fancied their brief past.

Her chin braced between her palms, she watched her husband's strong fingers slide away *Moby Dick* and pull out Hemingway's *The Old Man and the Sea* from the shelves laddering up the wall. Book by book and row by row, he examined the collection. Whether Lucille's old decorating books, or Eric's grandfather Joe's anatomy tomes and volumes of Great Lakes' shipwrecks, he applied the same methodical, page by page pattern of examination as he did the fictional classics. Not fast enough to be scanning for something hidden among the pages, too fast to be reading.

Unless he *was* able to capture full pages of text like a camera. He did briefly focus on each page before turning to the next.

Beneath the absent sway of Rebecca's hips, the wooden swivel desk chair creaked. The seat was too deep for her, making her feet dangle inches off the floor. The first time she'd sat in it, she'd felt like a little girl and said so. Eric had laughed and shown her right then and there that she was no "little" girl. God, but he'd had the deepest, fullest, sexiest laugh she'd ever heard. She'd give anything to hear it once more.

But something told her she'd never hear that laughter again. Insane of her to wish it.

She was insane, wasn't she? Unable to accept Eric's death, her mind had simply conjured up this likeness of him right down to the illusion of wet footprints in the entry hall. Right?

A few frames of Jimmy Stewart talking to his imaginary *Harvey* rolled through Rebecca's head. She felt a lopsided grin tug across her lips.

Her make-believe friend was no invisible rabbit, though. The only thing comical about this apparition was her discovery that insanity wasn't pleasant. She'd expected it to be. Escape *should* be.

Another of her myriad flaws—an inability to execute a good insanity, to imagine a ghost that was happy to have been conjured. This one wasn't even friendly.

Rebecca fingered the bone fragment on the desk. She nudged it this way and that. She pushed it forward across the surface of the desk…toward the image of the man it supposedly had come from. She wanted him to notice the bone and recognize it…to notice her.

Never enough for you, is there? sounded a voice inside her head, too painfully reminiscent of Eric's.

Rebecca's hands stiffened against the edge of the desk. The chair rolled back and struck the wall. The muscles across her apparition's back bunched.

One calculating, cool-blue eye peered over one broad shoulder, one quick censuring jut of a razor-sharp jaw and he turned back to his book. *Whish, snap, thump, ump.*

He *was* aware of her!

Rebecca propelled herself out of the chair and across the room, scattering the dust moats floating lazily upon the beams of sunlight slanting through the panes of leaded glass. She stopped at *his* elbow, stared up into *his* passionless face at *his* motionless mouth. Had those keenly detailed lips spoken that damning phrase? Lips perfectly defined as a marble Adonis'. Lips full and firm. Lips guarding a mouth she could never get enough of.

"Is that why you're here, Eric?" she demanded, the truth like gravel against her heart. "Did you come back somber and silent because I wanted too much?"

The ice-blue eyes shifted from page to page. *Whish, snap, thump, ump.*

Rebecca molded her hands to fit around his arm, but held them a fraction from contact. She felt the heat rising from his flesh. She knew, should she touch him, she'd find him to be of solid matter. He had been last night when she'd thrown her body against his…when he'd spurned her with his lack of reaction.

"Are you punishing me? Or am *I* punishing me?"

Whiiish, snap, thump, ump.

She dropped her hands to her sides and took a step back from him. Rebecca stared at the man she'd prayed to be able to touch one more time, knowing once would never be enough. Knowing she couldn't bear another rejection.

But he couldn't prevent her from watching him. For as long as she succumbed to the insanity and played by her own inane rules, she at least had him to look at and memorize in ways she'd only thought she'd done before. Strange, the irrational way a mad mind choreographed its world. Tragic, the painful course a broken heart traveled toward its death.

If only he would touch her…one last time.

An air horn blared from the lake at the bottom of the bluff on which the house sat. The steely jaw lifted ever so slightly. She saw his interest even though the translucent-blue gaze never left the pages before them, even though the rhythm of turning pages never faltered. She saw the fractional movement. He'd cocked his ear in the direction of that noise.

The air horn blasted a second time, closer.

Whi-ish, scrape. The pattern altered even though the eyes did not so much as blink. Rebecca's gaze slid from her apparition's face to the window toward which he'd cocked his ear.

She looked through the wavy glass created in a less technological era, past the deck Eric had contracted to be built around the back of the house with its corner gazebo, and down the steep, rocky ledges of a glacially formed bluff. The steely waters of Lake Superior chopped violently in the wake of the Great Lakes' cruiser jockeying up to the dock below the house.

"It's Ben Jarvey," she informed the husband she knew couldn't really be there. "Must be a slow charter day if he's got the time to come visiting."

Visiting. Rebecca stiffened. She couldn't have Ben Jarvey coming into the house and find…

Find what? A week's worth of picked at food and forgotten clothes strewn, dropped, and abandoned wherever a numb mind opened unfeeling fingers. She hadn't even aired out the house yet. Hadn't wanted to. Eric was here amongst the dust and stale air.

Eric was here!

Seen only by her.

Would Jarvey's presence chase her imagined Eric away?

Rebecca bolted out of the library, through the hall behind the main staircase, and into the kitchen. Snagging a pair of denim cutoffs from the floor, she step-hopped into them.

Shoes.

By the door. She crammed her feet into the tennies and bolted out the back door onto the wrap-around deck.

She jammed the tails of Eric's oversized t-shirt inside her waistband as she hurried across the back deck, through the attached gazebo, and down the zigzagging steps of rain-soaked timbers linking house to dock. Her feet thumped down onto the dock just as Ben Jarvey straightened from tying up his boat.

Ben smiled one of his wide, boyish grins that stretched a face already growing leathery with the effects of working in wind and sun.

"A person could break her neck, galloping down those steps that way."

"Just saving you the climb, Mr. Jarvey," Rebecca panted out.

"I wasn't planning on making any." Ben's sun-bleached eyebrows wedged up beneath the brim of his Milwaukee Brewers baseball cap. "That's why I blew the horn. It's why I always blow it when I clear the point. So, don't you go risking that pretty little neck of yours racing down them steps."

Reflexively, Rebecca touched her fingers to her bare throat and crossed her arms over her braless chest. Ben Jarvey had a knack for noticing everything. It was part of why he made a good caretaker for houses used only seasonally, like the house on the top of the bluff behind her…where her dead husband lurked… she hoped.

"Sorry," she rushed out, afraid if she gave Ben Jarvey the space to offer condolences, reality would chase away her last fragment of insanity and hope. "I should've called ahead and let you know I was coming up to the house. It was kind of a spur of the moment trip. And once here, well, with the house phone disconnected and cell service all but impossible here…" Rebecca let her voice trail off, intimidated by Jarvey's silence.

Ben's grin twitched. "Lucille always was tightfisted with that fortune of hers."

Rebecca's gaze jerked from Jarvey's mouth to his eyes. She'd never quite gotten used to how clearly the people of Copper Ridge saw Eric's grandmother. She'd have liked to be part of the conspiracy of those who could look Lucille in the eye when they talked to her and shrug her off when she raised her nose at them. Eric had been able to shrug her off.

Had been. Rebecca's heart tripped against her ribs. What if he were gone when she returned to the house? Specter or figment of imagination, he wasn't doing as she bid. If he did, he'd have wrapped her in his arms, and never again let go.

Suddenly, she wanted to run up the steps and make sure Eric still lurked in the shadowed rooms of his family home. She wanted that reassurance more than she wanted to keep Ben Jarvey from witnessing her insanity.

"The Mister didn't come with you this trip?" Jarvey asked, stopping Rebecca in mid-pivot.

If Ben was asking about Eric, he didn't know about Eric's accident. And if the Jarveys didn't know, no one in Copper Ridge knew.

Benefit of a town with an economy too depressed to support a local newspaper?

Benefit of a family matriarch who never shared anything but disdain for simple folk? Rebecca settled back on her heels.

"Too bad." Ben sniffed, assuming his own answer in her silence…and not sounding the least sorry about Eric's absence as he continued. Ben had his own reasons for wishing Eric away. "Chinook are hitting good now. He'd have liked fishin' them."

"Yes, well." Rebecca forced a smile. "As you can see, everything is fine here. You can get back to your charters."

Ben shook his head. "Trip out here didn't take me away from nothin'. Business slacks off after Labor Day weekend. Was busy through the holiday, though."

An alarm sounded inside Rebecca's head. Ben also had a knack for conversation. And Rebecca didn't. Helplessly, she watched Jarvey fold his arms high across his chest and brace his legs apart like an old sea dog readying himself to ride out a rough sea…or settling in to tell a long tale.

"Families cramming in last minute vacations before the kiddies go back to school. Yup. Big shot Papa givin' his kids *quality* time."

Rebecca jammed the corner of an already gnawed thumbnail between her teeth.

"Drag 'em out in the middle of a big lake where they spend their day barfing over the side of my boat or grousing about the boredom while old dad complains about ungrateful kids who cost him an arm and a leg to hire a fishing charter, then just lie around in the sun. I'm grateful for every minute I have with my little Mandy."

Rebecca flinched at the reminder of Ben and Alice Jarvey's daughter, an automatic response born of insecurity and the knowledge that Ben's beautiful, blond wife Alice had been Eric's first love. Rebecca chewed at her finger, ripping at a hangnail, tasting blood.

Jarvey glanced at her hand. Rebecca dropped it and curled her fingers self-consciously into her palm.

"Anyway, the Missus sent me. A registered package come to the post office for you."

"I hadn't expected any mail." Never mind she'd outright forgotten to have her mail forwarded. "I'll be sure and get into town and pick it up."

"No need." Ben pulled a large red, white, and blue envelope from under his arm and fingered a pen out of the breast pocket of his t-shirt.

Rebecca stared at the envelope that was the size of legal papers in Jarvey's callused hands. She read the name on the return receipt requested slip attached to it. Lucille Tierney. Rebecca knew what had to be in the envelope. She knew what her husband's grandmother wanted. She wanted her grandson's widow gone.

"You gotta sign. Right there on that line." Jarvey tapped the point of the pen against the thick blue X at the bottom of the receipt attached to the package.

Numbly, Rebecca accepted the pen from Ben and scribbled her signature on the designated line.

He tore off the signed receipt, crammed it in his shirt-pocket, and shoved the envelope into Rebecca's hands. "There. Nice and legal. Just the way the Missus said it had to be done. Takes her job as post mistress right seriously, my Alice does."

One corner of the envelope dug into Rebecca's palm where the bone fragment had cut her. Hard fact. Like the fact that Alice Jarvey had once, a long time ago, been an intimate part of Eric's life. Like the fact that the contents of the envelope sent to her by Eric's grandmother would force her out of this place Eric had called home.

Like the reality that Eric was dead.

But not gone. Not as long as his ghost walked the rooms of the Tierney House on top of the bluff.

She couldn't leave this place. Not now. Not as long as Eric was here, whatever his form.

That is, if he were still there, in the house. What if leaving the house—leaving him gave him the opportunity to slip away?

Panic flared through Rebecca. Ben, tossing off the mooring lines from her dock, vaulted onto the deck of his boat, lifted his chin at her, and knuckled the brim of his baseball cap, his usual farewell gesture.

A few more seconds and the man would be gone. Just a minute more and she could be back in the house. Where Eric *had* to be waiting!

Where he must be!

Jarvey's sky-blue eyes glanced up over her shoulder and he nudged the brim of his cap higher on his forehead. Rebecca froze as Ben's eyes scanned from the house to the hasty tuck of her nightshirt into the waistband of her shorts, as his grin turned sheepish and he tugged his hat brim down over his eyes. "You and the Mister make like I was never here."

Rebecca spun on her heel, her chin duplicating the angle Jarvey's had tilted while the rumble of the boat motor behind her counter-scored the dead stillness of her heart. She saw what Ben had seen. Beyond the latticework half wall of the gazebo jutting above the rocks stood her apparition.

Except, he couldn't be a ghost, a figment of her imagination…not if Ben Jarvey had seen him.

Rebecca charged up the steps. The naked man standing in the shelter of the gazebo at the top of the stairs was real. Jarvey had seen him, had even mistaken him for Eric.

But from forty feet away, logic argued as she flung herself past the bench built into the landing at the mid-point for those winded by the steep climb and up the next flight of steps.

She wanted him to be Eric, and she had seen him from afar and close-up, countered hope.

Inside a dim old house, raged reason.

Rebecca stopped where the zigzagging steps broached the gazebo. The mid-morning sun reflecting up off the lake sliced between the spindled posts supporting the structure's octagonal roof. In the sharp light, not even the minutest of discrepancies would be hidden from her.

He turned toward her, slowly, a measured rotation that didn't reflect the torrent of emotion rolling through Rebecca like a tsunami. The ice-blue gaze shifted from the departing boat to her. She raised her fingers toward the face she knew with wifely intimacy. He caught her by the wrist and held her fingers inches from contact.

"What did you tell him about me?" he asked in a voice that was gravel rough but, without a doubt, Eric's.

Chapter Two

"**N**othing."

Her answer puffed against his chin, a warm, soft breath. Softer than the lips she had pressed against his in the night. He hadn't been prepared for *that* kind of contact. He'd been caught off guard. But not today. Today, he'd stopped her before she could touch him.

Can't give her any edge. She was dangerous. Her with a softness he'd never before experienced. Her with an appeal that invited his fingers to linger upon the tender terrain of her wrist. Why hadn't he been properly warned about her sort?

Because there wasn't supposed to have been anyone here.

But there were. Two of them. This woman and the man she called Ben Jarvey who had given her a package, then looked up at him—seen him.

He tightened his grip on her wrist. "If you told him nothing, why did he look at me? Why did he raise his hand at me?"

"He was only waving." Her pulse bumped heavily against the silky skin beneath the pad of his thumb, echoing the uncertainty in her voice. An erratic heartbeat was a tangible he understood.

"Waving?" He leaned forward, using his size to intimidate her, a dictate of some instinct imprinted on an ageless brain.

She shrank back on her heels. Correct response.

"Just a friendly gesture." Her voice trailed off.

"Friendly?" he grilled in as low and menacing a voice as his body could muster, making her pulse skitter under his thumb. *Good.*

"Ben's a friendly guy. Y-you know Ben. You use his charter when you fish. He takes care of the house when no one's here."

He stroked his thumb across her wrist, testing. For what? The lie in her answer? Her kind were no doubt as adept at deceit as his could be.

He tapped the stiff edge of the envelope she gripped in her other hand. "What is this he gave you?"

Her knuckles went white against the envelope and the pulse beneath his fingertips sputtered. "N-nothing important."

Lie.

He eyed the package's label.

"It-it's just some legal papers from Lucille," said the woman he held now by both wrists. "A letter from your grandmother."

The label read *From Lucille Tierney. To…*

"Reb-ecca. Re-becca. Rebecca," he read aloud.

"That's me, Eric. Remember?"

The eyes, green as the horizonless lake, pleaded up at him.

Remember her?

No. She was not what he needed this body to remember.

Yet, some lingering impulse, some fragment of a memory made him circle his thumb over the pulse point in her wrist, circling and circling. The urgency in her eyes melted away. The tightness around her mouth eased. Her eyelids sank and her head tilted to one side.

"Aaaah, Eric."

Her words vibrated in her throat, a low-pitched sound that touched something deep inside him, something in the core of the primitive creature he'd become. Blood surged through him. The cords of his muscles tugged deep in his groin. Arousal. Inside his brain, some hardwired fragment of memory recognized the sensation, knew its compelling, physical danger.

She peered up at him from beneath her thick, copper-hued lashes. How did he know to name those lashes *copper*?

The same way he knew what to name each color splashed across the woods stretching to the horizon on either side of the house. Colors he'd only sensed, never *seen*. Brilliant greens, yellows, and reds. Such sensory overload had very nearly been too much for him to bear upon first sight. He knew their names and their varying shades because of the decorating books he had searched through with their *color palettes.*

The woman's eyes shimmered in the filtered light beneath the gazebo, an oasis in a world overwhelming with color. A cool, wet color that invited a man to slake his heat—that tempted a man beyond reason. A parched man could drown quenching such a thirst. Many of his kind had. The books of mythology from the shelves in the house further warned. Sirens, one passage had told, lured their victims to watery graves. A potent package, this female nearly a head shorter than he whose wrists easily fit within the circles of his forefingers and thumbs.

He wanted to release her—to distance himself from her touch. But such a retreat would be read as weakness, and he'd already been weak too many times in his life.

"Standing out here naked—" Her lulling voice wove around him like an invisible web. "—you'll catch your death."

Was that a warning or a threat?

Rebecca felt him pull back, a subtle shift in the weight of his fingers on her wrist. A living hell...to have the figment of your imagination reject you.

But he wasn't a figment of her imagination. Ben Jarvey had seen him. That made him real flesh and bone. Eric was real and he was back. That's all that mattered. Right?

He looked at her through cold blue eyes. No light of recognition warmed their chill. Not for Ben Jarvey. Not for her.

Amnesia would explain the lapse, she desperately reasoned. Amnesia could excuse the harshness of his questions. Amnesia justified his months of silence since the accident.

But amnesia did not explain the burned body found in the wreckage of Eric's plane.

An unlisted passenger?

But the DNA report...the ashes she'd brought here to scatter.

Mistakes were made all the time. All that mattered was Eric was here now. He'd somehow survived. Somehow, found his way back to her.

He'd found his way back to her.

Joy fizzed inside of Rebecca like soda in a can that'd been shaken. It spritzed from her in uncontrollable spurts, threatening to bubble over.

She twisted her arm within his grasp and closed her fingers on his wrist. He started and loosened his hold on her. But she held him firmly. She'd never let him go again. Not now when Eric needed her...at last.

She just had to make sure that he knew *he* needed *her*...before his grandmother got wind of his miraculous survival.

Rebecca wheeled from the shelter of the gazebo, towing him through the sharp morning sunlight slanting across the deck into the shelter of the house. "Let's get you dressed."

With the same single-minded devotion with which she'd plunged herself into despair, she tossed the special delivery envelope into the corner of the kitchen countertop, and led her no longer lost husband through the kitchen and up the back stairway to the second-floor bedroom that had been theirs.

She hadn't noticed the room's stuffiness before. Hadn't cared enough to let air into it. But everything was different now that Eric was back.

She shouldered open the swollen door to the little balcony across from their bed. She stood there a moment letting the stiff breeze off the lake wash over them. Unnecessary to close the essence of a husband in a musty house any longer, not now that he was no longer absent.

"You promised me you'd never leave." She faced him in the doorway between bed and balcony. "Right here. You promised me."

He looked at her through narrowed eyes.

"My poor Eric." She reached to touch his face and he jerked away. She dropped her hand to her side.

"I'm sorry. This all must be so strange to you." She glanced down his naked body, her voice trailing. "Very strange."

Amnesia could explain his not recognizing her. But it didn't explain why he came back naked, warned a little voice deep inside her head.

She shook away the nagging feeling that there was something far more wrong with him than amnesia, and turned to the dresser. "Good thing you kept a few clothes here."

From a drawer, she pulled a neatly folded pair of chinos, a polo shirt, and pristine white jockey shorts. For an instant, the pain of having the essence of the man laundered out of every article of clothing he'd ever worn shuddered through Rebecca. But that wasn't something she had to suffer any more. Eric was alive. He was here…with her.

She led him to the side of the ornately carved bed where they'd made love countless times and held the clothing out to him. "Here. Put these on."

He stared at the items in her hand like he'd never seen clothes before. But of course, that was impossible. Amnesia couldn't make a man forget what clothes were, could it?

Not a man capable of finding his way home.

No. Not home.

Reality check. Home was the executive condo in Park Ridge, Illinois. Home would have been the palatial colonial they'd been building in Wilmette.

Then why had she chased the memories of Eric to the Lake Superior house? Why, when memory failed him, had Eric returned here?

Because the happiest times of their three years together had happened here. For both of them, this old house built four generations ago during the boom days of copper mining had been a haven. For him, a place to heal after his parent's death. For her, the only secure home she'd ever known.

How right it was that he come back to her here. How right that she had been here.

How right that she be the one to help him recover.

Rebecca tossed the shirt and chinos onto the bed and held out the jockey shorts to him. He continued to stare dubiously at them.

"Like this," she said and shook out the briefs, stepped into them, and tugged them up her legs and over her shorts and hips. She stripped them off and held them out again. Still, he did not take them from her.

"I'll help you," she offered and dropped to her knees in front of him. But the instant she closed her fingers around his ankle, he jerked away, lost his balance, and toppled back onto the bed.

She rose…looked at him sprawled on the bed…raised on his elbows in a state of semi-arousal. Her cheeks warmed and her skin tingled. She wanted to stroke him. She wanted to press her cheek to his warm flesh. She wanted to shed her own clothes and crawl the length of his body, to feel him against her, in her.

She took a step toward the bed, toward him.

In one fluid movement, he was on his feet between her and the bed. She looked up into his blue eyes, his cold blue eyes.

Too soon.

She held the shorts up between them. "You need to dress so you won't catch a chill."

The cold eyes narrowed further.

"So you don't get sick," she explained.

Something flickered in his eyes. A memory?

In his oddly rusty voice, he said, "Sick, as in you'll catch your death."

She nodded.

He snatched the underwear from her hand and pointed over her shoulder. "Step back."

She did as commanded. She always had…though he'd never spoken to her before with such brusqueness.

He held the shorts in front of his face, stretched the elastic waistband between his fingers and frowned. He gave them a shake…like Rebecca had…lowered them, stepped into them one foot at a time, and pulled them up his long legs.

The cotton fabric brushed the dark hair on his legs. Their elastic snagged against that physical feature most defining his gender.

Rebecca giggled.

He frowned and tugged at the shorts.

"Let me," she said, stepping forward, reaching for him.

He slapped her hands away and glowered at her.

"It's okay, Eric. I'm your wife."

The expression on his face, the look in his eyes warned her any further attempt at touching him would net her worse than slapped fingers. Though he'd never handled her roughly, had never even threatened her in any way…before today, she stepped backwards once again.

"Tuck yourself in," she said, pantomiming the motion with her hands.

He mimicked her movements and tucked himself into the close-fitting briefs.

Rebecca smiled. "See, you're remembering already how to put on your shorts."

He eyed her from beneath lowered lids. He looked…suspicious.

Rebecca ached for the smiles of reassurance he'd given her even in her least refined moments. She ached for him to remember her.

She snorted. "What's wrong with me? Not half an hour ago, all I wanted from you was for you to notice me. And now that you have, I'm still not satisfied."

His dark eyebrows gathered above his staunchly straight nose. Disapproval would be more than she could bear right now.

Breaking eye contact with him, she grabbed the chinos off the bed, shook them out, and offered them to him. "They go on the same way."

He had trouble getting his foot through the long leg of the slacks. She had to instruct him about sitting on the edge of the bed in order to pull them up over his feet. He seemed to have figured out the concept of threading limbs through openings by the time he got to the pale blue polo shirt, though his movements were clumsy. What kind of brain damage made a man forget something as basic as dressing himself?

Brain damage?

Rebecca shuddered. She hadn't thought of any kind of damage until that moment.

She scanned the flesh disappearing beneath the descent of the pale shirt. Still the swimmer's torso, long and lithely muscled. Though it was devoid of tan lines.

And flawless.

How could a body wander naked for months without weathering? How had he traipsed from the smoking ruins of a downed airplane in an Indiana cornfield to the extremities of the upper Michigan peninsula without being noticed?

Something warned her that she might not like the answers.

Eric kept two pair of shoes at the lake house. She offered him the loafers and instructed him how to put them on. She watched him struggle with them until he gave up, sat on the edge of the bed, and let her take over the task. He didn't ask for socks. No surprise. Eric preferred to go barefoot in loafers and deck shoes.

"Do you remember the accident, Eric?" she asked as she slipped his foot into the first shoe, her curiosity getting the best of her.

"Accident?" he said.

Not an unusual answer for a man without a memory, Rebecca noted as she slid on his second shoe and pressed, "Do you remember how you got here?"

He pulled his foot from her grip and stood.

She peered up at him from where she knelt on the floor. The perspective added to his six-foot-two frame, a height that had always made her feel like he could protect her against anything. But she didn't know the man looking back at her through cold, slitted eyes; wasn't sure this man would protect her at all.

She climbed to her feet and backed away from him, suddenly desperate to ignore the oddities, the mismatched puzzle pieces that failed to fit the scenario of an amnesiac wandering hundreds of inhabited miles…naked. She fought the doubts chafing at the perimeters of her mind. What if this wasn't Eric?

A stiff breeze sliced up from the lake and through the open window. The curtains snapped against their rods, a fission of dust exploding from the loose weave of their fabric. A catastrophe of nuclear dimension to the microscopic universe expanding through the sharp beams of another world's mid-morning sun. The man in Rebecca's husband's body standing between her and their honeymoon bed sneezed. Eric was allergic to household dust.

Relief rushed through Rebecca, driving out her silly doubt. Of course, this was Eric. Who else could he be?

He followed The Woman out of the room with the bed and along the second-floor hall past the broad stairway that climbed from the center of the house. The shirt and pants confined his body, though their construction was flexible. The loafers, as the woman had called the rigid enclosures on his feet, made his toes feel claustrophobic yet protected. Bare, they'd registered every detail of everything he'd stepped on. Distracting yet useful, but also potentially dangerous.

He couldn't decide whether enclosing his feet was beneficial or detrimental, especially since *she* had instrumented the confinement. Her with her slim shoulders, narrow back, and gently flared hips. Her with her coppery hair brushing her neck with each step she took down the narrow, twisting steps on the far end of the house.

He felt himself tighten against the weave of the shorts. He gritted his teeth and forced himself not to think about her. Difficult, because she moved within easy reach just a step or two ahead of him, because his skin yet buzzed with the aftereffects of her touches.

He didn't trust how she made him feel.

He didn't trust how quickly she could change.

One minute she'd been staring at him, immobile save for the shift of her eyes as they studied him. The next, she was flying down the precariously pitched stairway. Would her gently curved mouth issue another warning like the one she'd made outside of the house, where her sultry voice had linked the words naked and death? Would she command him to do more of her bidding in her deceptively dulcet tone? Would she ask him more impossibly direct questions in her breathy voice?

This was a very potent species indeed, to be able to make a breeding male's anatomy respond with the most tenuous of touches…or without any at all. He'd reacted to the visual sway of her hips even. Potent and dangerous.

She released him at the base of the stairs, her energy spiking around her in brilliant rainbow hues as she moved through the room she called the *kit-chen*.

He already recognized it from what he'd viewed in the books.

She snatched up crumpled papers from the tabletop, lifted the lid of a contraption constructed of a composite plastic, and dropped the balled-up papers into the bin.

Gathering containers of various compositions from the surfaces either side of the sink, she likewise dumped their contents into the wastebasket. Yes, that was the word. Some cartons she sniffed and wrinkled her nose at before tossing them after the others. One, a tall, rectangular box she shook, fingered open its flaps, tilted back her head, and poured the contents into her mouth.

Hardly the pose of a vigilant woman, exposing her throat. A throat with an alluring curve, he amended. He suspected its flesh would be soft, softer maybe than the skin on her wrist above her pulse. That last was hardly the thought of a man in control.

Her pulse bumped against the skin two finger widths beneath the hinge of her jaw. Its rhythm reached across the room and echoed in his own veins. What was she thinking that pulsated life through her at a rate indistinguishable from his irrational lust?

She swallowed, lowered her chin in his direction, and said through an intriguing smile, "You'd think I'd be tired of cereal after practically living on it for five days."

He was capable of assimilating a page full of words at one glance. Yet he caught only the word on the tall box *flakes* before she dropped it into the wastebasket. What had she done to make his concentration fail?

She rubbed her stomach, again pressing the thin knit of her shirt against her ribs. A room apart and still her energy pulled at him, draining him of his power. *She* was the answer.

"You hungry?" she asked.

Another direct question and this one he didn't understand.

"Want me to fix you something to eat?"

She was pushing and he didn't know for what.

"Food," she said and rubbed her stomach again, pulling the cloth tight across the rigid points of her breasts. "Refueling."

He understood *refueling.* He had enough self-contained fuel to last the duration of his assignment…if he stuck to the plan.

"Can't run without fuel," she said, swinging open a small cabinet door.

She wanted him to run? Run where? And why?

"The cupboard is bare," she said, fingering through a half dozen metal cylinders sheathed in brightly colored paper printed with such words as tomato soup, cream corn, and pork and beans.

She turned with the soup cylinder in hand. "Tomato soup will get you going."

Going…as in to move along.

As in…to leave a place.

"Do not want to leave," he stated, suspecting he now understood her motive… to get him away from the house so he could not search it further.

Her eyes widened and the color drained from her face. "I don't want you to leave, either."

"Me thinks the lady doth protest too much," he recited.

"Excuse me?"

"Shakespeare."

"I know who wrote it. I just don't understand why you said it."

"It means you are guilty of something."

He was right. She was guilty. Guilty of needing too much of his love.

So she backed off…at least about food. When she'd followed him to the library and he'd given her an annoyed look, she'd left him alone with his books. No sense risking his remembering how much she'd clung to him—smothered him…not before he remembered how much she loved him and he her.

She'd left the library door ajar and had returned frequently to peek in on him as she dusted and scrubbed her way through the house. Couldn't have Eric sneezing and wheezing away their reunion.

She paused in her polishing of the marble-topped parlor coffee table and listened for the reassuring *whish* of turning pages. How she wanted to run down the hall to him. How she wanted to find in that library the man she'd fallen in love with the first time she'd looked up from her bank clerk's cubicle and met his wide, white smile set amidst a fresh Caribbean tan. Eric Tierney, a man strikingly handsome with Aryan eyes and ebony hair, had bothered to charm a freckle-faced waif of a woman. For that alone, she'd fallen in love with him. When he'd stood up to his grandmother after the woman had hired a private investigator to dig up every hideous fact of her heritage, she knew she would love Eric forever.

Rebecca looked up at the portrait of Eric's grandfather above the fireplace mantel. Eric had inherited Joe Tierney's strong jaw and welcoming smile…and the warmth that shone through the cool-blue eyes he'd gotten from his grandmother. "I'll put the warmth back in Eric's eyes, I promise."

Joe Tierney's gentle, hazel eyes peered back at her. Sad…as if he knew why she really hadn't notified Eric's grandmother of his return.

"Is it so wrong of me to keep him to myself for a while longer?" she pleaded, the portrait blurring through her tears. "You know how she is."

The compassionate eyes followed her as she paced the room. "Or maybe you don't. Maybe she wasn't as controlling when you were alive."

Rebecca stopped in front of the painting.

"Or were you some doddering fool infatuated by the girl you fell in love with?"

Joe Tierney's knowing eyes stared back at her. She reached past the mantel and touched the gold gilt frame. It was the closest she'd ever get to the gentle man Eric had idolized.

"I'm sorry," she whispered, her fingers curling away from the frame. "I can't share him. Not yet. Not until he remembers me."

She left the room and padded toward the library, a little quicker than she had the past trips but just as silently in her sneaker clad feet. She'd remove from Eric's hands whatever book he currently perused and make him remember. She'd shake him if she had to. That's what she'd do!

But the library was empty.

A flash of doubt that he'd ever existed at all shot through Rebecca. Maybe she had dreamt it all. Maybe she was just now waking up—just now hearing the grandfather clock in the hall ticking away the seconds.

Why then did the house smell of pine cleaner? Where were the cobwebs that had inhabited the corners before she'd fallen asleep?

If she wasn't dreaming, then where was he?

The snick of a latch turned her toward the door at the kitchen end of the hall. A cabinet?

Or the back door?

Her stomach rolled. She bolted past the closet built under the broad, main stairway and through the swinging door into the kitchen.

He stood in front of the sink, the sight of his solid profile thrumming her heart in her throat. God help her, she'd never survive losing him again!

That's when she noticed the writing on the box he lifted to his lips. *Flakes* the white lettering on its blue wrapper read, *Mothball Flakes.*

"Nooooo," she howled, lunging for him, slapping the box away from his mouth.

In one fluid movement, he turned on her, caught her by the throat, and slammed her back against the old fridge.

She'd have screamed if the air hadn't been knocked out of her. If the hand of the husband she loved so much wasn't crushing her throat shut.

Chapter Three

Her eyes rolled back in her head and she went limp. He hadn't planned to kill her. She'd attacked him and he'd reacted as ancient instinct dictated.

Removing his hand from her throat, he let her slide down the front of the refrigerator to the floor. Her head flopped sideways onto her shoulder, stretching her skin over the flutter of a pulse below the hinge of her jaw.

So he hadn't killed her after all. He supposed that was good.

Though he was better off without her incessant interruptions. Her disruptive energy had filled the library with pulsing light and muddy shadows each time she'd stepped into the doorway behind him.

Initially, he'd thought her to blame for causing his eyes to grow slow to focus on the pages of the books…until the words blurred at the edges of his creature vision, even when the female was not nearby. That's when he'd realized something more than her presence impeded his mind's photographic abilities— when he remembered her saying something about refueling. Low fuel could explain the inefficiency of his body.

He'd gone to the kitchen where she'd refueled, seeking the *food* she dumped into her mouth. He'd found flakes. Was about to eat them as she had when…

She'd attacked him and he'd very nearly killed her.

It'd been a reaction of self-survival. Survival hadn't had to be trained into him. He'd had a lifetime of protecting himself…one way or another.

What then had prevented him from eliminating her now? His body's limitations? Her body's enticements?

Might the silky slip of her curly hair brushing his knuckles as he'd choked her have persuaded him to release her throat a second too soon?

He stared down on the female slumped at his feet. When standing, the crown of her head barely reached his nose. Attacking him was a bold maneuver for one of such diminutive stature. But then, in his world, physical stature meant nothing.

She stirred, blinked, and peered up at him through huge pupils. He should feel satisfaction at the fear flaring from their dilated depths. He didn't. Why?

A breeze blew across the mothball flake dusted windowsill above the kitchen sink. He wrinkled his nose. He hadn't questioned the flakes pungent lack of appeal before she'd knocked the box from his hand. Palatability was not a consideration among those lacking olfactory senses. But he had a keen nose *now* and he understood its anatomy. The knowledge was imprinted into his being, even if its physical application was no longer of use. Just as he understood this antiquated form's need for ingesting fuel.

He plucked the container from the bottom of the worn enamel sink.

"Poison," she croaked up at him, her life force patchy with dark spots around her throat. "P-Poison," she stammered in her bruised voice, and he recognized the word her mouth had formed as he'd choked her. He knew its meaning. He'd seen it defined in *Webster's Dictionary.*

But why had she wasted her dying breath to speak that word to him?

He turned the box she'd slapped away from him, examining all its surfaces. On its backside, under the heading of harmful preparations, were the printed words "may be fatal if swallowed."

He sniffed at the box. His nostrils pinched shut. Perhaps he had been hasty to dismiss the usefulness of a nose. Seems it acted as an early warning system.

And the woman who had knocked the box from his hand?

He peered down at her. She hadn't been attacking him. She'd been saving him.

He snagged her by the upper arm and dragged her to her feet between him and the refrigerator. She flattened back against the appliance, her aura shuddering about her.

"I wasn't trying to hurt you, Eric," she said on a breath that trembled through the air between them.

He studied her, trying to understand her attachment to the man she thought he was, to understand her need to protect him, in spite of what he'd just done to her. With the tips of his fingers, he touched the purpling smudges marring the perfect, pale skin of her throat. She flinched.

"Pain?" he asked.

She swallowed hard. "I-It hurts a little."

He cupped his palm over her throat and her eyes grew larger. Why did he waste his energy fixing what would heal in time? Why waste the effort on a woman whose eyes were filled with fear?

Maybe he thought he owed her something for saving his life. Maybe he thought she was potentially useful.

Or maybe he simply wanted to feel her pulse skitter to his touch once more.

Her skin grew warm beneath his palm and her life light spiked around her. Amazing hues of color he'd never before seen bled from the contact of his hand to her throat, hues that made him want to keep touching her—keep giving her his energy. The dizziness that had threatened him in the library spun through his body, pulling the blood from his legs and head.

Her pupils pulsed, and he glimpsed a stark being of sharp contrasts mirrored in their dark centers, a creature with hair the shade of night and eyes the color of the sky in the morning. He recognized the creature reflected in her pupils... recognized himself in earthly form.

He recognized, too, that she was draining him...and he couldn't make himself let go of her.

Her face blurred before him, the box of mothball flakes slipped from his fingers, and darkness closed on him.

"Lean on me," she commanded, wedging her shoulder under his arm.

Why had she broken the connection of his hand to her throat? Why hadn't she finished draining him?

Why did she help him?

Her fingers were warm against his ribs and spine, her soft voice soothing in his ear as she guided him to the table tucked against the opposite wall. "Sit here."

The edge of the chair at the end of the table cut into the backs of his knees and he collapsed onto its yellow vinyl cushion.

"If you feel dizzy again, put your head between your knees."

Put his head between his knees? Was that possible?

"It's your blood sugar level, Eric. It's dropping." Her voice sounded slurred in his ears. "You've always had trouble keeping it regulated. I'll find something for you to eat."

"Eat," he repeated hollowly, his whirling mind making the connection between *eating* and *refueling*.

She moved away, leaving him feeling oddly cool. Not comfortably cool. And not because she'd opened the refrigerator door and its chilled air spilled out into the room. Something was terribly wrong with the body he inhabited, something so debilitating he couldn't escape it. And the woman he did not trust, the woman he'd almost killed seemed to know the key to correcting it.

Through a shrinking tunnel of vision, he watched her come near again, an unsteady prism of light and dark. Her voice echoed hollowly in his ears. "Open your mouth."

He couldn't recognize the scent of whatever it was she held close to his mouth, but it smelled appealing. If his theory about the nose being an early warning system was correct, then appealing should be harmless.

He opened his mouth. Something metallic clinked against his teeth. Something cold slid onto his tongue. Cool and slick that made the back of his throat pucker. Was this good or bad?

"Swallow the jelly, Eric," she commanded. "It'll raise your blood sugar quickly."

He knew what blood was, knew its importance to the physical being. But sugar…

Sugar: A water-soluble compound that is sweet.

The back of his throat puckered again. Good or bad. He was in trouble if what she fed him was hazardous.

He was in trouble anyway.

He swallowed.

Her fingers tightened on his elbow, an anchor to which his slipping consciousness clung. The drumming in his ears faded. Her face, close to his, sharpened into focus. Her full, pink lips tugged up and back, just enough to notch little dents into her cheeks.

With infinite curiosity, he watched the lips she'd pressed against his mouth last night now move around the words, "That's better."

Agreed, he might have responded, were he a man of words. Were he not preoccupied with the tentativeness with which she touched the backs of her fingers to his brow and cheek. They were warm and reassuring against his skin.

"But not a hundred percent yet," she said, her voice trembled like icicle-draped branches in a gentle breeze, a musical sound he'd once heard via mind-link and never forgotten.

Their eyes met. Fear swam in her dark pupils. She dropped her hand from his face and backed up a step. "Y-you do understand why I knocked the box out of your hands, don't you, Eric?"

"Flakes not good?"

Her fingers fluttered at her throat where the purple bruises had been. She nodded.

"But you eat flakes," he said.

Her eyebrows bunched together above the bridge of her nose, a small appendage that tipped ever so slightly upward at its tip.

"Earlier," he managed, resisting the urge to trace her nose with his fingertip. "From a box."

"Oh. The *corn*flakes."

"All flakes are not the same?"

She rubbed her throat, something sad in the way her lips pulled at their corners. "No."

She sighed and let her arms fall to her sides. "Cornflakes are made from corn. Mothball flakes are meant to keep moths away."

"They are made from moths?"

A smile twitched at the corners of her lips that telegraphed a sense of sadness to him. "No. Mothball flakes are not made from moths."

"And they are poison?"

Her fingers curled into the fringe of her cut-off shorts and her sad smile trembled across her lips. "Yeah. Mothball flakes are poisonous to eat."

She turned away, quickly, churning up the air between them. "I better get some protein and carbohydrates into you."

He shivered against the breeze she created across his chilled flesh. A reminder that he shouldn't be wasting energy memorizing the taper of her legs where they narrowed to her ankles, or how they dimpled behind her knees with each stride, and disappeared beneath the frayed edges of her short pants. He should not be contemplating the fit of his hands over the flare of her hips and into the dip of her waist. He shouldn't let the protrusion of her shoulder blades beneath her cotton t-shirt as she picked up the mothball flakes box he'd dropped concern him.

"Bread's moldy," she muttered, tossing a plastic bag containing something fuzzy and green into the wastebasket along with the box.

"Not good fuel?"

"Not good fuel," she confirmed, giving him a glance that made him sense pain in her.

She opened the refrigerator and took out a tall, wax-coated carton. She opened the spout at its top, sniffed, and wrinkled her nose.

"Definitely never drink chunky milk," she said, dumping the contents of the carton into the sink.

Silently, he filed away the information for future reference.

She swung the refrigerator door shut with her thin fingers. "Bare as Mother Hubbard's cupboard."

He made a mental note to find out who Mother Hubbard was as he watched the female scurry between the cabinets on either side of the sink. At least that word seemed to best describe her quick movements. But that haste, her darting this way and that, made it difficult for his eyes to focus. The room tilted.

He grabbed the edge of the table. It was cold. Enamel, registered the fact in his head. Something more he'd taken from the dictionary? Or had this fact come from one of the encyclopedic volumes, or one of the books on furniture?

Whichever, he did not like how enamel drained away his heat—his energy, made him feel...

Dizzy. She'd used that word before she'd given him the jelly.

Dizzy: 1. Silly.

That did not fit.

2. A whirling sensation a tendency to fall.

That one fit.

What had she said if he felt dizzy again?

Put your head between your knees.

He looked down at his knees. Even if he dared release the table edge, was it physically possible to put his head between his knees?

"Sorry," she said, her legs coming into focus beyond his knees. "Crackers and peanut butter seem to be the only safe food left in the house available on short notice."

He peered up at her.

"Eric?" The name was a breath across her pretty pink lips. "What is it? Do you remember something?"

He shook his head, not knowing how else to answer.

A sheen of moisture glazed her eyes and she set a brightly labeled jar and a box with bold blue lettering on the table. She didn't look at him as she fingered a square wafer from the cracker box and scraped the blunt blade of a knife down the interior walls of the jar labeled peanut butter.

She shifted from one foot to the other, the frayed edges of her shorts brushing her thighs. He wanted to know what that fringe felt like moving across his skin—wanted to know what her skin felt like. He slid a finger under the fringe along her inner thigh.

She went still.

"Re-bec-ca," he said, his voice sounding oddly husky in his ears.

The knife in her hand slipped against the wall of the jar.

"Rebecca." He rolled the syllables around his mouth and off his tongue, his finger stroking fringe and skin.

She trembled beneath his touch, the knife ticking against the side of the peanut butter jar. The beat of that knife, the pulse of his blood, the charge crackling from her skin to his seemed to speak to something ancient within the cells of the body housing him.

Danger, prickled the warning at the back of his neck. He suspected he knew what danger made his nerve endings stand at attention, and he pulled his hand away from her.

She teetered momentarily as though his touch was all that held her upright. Eyes lowered, she drew the knife from the jar, spread peanut butter across the cracker, and held it out to him. "Here. Eat."

He stared at the faint impressions her fingers left in the creamy coating.

"Like this," she instructed in a quavering voice. She popped a peanut butter coated cracker into her mouth and bit down.

He accepted a coated wafer from her and followed her example. The hard edges of the cracker poked his gums and the peanut butter pasted itself to the roof of his mouth. He frowned.

The corners of her mouth twitched, but without a hint of sadness this time, and the pooling moisture in her eyes evaporated. "Use your tongue."

She tipped her head back and demonstrated how she stroked the tip of her tongue over the roof of her mouth.

He mimicked the gesture, the spread coating his tongue and the inside of his mouth. He liked the creamy texture and the *sweet* flavor.

She handed him another peanut butter coated cracker, and another, and another. He ate with relish and Rebecca seemed pleased with this. This was good. Peanut butter made his mouth feel good and Rebecca's smile pleased him.

The dents were back in her cheeks, too. He wanted to touch them with his fingertips…and his mouth.

Earthly delights. No wonder others had succumbed.

No wonder he was tempted. Oh, so very tempted.

He leaned across the corner of the table, flicked a crumb of cracker from the corner of Rebecca's mouth with his forefinger.

The smile on her lips slipped and she went still again. But the moisture did not return to her eyes.

Something told him this was okay, good even. Maybe it was the scent of her exploding pheromones. Maybe it was the heightened level of her breathing.

Or maybe it was the light brightening the edges of that black hole over her heart.

Her lips parted, and that ancient need in the beastly body he inhabited made him lean close and brush his lips against hers. Her mouth smelled of peanut butter. He wanted to know if she tasted as good.

He stroked the tip of his tongue along the part in her lips, exploring. Slipping his tongue between her lips, he probed her mouth as he had his own.

She tasted sweet and nutty…and of a hunger he recognized. A primal hunger he knew he shouldn't explore. A hunger the urgent spread of Rebecca's fingers through the hair at the nape of his neck fed into. A hunger that eluded the reason battling through his surging senses.

If only she hadn't closed her eyes. If only he could search their depths for treachery.

"Eric," she murmured, sweetly, seductively, distractingly.

It wasn't his name. He wished it was. And there was the danger. She thought him to be another. For this reason, he must keep her close.

She pulled a shuddering breath in through her parted lips, a cooling trail across a heated path. She didn't want to lose the lingering heat of Eric's lips heavy upon hers. She didn't want to let go of the tingling memory of his tongue slowly sweeping the interior of her mouth. But he'd pulled away.

Slowly, reluctantly, Rebecca's eyelids lifted. His pale eyes came into focus, sharp now…and wary. These were not the eyes of the man who'd just kissed her like only a lover could. These were the eyes of the man who'd choked her.

Her elbow jerked, striking the peanut butter jar on the table. The protruding knife rattled against the empty glass. She steadied the jar with an unsteady hand when every nerve ending in her body screamed for her to run.

From Eric, her husband, the love of her life?

…Who had choked her unconscious.

No. The air had just been knocked out of her. She'd blacked out from lack of oxygen. That's all.

Eric would never have intentionally slammed her against an appliance, a wall, or anything.

Though the Eric she had known hadn't experienced a plane crash. He hadn't experienced near death. He hadn't wandered the countryside for months, not knowing who he was.

…Not remembering how to eat or dress himself.

What kind of amnesia caused that much damage? It was as if he had no human frame of reference.

She blinked at the man who looked so much like her Eric, yet…

She gave her head a shake. She didn't want to revisit the questions his odd behavior raised…this man who acted so unlike her Eric.

Stranger, nagged the doubt pushing its way through her hope.

She took a step away from him. The cold blue eyes followed her. Not Eric's eyes. A stranger's eyes.

He curled his fingers against the surface of the table, fingers that had stroked the inside of her thigh…and closed off her airway.

Reflexively, she touched her throat.

What if she so badly wanted Eric back, she saw in a stranger only how alike he was to her husband, rather than how different? It would explain his oddities, like how he'd been able to choke her unconscious, how he could look at her with eyes the color and shape of Eric's, but cold as Eric's never had been. It would explain the apprehension dancing up and down her spine, the danger pulsing through her veins and her sudden need to escape.

"We're out of peanut butter," she forced out around the bubble of air lodged in her throat, around the lump of fear threatening to choke her…as he had…as Eric never would have. "I'll go to the grocery store and get more."

She headed for the back door.

"Rebecca."

She didn't stop. Maybe if she pretended she didn't hear him, she could escape.

"What is groc-er-y store?" he asked in his oddly cadenced voice.

"A place where you buy food," she answered, snatching the car keys off the rack by the door and turning the doorknob.

"Food. Fuel," he said.

"Yes, fuel," she said.

"Where is grocery store?"

She went still and closed her eyes, willing him to let her leave. "In town. In Copper Ridge."

"I will go with you."

She heard the skid of chair legs and jerked the door open, saying as she stepped out onto the porch, "No need for you to interrupt your reading. Stay here. I won't be long."

She pulled the door shut behind her. Beneath the soles of her sneakers, the porch steps creaked and the gravel in the driveway crunched. She flung open the garage door and stepped into the dankness of the stone out-building.

She shivered from the coolness and from the sense of foreboding making the hairs at the nape of her neck prickle. Reaching for the door handle of the canvas-capped Jeep, she glanced at the rear of the narrow garage.

Had she expected to see him there, framed in that yawing opening and backlit by the bright afternoon beyond the dark stones? Hope or fear?

Fear of course.

She opened the canvas door with its plasticized window and stepped over the red metal running board onto the rubber-matted floorboards of the Jeep. The chilled leather seat cover sent another shiver up her spine.

She turned the key in the ignition. The engine, slow to turn over, cranked twice before firing. She jammed the stick shift jutting from the floorboards into reverse, her feet working the clutch and gas pedals.

She saw him then, framed in the rearview mirror, a silhouette in the doorway beyond the Jeep's blurry, plastic back window. Her right foot jumped from the gas pedal to the brake. Her left slipped off the clutch. The vehicle bucked and the engine coughed and quit.

Hands white-knuckled on the steering wheel, she stared at the mirrored figure shaped like her husband. Was she in danger?

She dropped her hand from the steering wheel, unerringly finding her cell phone on the console. She'd left it in the Jeep so she wouldn't hear it ring if Lucille called…even though cell service on the ore rich bluffs of Copper Ridge was questionable. She hadn't wanted to hear what Lucille had to say…just as she hadn't wanted to see how very unlike Eric the man standing in the garage entry was.

She eyed his silhouette in the mirror, saw Eric's broad shoulders, his tapered hips…his stance identical to the one Eric's grandfather posed in his portrait above the fireplace. Lucille had always said he had Joe's mannerisms.

What if Lucille had been trying to call her to tell her about this man, this Eric look-alike?

Maybe Lucille's special delivery envelope wasn't filled with eviction notices, but an explanation about a long, locked-away twin brother, or cousin with an uncanny resemblance to Eric. Or maybe her letter explained a brain-damaged Eric. Maybe Lucille had hidden him away all these months and he'd recently escaped. That would explain the lack of weathering to his naked body.

It was the sort of thing Lucille would do to get rid of an unwanted granddaughter-in-law. After all, what proof did she really have that Eric was dead? Lucille had been the one who'd delivered the dreadful news. No one *official* had come to her. Just Lucille, who'd stood in the foyer of hers and Eric's Lake Shore condo and stated the details of Eric's death with no more emotion than if she were reporting the closing figures of the Chicago Stock Exchange.

Why hadn't she seen that woman's lack of grief before—seen that Lucille hadn't grieved. She had nothing to grieve. She'd had her grandson to herself all this time.

Rebecca could understand that. She had wanted Eric to herself, too.

She stared at the man reflected in the rearview mirror. Of course, he was Eric. A little damaged. But she could fix him. She'd make him remember. Something Lucille apparently hadn't been able to accomplish. She'd prove herself worthy of the Tierneys…of Eric.

An instinctive fear crawled up her spine.

Surely it was no more than her usual insecurity. The fear that, if she let him come to town with her, he'd remember someone else before he remembered her. Besides, there were people in Copper Ridge she'd rather he not remember.

Just as she now feared that, if she left him behind, he'd walk out of her life as easily as he'd materialized back into it.

Cell phone in hand, Rebecca climbed out of the Jeep and strode toward Eric.

She stopped in front of him, close enough that, when she inhaled, her rising breasts almost brushed the breast pocket of his crisp blue polo shirt. She looked into his eyes, eyes of a stranger. But a stranger only because the man watching her through them wasn't the man she had known. He couldn't be. He had amnesia, had no memory of her.

And he didn't fully trust her. She saw that too in their narrowed depths.

But then, only moments ago, she hadn't fully trusted him, either.

She raised the phone until the wary eyes glanced at the apparatus in her hand.

"I'll phone in our order," she said.

"Phone?"

"Telephone."

A glimmer of recognition registered in the cold blue eyes. He nodded. Strange, how he recognized the word but not the object.

"They'll deliver the groceries to us. Small town living at its best." *If the cell phone will transmit from here.* She forced a smile.

"Peanut butter?" he questioned, a spark of interest warming the cool eyes.

"Yes. And other food."

"Fuel," he said as though registering food and fuel meant the same thing.

The muscles in her cheeks jumped against the force of holding a smile. Why couldn't she be happy? She had her Eric back.

She did, didn't she?

Chapter Four

She ushered him ahead of herself into the house. Of course she had her Eric back. She just needed to think—to figure out how to get him to remember her before anyone else got to him.

Pictures would be useful. But any photos of her and Eric were back in Chicago…in their condo. Lucille didn't allow reminders of Eric's *mistake* in her world, and The Bluffs was still hers. There weren't even any letters to jog a reluctant memory, she and Eric had never been long enough parted during their short courtship to merit anything longer than text messages.

All they had here at The Bluffs were memories. But *Eric* had no memory… unless she could make him remember. How could she unlock a memory when all she had to work with were memories?

Memories of hungry love and eager hands exploring urgent bodies. How she longed for just one more such touch. Touch. That was an option.

Halfway through the kitchen, she caught him by the elbow. He spun at her and caught her wrist in a bruising grip. She peered up at him, saw the way he studied her with open distrust. Her heart ached.

"You used to like me touching you, Eric," she said in a small voice.

"Touch," he enunciated as though the word was foreign to his tongue. "Touch," he repeated. "A tactile sense."

His fingers loosened around her wrist a moment before dropping away. For several seconds, they stood standing so close to one another that Rebecca had to crane her neck to see into his eyes. No hint of any memory in those eyes…

How could she make him remember if he would not allow her to touch him?

Unable to bear seeing the stranger in his eyes, she turned toward the cabinet beneath the disconnected wall phone by the door and retrieved paper and pencil from its top drawer. "I better write up that grocery list," she murmured.

He must've moved with her. She could feel him at her back, a comforting heat…from a man who'd forgotten he liked her touch.

Rebecca winced. She wanted so badly to sink against his chest and into his arms. But his arms would not welcome her contact…as he had already demonstrated more than once.

She sidestepped toward the long wall housing the sink to avoid turning into him. The sharp scent of the mothball flakes still dusting the countertop pinched at her nostrils, and the memory of his emotionless face as he pressed her by the throat against the refrigerator.

She closed her eyes against the image. But it was etched across the backs of her eyes. She wheeled away from the mothball flake peppered countertop, the odor wrapping itself around her, suffocating her.

The blood drained through her and she wobbled. A strong hand caught her by the upper arm, steadying her. She opened her eyes and found Eric looking at her curiously.

"I'll be okay if—" *You just take me in your arms and hold me forever.* "—if I can just sit down."

He guided her to a chair at the table…took care of her the way he used to do. At least that much of him had survived.

She blinked up at him, a lightness lifting through her. "Eric—"

"Sit," he commanded, all but pushing her down on the chair seat.

The impact jarred her back to reality, a reality that included the brain damaged husband staring down on her through narrowed eyes and the notepad and pencil still clutched in her hand.

She blinked from his unwavering gaze, and waved the pad of paper. "I better get started on this list."

"More peanut butter," he said and swiped a dollop of peanut butter from the rim of the empty jar.

Yes. That was it. Food. She would reach him through food. She'd buy all his favorites. Cook all his favorites. Serve him all his favorites.

He would remember his favorite foods…and then he'd remember her.

She needed watching, this woman who'd almost escaped into *town*. This woman whose breaths came in shallow gasps, whose aura flared red and ragged.

This *Rebecca* who touched him far too much.

But then, this was a tactile species. Maybe she didn't touch him too much… for her kind. He had to admit there was a pleasantness to the contact.

And his own touches of her?

He licked his lips, testing if he could create the sensation he'd experienced when brushing his lips across hers. It tickled. But it wasn't the same.

He wondered, if he touched his lips to hers now, he could recreate the pleasant sensation. Her colors were different now. Muddy. Dark. Not at all pleasing to the eye—or inviting.

Like the colors that had rolled off her after he'd removed his lips from hers, when she'd opened her eyes and looked into his. These colors were more like those that had trailed her out the door and climbed into her Jeep transport. These colors were dotted with black and warned him whatever instinct had prompted him to not let her go to town alone were right.

She needed watching.

Rebecca finished the grocery list. Now all she had to do was call the order in to Copper Ridge's one and only grocery store, a store more like an old-time general store that offered everything from food stuffs to socks. A benefit of a small town isolated from the world.

Leaning against the kitchen sink, she fingered her cell phone, delaying the call. What if she turned the cell phone on and it rang, Lucille on the other end. She could hope they were out of cell tower range.

She glanced across the table at Eric. He looked at her with that expressionless gaze she didn't like. He wouldn't let her leave without him and she couldn't take him with her. Better she hope for reception.

She flicked on the cell phone. The system powered up. She held her breath. A quiet blip told her she had voice mail. No surprise. She knew who it was from. But no shrill ring of an incoming call. Quickly, she punched in the number for the store.

Flora Lindstrom answered on the third ring, Flora, who'd been born in Copper Ridge, grown up, married, raised a son and buried two husbands here. "Howdy doodie. What ya need?"

Rebecca needed the past nine months to be rewound. She needed for the husband she loved not to have flown off in his plane that fateful day so many months ago.

She needed someone to hold her and comfort her.

"Hi, Flora," she managed in a small voice.

There was a second's hesitation on the other end of the phone, then, "Rebecca? Is that our Eric's Rebecca?"

A smile pulled across Rebecca's lips and tears slipped from her eyes. She and Eric visited Copper Ridge only two or three times a year, yet Flora still recognized her voice. Dear Flora.

"It's me," she confirmed in a tight voice, an ache in her chest so bad she wanted to weep out her whole story.

"I heard Ben had a special delivery for The Bluffs this morning," Flora said.

The breath shuddered from Rebecca at the reminder of Ben Jarvey's visit, Ben, who knew everybody's business, yet knew nothing of Eric's accident. Much as she'd like to unburden herself to Flora, she couldn't risk spilling her grief to anyone in a small town where everyone would know her business in a heartbeat. Clearly, everyone in Copper Ridge already knew about that package from Lucille Tierney.

"Yeah," Rebecca murmured. "Ben was here a bit ago."

"How long you visiting for?"

How long? She glanced across the kitchen table at Eric who still sat in the same pose he'd held all the while she wrote her list. How long dared she keep him here?

"Long enough to need some groceries," she answered for herself and Flora.

"Sure enough," Flora said. "Just let me get my pencil here. Okay, whatcha need?"

Rebecca read off her list, finishing with, "Could you have that sent up to the house?"

"Sure thing. You'll have your groceries soon as I can pack them up and pry Sonny off his computer. That boy can't seem to stay in one spot for more than a minute unless he's on that computer of his. Then it's like his butt's glued to the chair."

The mention of Flora's son drew Rebecca's gaze out the window above the sink to the dark green water of the lake beyond the bluff.

What if Eric remembered his childhood friend when he saw him, remembered the dare made by two boys who lacked the proper respect for Lake Superior, a lake so cold it never gave up its dead?

Almost never.

There'd been one.

Sonny.

Something that traumatic could jog his memory.

Or Eric might not remember him, and, if the boy that Sonny had never grown out of tried to get too familiar with the man that Eric had become, what would he do? She touched her throat where Eric's fingers had all but squeezed the life out of her.

"Rebecca?" Flora said, she apparently having been silent too long. "Something wrong, dear?"

"No," she breathed out. "Just making sure I didn't forget something," she covered. "Just send up the groceries."

She finished the call and spoke into the still air of the kitchen, "Please go read in the library."

Eric narrowed his eyes at her. "I will hear the door open."

She blinked, confused. "I don't understand what that means."

"It means, I will hear you if you try to leave the house."

She snorted. "Is that what you're concerned about, Eric?"

"Do not try to leave," he said with dead calm.

If only that was the worst of her worries. "I won't leave you, Eric. I'll never leave you. Promise."

"A promise: One. a declaration that something specific will or will not be done. Two: an assurance of future excellence or achievement. Three—"

She chanced a light touch to his arm, stopping him. "In this case, it's number one. You have my *assurance* I will not leave you."

He studied her for a moment, looking her in the eyes, then scanning the space around her. He rose, nodded, and exited the kitchen.

She was wiping away the last of the mothball flakes when she heard the crunch of tires rolling into the gravel driveway. Sonny.

Rebecca dropped the dishrag into the sink and opened the swinging door between the kitchen and hall just enough to listen. The quiet *whish* of turning pages drifted from the library. Everything was as she'd hoped it would be.

Footsteps sounded on the porch. Rebecca jumped and hurried toward the side door, hoping to head off Sonny on the porch. She wasn't quick enough. The screen door creaked open, a shock of carrot-colored hair bobbed beyond the glass, and a pair of bright blue eyes peered in at her where the curtains didn't quite meet.

She'd forgotten how nosy Sonny could be, a trait people didn't call him on because of his child-like demeanor ever since the *accident*. Besides, gossip was the favorite form of entertainment in a place isolated from the world by ore-rich bluffs that defied television and radio signals alike; and who better to gather information than a man with a simple mind.

A foot thumped against the storm door, rattling its windowpane. She opened the door before Sonny knocked again. Hopefully, Eric hadn't heard anything in spite of what he'd said earlier about hearing if she tried to leave.

She reached through the partially open door for the bags filling Sonny's arms. If she didn't invite him in, he and Eric wouldn't have to meet. But, Sonny elbowed his way past her, chirping, "Heavy bags. Make way."

He set the bags on the table and faced her with his perpetual grin. "Did you hear the sirens?"

She shook her head, wishing she'd remembered to have a tip ready to give Sonny. Snatching her purse off the kitchen counter, she rummaged through it for a tip.

"Something big's happening," he said, bouncing on the balls of his feet.

She pulled out the smallest bill she had, a ten and held it out to him. He bounded past her, leaned over the kitchen sink, and peered out the window toward where the bluff met the woods.

"Sheriff and State Police cars were parked on the side of the road coming up here. Saw them come through town a bit ago. Lights flashing and sirens wailing. You didn't hear them?"

"No."

"Woulda followed 'em except Ma was still puttin' your order together. But I kept track of 'em." He settled back on his heels and tapped an earplug that was attached to a device the size of a smart phone in the pocket of his plaid flannel shirt. "I haven't heard anything yet, though."

"I heard the door open," delivered the deep voice from where the door between kitchen and hall swung on its hinges.

Rebecca looked from Sonny to Eric. Before she could say anything, Sonny spun on his heels and greeted Eric with his eternal enthusiasm.

"Eric-my-main-man." He stepped toward Eric, one hand raised for a high five.

Rebecca stepped between him and Eric, blurting out, "Eric had an accident."

Sonny blinked from her to Eric, giving him a once over glance. "What kind of accident? He doesn't look hurt."

She glanced over her shoulder at Eric. He was studying her again, this time with an almost casual curiosity. At least he didn't look hostile, nor disputing what she said about him having an accident. Did that mean he remembered at least that much of his past or that he knew to play along?

"Did he hurt his head like me?"

"Something like that," she answered Sonny, watching Eric for any sign he was getting ready to pounce. But he held her gaze, a quizzical crease pinched above his nose.

She faced Sonny. "He doesn't remember things…people."

A grin stretched Sonny's lips and he raised his gaze to Eric. "I don't remember things the way I used to, either. You get used to it after a while."

Do you, she wanted to ask but didn't. Sonny had never changed after the day he dove off the Tierney's dock and drowned in cold Lake Superior. Oxygen deprivation, the doctors had diagnosed. Could that be what happened to Eric? Oxygen deprivation?

A permanently damaged brain.

The possibility that Eric would stay forever as he presently was, suspicious and not knowing her, sent a shiver through her.

"I bet I know what the cops found," Sonny said in a rush, as though he hadn't just been told his best boyhood friend was brain damaged. "I bet they found the wreckage."

"What wreckage?" Rebecca asked.

"UFO," Sonny replied.

Rebecca almost groaned, in no mood for Copper Ridge's second favorite pastime, UFO hunting. She blamed it on the lack of recreational occupation, Michigan's Upper Peninsula vantage point to the Aurora Borealis, and the nearby US Air base.

At least the Air Force had served as an explanation for non-believers whenever odd lights whizzed through the night…until the base closed. Cutbacks. More economic disparity for a tenacious community carved out of the foot of a copper-filled ridge that had once been its life's blood. But then the copper became too expensive to mine and the mining companies moved on as well.

She thrust the ten-dollar bill into Sonny's hand and pressed her hand against his back. "You better get back out there then and find out what the sheriff and State Police are up to."

"Got 'em covered," he said, tapping the device in his breast pocket.

"That's some special radio, if it gives live updates on police activity," she said, ushering him toward the door.

"Not a radio," he said. "A scanner. Got it tuned to the police frequency."

"You can get the signals for a police scanner here?"

He nodded. "And good radio reception. We even get more than two television stations since we got *the dish.*"

Rebecca forced a smile. "You and your mother got a satellite dish."

"Most everybody in Copper Ridge got satellite dishes," he returned.

She reached for the doorknob, only half listening to Sonny.

"Didn't you see the lights last night?" he asked.

She shook her head, her fingers closing on the doorknob.

"Lights so bright you couldn't look at them."

Her hand froze in mid-turn.

A light so bright it blinded.

She'd been awakened by such a light. She'd followed it to the sitting room… to Eric.

Eric, who had a pilot's license. He could have flown here. That would explain how he got to The Bluffs…though the nearest landing field would've been at the abandoned air base on the far side of the ridge, and he hadn't looked like he'd walked that far.

Nor could it explain that light that had blinded her seconds before she'd found him…unless the plane had crashed somewhere on the bluff.

She winced at the thought of him in another plane crash. Though it could explain some things…like his nakedness. His clothes could have been burned off him.

Without burning him?

He could have bailed out before the plane crashed and parachuted into the lake, then discarded his drenched clothing.

Into a lake that never gives up its dead.

But he wasn't—isn't—dead.

Explain how he could appear instantly in the bluff house's sitting room after the light disappeared.

"Did you see the lights?" Sonny asked, ducking around Rebecca toward Eric.

She didn't like the speculative way Eric looked at Sonny. Letting go of the doorknob, she caught Sonny by the arm and tugged him back to her side.

"It was raining last night, Sonny," she said. "Overcast. You couldn't have seen anything through the cloud cover."

Sonny met her gaze, for an instant his eyes as knowing-looking as any she'd ever seen. Then, in the next instant, that flash of intelligence was lost in the wide eyes as he insisted, "Flashes through the clouds. First high then low, east then west."

"Lightning," she offered, something telling her it was important that Sonny dismiss the lights.

He shook his head. "I followed 'em."

"A plane then," she reasoned. "Or a helicopter."

"I followed one of them up here to the top of the bluff."

She forced a smile. "It would be a good idea for a plane or helicopter to fly *over* the bluff."

Sonny grinned and rocked back on his heels. "Didn't fly over."

Rebecca fought to hold onto her forced smile as she murmured, "Hence the wreckage."

If there was indeed a wreckage and the police did find it, they would track down who was flying the plane. Then they'd come here and want to talk to Eric about it. They'd find out he was supposed to be dead. Someone would notify Lucille, and she'd come and take Eric away. Could things get any worse?

Sonny cupped his hand over the earplug. "They found a body."

Chapter Five

R ebecca gaped at Sonny. "The police found a body?"

"The Coast Guard. They're radioing the cops that—" He paused, hand cupping his ear, listening. "It's a man's body."

She glanced at Eric. She didn't like the way he watched Sonny.

A terrible possibility crawled up Rebecca's spine. Was her thought-to-be dead husband who'd returned in a blaze of light, the gentle lover who'd nearly choked the life from her, linked to the dead man?

Her hand was halfway to her throat before she caught herself.

Sonny needed to leave before Eric determined him a threat and did something about it. But Sonny might be able to answer some questions. She strode toward Eric in case he went for Sonny.

"What about the wreckage?" she asked, watching Eric for a reaction.

"Nobody's saying nothin' about any wreckage," Sonny said.

Eric tilted his head. She stopped in front of him, willing him to look at her instead of Sonny.

"The Coast Guard couldn't have found just a body floating," she said, torn between wanting Sonny to leave and getting information from him. "Bodies sink in Superior and they don't come back up."

"Body ain't in the water," Sonny chirped. "Body's on the rocks at the bottom of the bluff."

She spun at him. "*Our* bluff? The body is at the bottom of *our* bluff?"

Sonny grinned and rocked back and forth on his heels. "Yup. On the other side."

Rebecca reached back—gripped Eric's wrist, readying herself to protect Sonny. But Eric didn't move.

"Gotta go," Sonny said, bounding out the door before she could ask him anything else.

She let him go. In the end, the questions she needed answered could be answered only by someone who'd been there.

She watched Sonny's rusty truck ramble off down the road, fueled as much by boyish morbid curiosity as gas. She waited until he was out of sight before turning to Eric whose attention had turned to the groceries on the table.

"Did you fly here?"

Eric lifted his nose from the grocery bag. "Fly?"

She moved to his side, looked him in the eye. "Did you fly an airplane here?"

A snort that was almost a snicker burst from him. "Not an airplane."

"Did you fly here in something else?"

The amusement that briefly flitted across his face evaporated. He reached into the grocery bag, pulled out a jar of grated Parmesan, and sniffed at it.

"Is this edible?" he asked.

"Yes." She closed her fingers over the vinyl padded back of a kitchen chair to keep herself from grabbing him and shaking him. "Eric, did you fly up to Copper Ridge, to the bluff house?"

He turned the jar, examining it.

"Eric, were you in another accident?"

He shook the jar and bared his teeth as though he was about to bite the container.

She snatched the jar from him, twisted off the cap, removed the protective paper seal, and dumped some Parmesan into his palm. "There. Taste it."

He stuck his tongue into the grated cheese and drew it into his mouth. He smacked his lips and rolled his tongue, declaring, "Arid."

"I think you mean dry."

"Aah, yes. Dry." He licked the remainder of the grated cheese from his palm, tasting further. "Salty." He tipped his face toward her. "Is this why you eat Parmesan, for its salt?"

"Not exactly."

"The human body needs salt." He stuck his head back in the grocery bag.

"Eric, I'm trying to talk to you."

He pulled out a head of cauliflower. "Organic substance. Is this edible?"

"Listen to me."

He brushed the nubby surface of the cauliflower across his lips before taking a zucchini from the bag. "And this?"

"It's edible." She took the vegetables from his hands and set them aside. "Listen to me, Eric. There's a dead man on the other side of our bluff. The police are going to be asking everybody in the area if they know anything about that man."

He nodded and returned his attention to the grocery bags. This time, he lifted out a bag of licorice and held it up to her.

She sighed. "It's candy. Licorice. Your favorite."

He peered at one sealed end, then the other. It appeared the parmesan jar had taught him to be mindful of containers and wrappers.

"You have to open the bag. Like this." She ripped open an end for him, pulled out a licorice whip, and handed it to him before continuing. "Do you know anything about the dead man on the other side of the bluff?"

He dangled the licorice whip in front of his face, tipping his head this way and that as though he'd never seen licorice.

"Were you in another accident, Eric?" she pressed. "Do you remember?"

He tipped his head back, spread his lips, and fed the licorice whip into his mouth.

"Eric, please. To help you, I need to know what you remember."

He'd chewed only a few seconds when his eyes widened in horror and he spit the licorice out on the floor.

He wiped his tongue with his fingers and declared, "Licorice burns." He looked at her. "I am supposed to like this?"

She sighed. "Apparently you don't anymore."

He swiped a couple more times at his tongue. "How do I know if I like a food or not?"

"Keep tasting, I guess." She wiped up the licorice with paper toweling, the fact that she couldn't even please him with his favorite candy any more dragged at her shoulders.

She tossed the paper toweling into the trash can and turned just in time to see Eric peal back the cellophane from a pound of spaghetti and take a bite.

"You can't eat that." She cupped her hand under his mouth and he spit the brittle pieces of pasta into her palm.

"I removed its container first," he insisted.

She groaned. "Pasta needs to be cooked before you eat it."

He scowled. "This eating business is complicated."

"Eric, please stop with the food for a minute. There is a dead man on the other side of the bluff. The police are going to come here and they are going to ask us questions about him. Do you understand, Eric? The police are going to ask *you* questions."

"Police," he said. "Law enforcement. Peace officers. This is good, no?"

She slumped onto a kitchen chair, shaking her head. "No, this is not good."He stared down on her bowed head. Where he came from, The Protectors made sure rules were followed, made sure society operated smoothly as it should. Apparently, this was not the case in her world.

One more way in which his kind were superior to hers. Were she a worthier adversary, he'd have debated the issue with her.

But she knew more about food than he did, far more, and he needed food to fuel this primitive body. This was the issue he needed to address with the woman whose name rolled off his tongue and touched his lips in a most appealing manner.

"Rebecca, how do I know what is edible and what is not?"

She peered up at him, her brow creased and her aura dim. "You don't need to worry about that, Eric. I'll feed you."

He pondered her proposal a moment. The issue was trust and whether or not he could trust her to feed him *good* fuel. Evidence, the licorice she'd given him.

But she'd also fed him peanut butter that was most pleasant to his mouth and knocked mothball flakes that were poisonous from his hand, warning him with what nearly had been her last breath. He concluded he could trust her not to poison him, at least as long as she thought he was her Eric.

Still, logic dictated he form a back-up plan, in case something happened to the woman and he was left to fend for himself…or she found reason to feed him something as foul as licorice.

"How do I learn about food?"

"I told you I'd feed you. You don't need—"

She met his gaze, and stopped. The breath went out of her and her shoulders drooped. "You mean like recipes?"

The preparation of something to eat or drink. It wasn't quite what he had in mind, but it was a place to start. He nodded.

She glanced at a small shelf above the chrome edged table. It held a few books of assorted sizes, their bindings well creased. "You might start with the cookbooks."

More books. What he'd already scanned had yielded little use to his mission, though the text dictionary had given him a fuller comprehension of her language. The rest had offered little more than a hodgepodge perspective on her world, a hint at their psychology, and useless facts about indigenous plants, Great Lakes' shipwrecks, and the local mining industry. Even the books about space exploration and their pictured galaxies were laughable.

"Books are a very inefficient way to store information," he said, fingering one of the cookbooks from the sunshine yellow shelf.

"What do you want?" she said in a voice edged with frustration. "Cookbooks on microfilm? Audio CDs? Maybe in digital download?"

He began flipping through the pages of the book. "You limit your thinking to the physical."

"What I limit myself to at this moment is the fact that the police are going to come here with questions about the dead man on the far side of our bluff."

Having scanned the thin cookbook, he closed it, placed it back on the shelf, and pulled out another.

She rose with a force that made her chair skid noisily away from the table. "Eric, is there anything I need to know about that dead man?"

"Need? No," he answered and flipped open the second book.

She paced between the table and the sink, back and forth, stirring up the air in the kitchen. That air bumped against him and brushed over him, cool and scented with…

What were those smells? Peanut butter, mothball flakes, spoiled milk, and… her. Most distracting. But he managed to complete the second book, and now knew a zucchini could be baked with parmesan cheese.

"We need to figure out what to do," she said on one of her passes.

He exchanged book two for a third. This one was thicker and had a hard cover, like most of those in the room lined with shelves of books. He flipped it open, noting that it, like the first two, had been inscribed in the front by hand with a name. He traced the looping script with a fingertip. Writing might be an archaic means by which to document information, but its loops and angles did have an appeal to the eye.

"Sonny was easy to fool," she said on her latest pass, pausing at his elbow and peering up at him. "Do you remember anything about Sonny?"

He flipped the well-worn pages of the cookbook cradled in his hands. "Red hair. Blue eyes. Eric, my man."

She groaned. "I meant from the past, from when you two were kids."

She chewed at a fingernail as she waited for him to respond. He continued flipping pages, scanning information.

"Do you remember anything about Sonny's accident?"

How could he, he thought, not without some annoyance. He wasn't here.

She leaned close. "Do you remember the two of you swimming in the lake, swimming away from land? Do you remember Sonny going under?"

He paused in his scanning, a fragment of memory seeping through his veins, like water from a lake whose average depth was five hundred feet, whose horizons stretched three hundred fifty miles east to west and one hundred and sixty north to south, whose mean temperature could sap the heat from a body almost as fast as any arctic ocean.

"You're remembering something, aren't you?" she demanded.

He remembered the red-headed boy slicing through the water away from him. He remembered the red-haired head disappearing from the surface of the lake. He remembered cold, cramping legs and dark, murky water as he dove and dove in search of the red-haired boy.

"Do you remember calling for help? Do you remember your grandfather diving into the water and bringing Sonny out?"

"Grandfather. Father of one's father or mother."

"That's right," she said, a hopeful note to her voice. "You and Sonny made a dare. The first one to turn back was a chicken."

"Dare. To challenge someone."

She clutched his arm. "You remember."

"A dare is foolish." He looked pointedly at her hands on his arm.

She released him and sank back on her heels. "You were just boys. Boys make mistakes."

Didn't he know it? In his adolescent period, he had brashly disobeyed the rules of his society. The Elite hadn't been as forgiving as this Rebecca seemed to be of the boys Sonny and Eric. They'd put him on a probation that greatly curtailed his exploring.

Though it had barely curbed his curiosity…back then. Only maturity had tempered that failing of his, maturity that had enabled him to focus on his responsibility to the society that had chosen him for this mission. As tempting as it was to explore the five senses of *this* body he possessed, to take advantage of an opportunity few of his world had ever been allowed; tasting peanut butter on his tongue and The Woman's mouth on his were a waste of time. There was good reason his kind had moved beyond the distraction of such senses. His focus must remain on finding and retrieving The Capsule. The future existence of an entire society depended on his success—on his returning the element encased in it.

His future as well. With this single act, he could make up for all the errors of his ways. He could prove his mentor's faith in him justified. He could prove Merlin's methods viable; Merlin, as The Wise One had fancied calling himself after a character from an ancient legend.

If only this body he'd cloned would give up the memory of The Capsule's location. Providing The Elite, who assumed the memory he needed would be found in the body he'd reconstruct, were correct. Digging through the ashes of the dead hadn't given him any clues.

Good thing he had Merlin's unique mentorship to educate him in other means of investigation…such as books. He'd make sure this fact was well documented in his report.

He focused on the book in his hands, a hard thing to do what with The Woman close beside him, her bright curls a haloing aura of their own. If only the books would yield a clue. But these didn't seem to be the right kind of books to reveal what he needed. He closed the cookbook.

The woman with the name that rolled off his tongue shifted in front of him. She shook a finger in his face. "Lucille isn't going to be able to control this investigation the way she did the one into Sonny's drowning."

He blinked at her. "Lucille?"

"Your grandmother."

"Mother of one's—"

She threw up her arms and wheeled away from him, her curls whipping about her head, tempting him to reach out and touch them. No wonder those in his world had likened a woman's touch to the call of ancient Sirens. Capable of luring a man into giving up his immortality, many had warned. The proof was in the failure of a handful of male entities to return to his world.

It was imperative that he return. Lives depended on him.

He curled the fingers of his free hand into his palm to keep from reaching for that shiny, copper-hued hair, the other safely occupied holding the cookbook. Touching this Rebecca was not safe.

"Lucille won't be able to sweep away any investigation involving a dead man," she said.

He wished she would be silent. He had more pressing matters to attend to than a dead man and this Lucille she kept referencing. He needed refueling, not a woman who tempted and cookbooks that yielded nothing more than food preparation and nutritional charts…and that hand-written name that appeared in the front of them.

As did many of the tomes in the book-lined room. Was this link—this name—important?

He looked into the woman's eyes, those thirst-quenching, sea-green eyes. "Who is Joe Tierney?"

Her eyes brightened. "Why do you ask about Joe?"

"His name is written in script in many of the books I scanned."

The light dimmed from her eyes. "They were his."

"And he is?"

Her eyes grew shiny with moisture and she spoke in a hollow voice. "Joe Tierney is—was your grandfather."

"Grandfather," he repeated absently, calculating Earth years in his head and realizing he may have reconstructed the wrong body.

Rebecca's fingers itched to touch Eric, to take him in hand and shake the memories back into him. Memories of her or Joe. Joe, he'd told her, had been the most influential person in his life. Joe, who'd been more father than grandfather to him, who'd made Eric the kind of man who'd love a girl as flawed as she.

She chanced a touch to his arm.

He jerked away and frowned down at her.

"I need fuel. You will cook the spaghetti first," he commanded, flipping open the cookbook he yet held and thumping a knuckle against a chart. "The food pyramid of nutrition states pasta is the foundation of healthy eating."

Food. He was thinking of food when it was just a matter of time before the police found their way to The Bluffs, to Eric. At least no one could blame him for anyone's death, accidental or intentional. Not in his current state.

If he even had anything to do with the dead man. He might not.

Hope inched through her as she dug a pot out from the cabinets by the stove. But it was a short-lived hope. Connected to that dead man or not, the end result would be the same. Lucille would find out about him and come for him. Rebecca didn't want to share Eric with anyone just yet, especially his grandmother.

She was helpless to stop the impending chain of events. The only task that seemed within her power was to cook for him.

"There should be a couple cans of tomato sauce in one of those bags. Get them for me," she murmured as she gathered garlic, oregano, and bay leaves from the cupboard.

"Tomato sauce?" he questioned.

She felt him at her back, a heat that she wanted to sink into. But this Eric would not hold her. He would likely push her away and she couldn't bear that on top of the fact that she'd again soon have to share him with Lucille. If only a body hadn't been found on the far side of their bluff. If only the police wouldn't have to come here.

If only Eric's grandmother didn't have to find out he was here.

"Spaghetti needs sauce," she said. "You won't like it plain."

"You said I would like licorice and I didn't." His breath puffed against her ear as he leaned close.

How she ached to feel more of him, to have him hold her and caress her.

Never enough for you, is it Rebecca?

She winced at the memory of the last words Eric had spoken to her before he'd left her for that fateful last flight and she murmured, "Maybe you will like it plain."

"But you think not," he said in a low voice that reminded her of the old Eric whenever he'd prod her out of a funk.

She turned between the stove and him, careful to keep her elbows close to her body. For the first time, the blue eyes looking back at her weren't cold. A breath shuddered from her.

He turned toward the table where the grocery bags sat. "Make the sauce."

A concession. His believing that she knew best, at least about spaghetti sauce. A small concession, but progress just the same. If only she could have more time alone with him to make him remember her before the police came and found him…before Lucille Tierney sank her claws into him again.

But she couldn't stop any investigation. Only Lucille had that kind of clout.

The realization hit Rebecca like a load of bricks. Lucille Tierney had the kind of clout to stop an investigation…even one that involved a death…Joe's death. Somehow that woman had arranged for the death certificate to read pneumonia, even though old Doc Sumner had sworn there was no fluid in Joe's lungs.

Rebecca wanted to ask Eric about those days following Sonny's drowning, days Sonny spent comatose in a hospital. Joe's last days of life. But this Eric couldn't even remember food, let alone the grandfather who raised him…and died as the result of saving Eric's best friend.

She watched Eric move toward the table. He moved like a man ready to strike at anything that threatened him…this man who had struck out at her… this man who had not known how to dress or feed himself mere hours ago. He'd relearned a lot in a short time.

Me thinks the woman doth protest too much.

A promise: One. a declaration that something specific will or will not be done. Two: an assurance of future excellence or achievement. Three—

Mostly from books. What he had relearned was mostly from books.

What kind of amnesia wiped away the most basic knowledge yet left a man the ability to read the pages of a book at a glance, then retain everything he'd read?

Unless he hadn't been relearning but rather *recovering* his knowledge. What if when he'd been pulled from that plane crash nine months ago, he had been so badly injured that he'd had to be medicated with drugs that caused a strange type of amnesia. They sometimes put people in comas to give their bodies time to heal.

But, if he'd been in a coma, why weren't his muscles wasted? If he'd survived a fiery plane crash, where were the burn scars? There had to be scars of some sort. Yet there hadn't been a single scar on him when he'd stood naked before her.

He turned to her, both cans in one hand…those beautiful, broad, unmarked, untanned hands. Maybe she'd been in too much shock to notice scars. Maybe her state of euphoria as she'd dressed him hadn't let her see the damage.

Or…

Maybe he hadn't been on that plane that crashed.

Maybe the crash had been an elaborate hoax. That he'd been hidden away from her these past nine months, a captive kept subdued by drugs.

But, would Lucille go to such lengths to separate them? Was she capable of murdering a man just to have a body to put in Eric's airplane?

Unless there hadn't been any body at all. She had only Lucille's word that there had been, that Eric had died in that crashed plane.

He held the cans out to her.

She shook her head. "Tell me Lucille didn't do this to you. Tell me she isn't this cruel."

He frowned.

"Did she hide you away from me? Did your grandmother drug you?"

"Grandmother: mother of one's mother or father."

She knocked the cans from his hands, grabbed him by the wrist, and towed him toward the door. "We have to get out of here."

"Out of the structure?"

She snatched her purse from the countertop, Lucille's special delivery letter taunting her from the corner. "Out of the house, out of Copper Ridge, out of the country."

She opened the side door and hauled him across the porch and toward the garage.

"No," he said, dragging against her.

She tugged him into the garage and along the dank stone walls. "We have to, or Lucille is going to come after you and take you away." She released the latch on the passenger side door of the Jeep. "Get in."

"No."

She gave him a shove. He didn't budge.

"Please, Eric. If Lucille gets her hands on you again, she's going to drug you."

"Drug: a chemical substance used to cure a disease or improve health."

"Or to stupefy," she said.

A line of confusion pinched across his brow.

"Poison," she explained.

Understanding lifted across his features.

"Now will you get into the Jeep?" she pleaded.

"No."

"We don't have time to argue. Get in the car." She gave him another shove.

He pinned her between the Jeep and its open door. "I cannot leave here."

"You aren't going to have a choice if Lucille finds you here. She'll take you away."

"She cannot."

"Don't bet on it."

"Bet. A pledge one loses should he not correctly predict the outcome of an event."

"You got it. Get in the Jeep."

He hooked one arm over the Jeep door and the other across its canvas top and looked her in the eye. "I can correctly predict the outcome of anyone trying to take me away from here."

A chill skipped up Rebecca's spine that had nothing to do with the cold stone wall enclosing them, a chill that made her think of a hand at her throat and a dead man on their bluff. Much as she knew she did not want to know the answer, she asked the question.

"How can you know for certain that no one can take you away from The Bluffs?"

"Because I am authorized to kill anyone who tries to make me leave before I complete my mission."

Chapter Six

Mission? He believed all this was some mission?

This whole thing was escalating into a nightmare. As if she hadn't already been living a nine-month long one. If he repeated to the police that business about being authorized to kill anyone who tried to make him leave—about being on a mission—if he tried to kill any officer attempting to force him away from The Bluffs, Lucille finding out where he was would be the least of their problems. He'd become suspect number one regarding the dead man and she doubted even Lucille could help him then.

"Did you have anything to do with the dead man they found on the other side of our bluff?" she asked.

His eyes narrowed at her.

"Did the dead man on the bluff try to make you leave?" she pressed, needing to know just how much trouble she needed to protect him from…even though she would rather not know.

He gazed past her through the open garage doors, his brow creased with thought. "The needs of the many supersede the needs of the few."

"Are you the many, Eric?"

He looked at her as though she'd just said the most absurd thing. "I am only one."

Did that mean he didn't have anything to do with the death of the man on the bluff? She wanted to believe he was still the gentle Eric she'd married. That he wasn't capable of killing a man…or choking his wife.

She shook off the damning thoughts. She was jumping to conclusions. A dead body didn't mean murder. Nothing had been said to indicate the man's death was anything other than an accident.

Still…

The needs of the many supersede the needs of the few.

I am authorized to kill anyone who tries to make me leave.

She peered out into the gravel driveway that twisted its way down the bluff… past where a dead man had been found. If there was the slightest chance the man's death was not an accident, if the police even tried to take Eric away…

If he fought them, they could kill him. She could not—would not—lose him again.

She had to hide him. But, between Ben and Sonny, all of Copper Ridge would know Eric Tierney was in residence at The Bluffs.

Copper Ridge, where the folks lived closed away from the rest of the world… folks who did not trust outsiders. Here, even the county sheriff was an outsider. Maybe…

She motioned him out of the garage, followed him back into the house, and closed the kitchen door behind them.

"If anyone drives up to the house, you are going to have to hide. Do you understand, Eric?"

She had taken him to a place in the top of the house with musty air that made him sneeze. At first, he'd refused to stay in this place she'd called an *attic*. She'd argued that it was the safest place for him to hide. She'd insisted the police were dangerous to him. What convinced him to stay was that nagging sense that he was in the wrong body and that those things belonging to the right one lingered in the many dark corners where the angles of the various roofs came together.

But, by the time he'd scanned half the books stacked in the attic, his head ached and his nose itched. He found the Rebecca woman mopping the floor around the base of the wide stairway descending the center of the house. Her fiery hair had been tied up atop her head, revealing the appealing curve of her neck. A frown puckered her brow and her aura was frail. Something troubled her even before the step squeaked beneath his foot, making her glance up.

"What are you doing down here?" she demanded, red bursts rimming the dark spots mottling her aura.

"My head does not think clearly," he said.

"You sound stuffed up." She leaned the mop against the wall and climbed the stairs to him. He prepared himself for her to touch him, but she continued past him up the steps. "Let's see if there's any antihistamine tablets in the medicine cabinet."

He followed her up the steps and into what he recognized from *The Complete*

Guide to Home Decorating as a bathroom. She opened the door of the cabinet above the sink and poked around an assortment of bottles and tubes before lifting one from its shelf.

"This one isn't beyond its expiration date." She filled a glass with water and handed it and a pill to him. "Put the pill on your tongue and drink it down with the water."

The pill melting on his tongue did not taste good. The water did, and he drained the glass.

She raised her eyebrows at him. "When did you last drink anything?"

"Drink?"

"You have to drink fluids, preferably water, or you'll dehydrate."

"Aaah." He'd read about dehydration. "How much must I drink?"

"Sixty-four ounces a day are recommended."

He handed her the glass. "More water."

She refilled the glass and gave it back to him. He drank it down and held out the empty glass to her again, requesting another refill.

"You shouldn't drink all sixty-four ounces at one time," she said. "Better to spread your drinking out through the day."

He nodded, but didn't move out from between her and the door. For some reason he couldn't fathom, he found himself wanting to know what had turned the beautiful colors of her aura muddy. Perhaps it was the business of the dead man. Her colors had flashed with the dark reds of turmoil when she'd towed him out to her Jeep. He was about to question her when his stomach rumbled.

She glanced at his mid-section. She'd heard it, too.

"What does it mean?" he asked.

She looked up at him, her sea green eyes sad beneath their heavy lids. "It means you're hungry."

"Eat spaghetti?"

"The sauce is still simmering."

"Simmering, to stew below or just at the boiling point," he recited with a pride that took him back to his days apprenticing with Merlin. He'd liked showing Merlin that he'd learned his lessons.

But, the woman Rebecca didn't seem to like it. Her aura shuddered and she looked away.

"I'll make you a sandwich to hold you until supper."

"Supper: a meal eaten in the evening. Meal: food portion eaten to satisfy appetite."

"Yes," she said, brushing past him into the hall without meeting his gaze.

Her bare arm was almost cool to the touch, yet she emitted a heat as she passed, a pleasant, inviting heat. He followed her down the hall to the narrow back stairs.

She paused on the top step and spoke over her shoulder. "You don't have to come with me."

But something urged him down the steps after her. Maybe it was the dark red bleeding once again into the grays of her aura. Or maybe he just wanted to get out of that attic with its dusty air for a while. He was already breathing better.

She hurried ahead of him through the kitchen to the side door and peeked out between the window curtains before facing him. "You can go back to your reading in the attic. I'll bring a tray up to you."

He drew in a deep breath, the aromas of the kitchen tickling his nose in a way that made his mouth water. "The air smells better down here. I will stay in the better-smelling air."

"You remember what I said about the police, don't you, Eric?"

"Police here are not Protectors. Police could try to take me away. Therefore, I must hide in the attic if the police come."

"And you have to be quiet up there."

"I will be quiet," he answered, sniffing the rich, acidic scent filling the kitchen. "What is that scent?"

"The spaghetti sauce."

"An edible," he said, following his nose to the pot of thick, red liquid bubbling on the stove.

She caught him by the arm and steered him to the kitchen table. She motioned to a bowl of round, red objects. "Have an apple."

He plucked one of the apples from the bowl and held it a moment in his palm. "Organic."

"Edible," she said.

"Raw?"

"Yes. Just bite into it."

The skin of the apple snapped as his teeth punctured its skin. A favorable juice flooded his tongue and filled his mouth. An entirely different sensation than peanut butter. This one didn't cling to his tongue or the roof of his mouth. This one was more transient, thin like water, but much tastier.

"I like this," he said.

"It's sweet," she said, folding her arms across her stomach, backing away from him, a dark red color spiking around her. "You always had a sweet tooth."

"Yes, pleasing to the taste," he said, watching her turn to the cabinet, her aura still troubled. "A need has been fulfilled."

She nodded absently as she gathered bread, peanut butter, jelly, and a knife. He bit off another chunk of apple and chewed as he strolled to the stove where the rich red spaghetti sauce bubbled.

Red sauce. Red apple. Red hair. Red aura. All these shades of red, some good, some not. Which was the sauce?

He swallowed his bite of apple and stuck a finger into the spaghetti sauce… and immediately drew back with a yelp.

Rebecca spun on her heel to find Eric in front of the stove, apple in one hand and the other shaking a sauce-coated finger. She grabbed him by the wrist, turned on the faucet and stuck his sauce-coated finger into the stream of cold water.

"What possessed you to stick your finger in hot spaghetti sauce?" she demanded.

"I wanted to taste it."

"It's hot. It burns."

"I know that now."

"I bet you do," she muttered, turning off the water and checking his finger. "No blisters."

"That is good?"

"Very good."

He shifted behind her, his arm, which she held between hers and her side, pressing against the side of her breast. It was the most touching he'd allowed her and she was reluctant to let him go.

She slid her hands over his, lingering under the guise of studying his scalded finger, when it was really the strong angles of his knuckles she explored and his smooth, firm palm her fingers stroked. She wanted his long fingers to thread between hers. She wanted his strong hand to close over hers. She wanted his hot palm to slide across her stomach and press her back against him.

"How do I eat hot sauce?" he asked, breaking into her wishful thinking, pulling his hand from hers.

"Very carefully," she murmured, and turned between him and the edge of the sink. He stood there, too close for comfort, yet not as close as she needed him, water dripping from his fingers onto her toes. He looked at her as though he knew everything she was feeling.

She grabbed a towel from the drawer handle at her hip and shoved it into his wet hand. He glanced at the towel.

"Wipe your hands," she ordered in a voice more broken than commanding. How she wanted to throw her arms around his neck and kiss the memories back into him…memories of them…the good ones. But it wouldn't work that way, she knew. Nothing had ever come easily to her.

He held the towel up without comprehension.

"Use both hands."

He raised the hand with the apple in it. She took the apple from his fingers, from his cool, damp fingers, and set it on the countertop beside her.

"Like this," she said, sinking her hands into the towel dangling from his fingers and drying her hands.

He gathered the towel between his hands trapping hers between them.

"Among your muddy colors are slivers of brightness," he said as he wiped his hands, his eyes seeming to study the space around her.

"Among my what?"

"Your spirit ails. But there are bright specks of healing among your muddy yellows of fear, dark blues of rejection, and orange stress. Your aura tells all."

"My aura?"

His gaze shifted from the space around her to her face, their hands still caught together in the towel between them. "Everything living has an aura. Color is light and light is the mark of creation. Without light, there is no life."

He slid his hands from the towel and from around her hands.

Immediately, she felt the coolness of loss, saw the curious disquiet pinch at the corners of his eyes. He pressed one hand to the center of her chest.

"You are dying…here."

She leaned into that hand pressed to her chest. He could give her life, renew her will to live…restore her heart. Did he know that? Did he see that too in her aura? She was about to ask when she heard the crunch of tires rolling into the gravel driveway.

She jerked away from his hand, ran to the door, and peeked through the curtains.

"It's the police. Get up to the attic," she ordered from the door. "And keep quiet."

Rebecca moved away from the door. No sense looking like she was expecting them. Besides, the more time it took her to open the door, the more time Eric would have to get to the attic and close himself away. She wasn't certain he fully understood the need to do it quietly.

She stood at the bottom of the back stairs, listening. She heard nothing other than the closing of a car door in the driveway. She moved away from the steps and waited for the sound of booted feet on the side porch. Silence…save for the faint tick of the grandfather clock echoing from the front entry hall and the quiet *plop, plop* of the simmering spaghetti sauce. She should have turned on a radio to mask sounds.

But she didn't know where in the house there was a radio. Radios didn't work well here among the bluffs.

Or rather, they hadn't. Such things had changed in the year since she'd last visited. Copper Ridge had satellite dishes now, as Sonny had pointed out.

What was taking that officer so long to get up to the house?

She went to the door and peered out the window. One sheriff's car, but no sheriff or deputy. Then, a white-haired man in khaki slacks and wearing a chocolate brown jacket imprinted with Keweenaw County Sheriff's Department stepped out from behind the garage. He'd been checking out her Jeep. Suspicious even before he questioned her. What chance did she have against a pro if interrogated?

Whatever chance she made for herself. Hers and Eric's future together depended on her convincing him she was alone here and had seen nothing that would be of help to any investigation. She could do it. She'd lived a lifetime of pretending to be what others expected her to be. That's what she had going for her. She'd start by keeping as close to the truth as she could.

She opened the door as the Sheriff stepped onto the porch and stepped outside to meet him with a smile. "Something I can do for you?"

He gave her a nod and stuck out his hand. "I'm Sheriff Wickes, ma'am. Would you be Mrs. Tierney?"

She shook his hand. "Yes, I'm Mrs. Tierney."

No lie yet.

Still, she felt the slight hesitation with which the sheriff released her hand, and he let her answer hang between them. It made her want to move things along, to get this thing over with…to fill the silence.

"Is there a problem?" she asked.

"No. No. I just expected Mrs. Tierney to be a bit older."

The corner of Rebecca's fixed smile twitched. "Perhaps you were expecting my grandmother-in-law. She too is a Mrs. Tierney. She grew up here. Lived here until…her husband died."

He nodded. "Guess that's the case."

"Is that what's brought you up on the bluff, reports that someone other than the elder Mrs. Tierney was in the house?" She chuckled and gave herself a mental pat on the back for managing to sound so casual.

"No. No one's sounded any alarms about a stranger in the house. Copper Ridge folks are a closed-mouth bunch with outsiders. They often take care of things themselves. I expect you know that, being an outsider yourself."

She struggled to maintain the smile. "What makes you so sure I'm not a local myself?"

"Lucille Tierney would never have let her grandson marry a local girl."

Rebecca blanched. Sheriff Wickes knew more than he was letting on. She let her smile slip. "You've done your homework, Sheriff. Is there something I've done that I should be concerned about your visit?"

He smiled back at her, a friendly smile that didn't quite reach his eyes. "Think we could go inside and talk, Mrs. Tierney?"

She wanted to say no, to remind him he couldn't force his way in without a warrant, but that would only raise his suspicions. Then, he was sure to come back with one.

"Sure," she said, stepping aside and motioning him into the house.

He strolled through the kitchen, his eyes taking in everything. His gaze settled on the half-eaten apple by the cutting board near the stove. Eric's apple.

"I'm afraid you caught me in the middle of my afternoon snack," she said, hurrying past him and picking up the apple.

His gaze strayed to the sandwich fixings to the near side of the sink.

"I missed lunch," she volunteered, hoping to waylay any suspicions he had.

"Go ahead and finish your *snack,* Mrs. Tierney."

She was about to bite into the apple when it struck her that her teeth marks wouldn't match Eric's. Just how much would this guy notice?

A lot, judging by the way he watched her.

She lowered the apple from her mouth. "Can't very well answer questions with my mouth full. I'll finish it later."

She put the apple down and strode toward the table, motioning him to join her. But he didn't accept her invitation to sit. She didn't sit, either.

"How long you been up here visiting?" he asked, strolling around the big kitchen.

"Just a few days. Why?"

He paused at the sink and peered out the window. She hugged her arms across her stomach. She hoped she'd gotten all the mothball flakes wiped up. Not that mothball flakes should make him suspicious of anything. It was just…

She was being paranoid. She drew a steadying breath.

He looked over his shoulder at her as though she'd just cocked the hammer of a pistol. "Notice anything unusual around here in those few days?"

"No."

He tipped his head at Lucille's Express Mail envelope in the corner of the countertop as though he were reading the name on the envelope. No doubt he was. She itched to chew at a fingernail.

"Any strange cars on the road?" he asked.

"I haven't left the house since getting here. I couldn't say."

Slowly, he circled the room once more, peering out the window in the door, eyeing the phone by the door, perusing the shelf of cookbooks above the table, nudging open the dining room door on the far side of the back staircase and eyeing the space beyond. He let the door swing closed and moved to the back stairs.

"Would you like a cup of coffee, Sheriff?"

He gave her that half smile that didn't reach his eyes. "Don't touch the stuff anymore. Gives me acid."

She nodded and glanced away from his probing gaze.

"Anybody come up to the house with you this trip, Mrs. Tierney."

She almost smiled. She didn't have to lie to answer this question, either. "No. I drove up alone."

"That's a big pot of sauce on the stove for one person."

She blinked. "I never quite learned how to make spaghetti sauce for one. Besides, it freezes well."

He nodded and sidled past the stairs to the hall door. He nudged it open halfway. "Mind if I ask what brings you up here this late in the season?"

Yes, I mind.

"What season would that be, Sheriff?"

He faced her, the door swinging shut behind him. Back and forth. Whish, whish…like the pages of a book turning.

"Fishing season," he said.

She grunted. "I don't fish."

"So, you came up here to…"

He let the question trail. She'd had enough time to anticipate such a question and consider several answers. She'd rejected any of the options that included mention of a husband. Given the sheriff's apparent knowledge of the Tierney family, she was glad she had…just in case he knew about Eric's *death*.

"I just came up here for a little peace and quiet."

He nodded at the still swinging door behind him. "Mind if I look around?"

Her fingers dug into the sides of her breasts. "Of course not. But, what is this all about?"

He was halfway down the hall before she caught up with him. He didn't answer her until she'd caught up to him at the foot of the main stairway.

"We found a body below the bluff this morning," he said, watching her.

Maybe it was because she hadn't expected him to answer so bluntly. Up until now, he'd evaded her questions. But he had stated the blunt fact of his business this time and she started. "A body?"

She sounded shrill, anxious. But that was okay, right? She was supposed to be surprised, shocked even.

He headed for the sitting room…where Eric had come back to her in a blinding light.

Where the urn of ashes still lay on its side on the tea table on the far end of the couch. She hadn't gotten that far in her cleaning yet; and she didn't want him to see those ashes and ask about them.

"I haven't even opened up that room," she said, hoping she didn't sound too urgent. "There's nothing to see in there."

But he already had the door open.

She held her breath as he glanced around the dark interior of the sitting room. Thank goodness, she hadn't opened the drapes.

He closed the door and stepped around her toward the back of the house, opened the deskside door, and stepped out on the deck. But it was the woods across the side yard he seemed to study.

"You've got some view here," he said.

She should comment how most people are more interested in the view of the lake. She should be making small talk. She should be acting more curious about that dead body. Not just standing there on the doorstep hugging her arms around herself. But her mouth was so dry, she was afraid anything she tried to say would stick on her tongue.

He scanned the side of the house, his gaze seeming to pause on each window before he stepped inside and turned to the door along the hall behind the stairs.

"That's the library," she managed to get out. *Where Eric had spent the night going through every book. Please let him have put everything back where it belonged. Please let there be no man-sized, bare footprints she'd missed wiping up.*

Sheriff Wickes opened the library door a foot and gave the room a quick glance. Someone had closed the drapes in there. She knew who.

Feeling more confident, she started to ask how the man died, but caught herself. The sheriff hadn't mentioned the sex of the body. "How did this person die?"

"That's what we're trying to figure out, Mrs. Tierney," he said and started up the stairs.

"The way you're acting makes me think there's something suspicious about this death."

He didn't slow in his climb toward the second floor…toward where he was sure to find the door to the attic.

She sprinted after him, catching up to him just as he opened the door to hers and Eric's bedroom. "Is there something I should be concerned about?"

He closed the door and looked at her intently. "Something you want to tell me, Mrs. Tierney?"

Had she left out a pair of men's shorts? Had she left Eric's dresser drawers open with some telltale article of clothing hanging out?

She took a gamble and borrowed from Lucille Tierney's autocratic attitude and raised her chin at the sheriff. "If there is something suspicious about that death, something endangering me, it's you, Sheriff Wickes, who has something to tell me."

He let his gaze linger on her a few seconds longer before nodding and moving on to the next door, his response trailing. "The body was found at the base of your bluff."

Sheriff Wickes was on a fishing expedition, and he was trolling into dangerous waters. She needed to distract him before he got to the attic door.

She sniffed the air as she'd often witnessed Lucille do. "And you're searching my house and scaring me half to death over someone falling off a bluff?"

He opened the bathroom door and glanced around inside. "Your bluff to be specific, Mrs. Tierney."

"And someone trespassing on my property and wandering through my woods and falling off my bluff merits you traipsing through my house?"

He pulled the bathroom door shut and faced her. "He didn't fall off your bluff."

"He jumped?" she ventured.

"He was thrown off."

She gasped. "Thrown off?"

"Thrown or chased off," he said, moving on down the hall. Just two more doors and he'd be at the door to the attic.

"How can you know that?" she sputtered, shaken by the evidence that the man at the foot of their bluff had been murdered…and the sheriff's relentless advance on the attic door.

"His body was further out on the rocks than could be accomplished by a fall," Sheriff Wickes said, opening and closing the linen closet door, fixing his gaze on her, "almost as though the intent was for it to be washed away. A person would have to take a good, long, running leap to land that far out…or have been helped off the bluff. Superior doesn't give up her dead, you know."

"I know," she said, tightening her arms across her stomach so she wouldn't chew her nails…which would be a dead give-away to the state of her nerves.

The sheriff studied her a moment before stepping across the hall and opening the door to the master bedroom, Lucille's room. He stepped inside.

"How can you be so certain he didn't run off the bluff by accident?" she all but pleaded, not following him into her grandmother-in-law's bedroom.

"Anybody running that blindly is being chased," he said, lifting the shade away from the window overlooking the back yard and peering out. "And then there are the marks on his neck."

"Marks?"

Sheriff Wickes turned toward her. "Choke marks."

"Choke marks?" The words croaked from her and her fingers fluttered to her throat…her throat that had felt terribly bruised after Eric had choked her, yet was unmarked. Her heart skipped a beat.

Still, she turned away from the doorway, away from Sheriff Wickes and away from his scrutiny. The sheriff skirted her into the hall and headed for the one door he hadn't yet explored. She rushed after him.

"That's just the attic," she blurted out, wishing she could grab him and pull him back. "Nobody's been up there in ages."

Too late, she wondered if there'd been enough dust on the stairs to mark hers and Eric's footprints.

The sheriff closed his fingers around the doorknob and turned it. Rebecca's breath caught in her throat. He'd opened the door barely an inch when his beeper went off. He released the doorknob and checked the readout.

"Could I use your phone, Mrs. Tierney?"

"You're welcome to," she responded with great relief, "but it's not connected." *Though, up here on the top of the bluff, my cell phone works. Not that I'm going to offer anything that might keep you here a moment longer.* "Sorry," she added.

"Guess I better get out to the squad car and answer this page before they send out a search party for me."

"Wouldn't want that," she agreed through a forced smile, closing the attic door, making a mental note to wipe down the attic steps so there would be no dust in which to leave footsteps.

She followed him down the stairs, through the house, and to the back door where he paused on the porch, turned halfway to her, and said, "I might have a few more questions for you, Mrs. Tierney. Mind if I drop by again if need be?"

"Of course not," she said through her fixed smile and closed the door between them, issuing a silent prayer that he wouldn't return.

From the small oval window in the peak of the gable overlooking the side yard, he watched the sheriff climb into his transport and drive away. Once the vehicle was out of sight, he turned his attention back to the footlocker he'd been searching through when he'd heard Rebecca and the sheriff at the bottom of the attic steps.

At that moment, he'd thought she'd betrayed him to her sheriff; and he'd prepared himself to do what he must to protect the mission. A couple of human lives were a small price to pay for the survival of an entire civilization, especially one that had progressed beyond the need for cumbersome physical forms and antiquated instinctual drives.

But Rebecca's aura had flared so brightly, the red of her alarm had shot through the gap between the door and doorframe and up the stairway. A warning?

In any case, the danger had passed.

He returned his focus to the sketchbook he'd found in the footlocker. It was still open to the drawing of a man on the deck of a ship firing a flare into the sky. *Like Rebecca's flare of warning?* The artist who had sketched the image had inscribed below it, "Mac and signal flare gun."

Like the way Rebecca had signaled him. Rebecca, who'd cleared his vision and restored his equilibrium with peanut butter, who'd made the pressure leave his head with a pill and water, then hidden him from danger. Among all the sad hues of her aura had been shades of trustworthiness.

Secure that those things he was familiar with made sense, even in this alien world, he closed the sketchbook and laid it in the footlocker next to a stack of letters that had been tied up with ribbon. They weren't tied together anymore. Little good they'd offered him even though they'd been written by the man who'd hidden what he sought. They had been full of foolish sentiments, promises to return soon, affirmations that the writer was renewing himself and vows of love. Still, he paused long enough to trace Joe Tierney's looping script.

He sighed at the old man's foolish sentimentality, closed the lid of the footlocker, and scanned the dim interior of the attic. There were so many dark corners and so many storage containers. The Elite had been certain The Capsule would be found in this house. His mentor had argued it would not be so easily recovered. In either case, he was convinced the key to finding the encapsulated element necessary to save his world was among those things belonging to the man who owned the trunk at his feet. This time, he used some of the resources natural to him to narrow his search to only those things belonging to Joe Tierney.

He closed his eyes, blocking out the visual sense and willing his higher senses to take over. It took greater effort, burned up more energy than he expected to block out the whistle of the wind through ill-fitting windows and creak of old timbers straining against that wind. He had to breathe through his mouth to keep himself from smelling the stale air and moldering dust.

Still, he found himself flooded with the composition of the cloth and leather touching his body and the molecular makeup of their former wearer's DNA. A fragment of a memory stored in those cells hit him. A woman's fingers stroking his bare chest and sliding under the elastic waistband on his shorts. Rebecca's hand. His body reacted much as it had when he'd licked peanut butter from her mouth.

His eyelids popped open. He needed to immerse himself in the DNA of the one who had hidden The Capsule, not that of the man who knew the intimate touch of the woman Rebecca. He reached into the footlocker, moved the sketchbook and stack of letters aside and pulled out Joe Tierney's jacket and knit cap.

Absently, he identified their makeup as wool. Using the man in the sketch as an example, he shrugged into the jacket and pulled on the cap.

Almost immediately, he felt the connection. He felt it in his muscles. The memories. Like how to sketch a man shooting a flare into the sky, or tie shoe laces, or slip the smooth plastic buttons through buttonholes to close the jacket against the elements of this world.

He could feel the chilly spray off a Lake Superior wave. He tasted tomato sauce on spaghetti.

He *knew* what a woman smelled like when she was in a state of arousal.

"Joe?"

Her voice sounded thin, fragile. So fragile he thought if he breathed too deeply he would disrupt the air currents that carried the sound of her voice and the sweet, amazed, musty scent of her.

He lifted his face toward the stairway. She stood there, on the top step, more tempting than any of the food he'd tasted. Dangerously tempting.

Chapter Seven

Rebecca wove her way through a sea of boxes and old furniture, reaching for the man silhouetted against the attic window. It couldn't be Joe.

She turned him into the light from a dormered window and tore the cap from his head. Black hair, not sable brown. Ice blue eyes, not gentle hazel.

"I-I thought you were Joe. I thought you were your grandfather. You looked just like him in his pea jacket and knit cap."

"You knew Joe?"

She shook her head. "He died before I met you. But, in that jacket and cap, you look just like him."

His gaze traced a path around her as he demanded, "How then did you know I looked like him?"

A nervous laugh escaped her. She wasn't ready to confess how she'd come to know Eric's grandfather. She shook her head. "I thought I was seeing a ghost."

"Ghost. A disembodied spirit," he recited.

"Right," she said, the word dying on her lips. What if Eric was a figment of her imagination after all…along with Ben Jarvey's visit, Sonny Lindstrom's delivery, and Sheriff Wickes searching her house. Maybe, in her grief, she'd conjured up the whole scenario, something absurdly troubling out of self-flagellation for always wanting more than Eric could give her. Like the issue that had dominated their arguments the last months of his life. She'd wanted him to plant in her the one thing that would have bound him to her forever.

She stared at Eric, framed by the dormer. If he were no more than an apparition…

She curled her fingers over her empty womb. Ghosts were spirits. Ghosts were not of the flesh. Ghosts could not fill a woman's womb.

But ghostly apparitions didn't stop light slanting in through a window and cast shadows. Ghosts didn't sneeze at dust. They didn't leave the impression of their lips on a woman's mouth.

Her fingers flexed in the air, wanting to touch the lips that had touched hers. But, he wouldn't welcome her touch.

She drew back her hand, her fingers finding their way to her own lips, a whisper of a touch…just like she remembered his lips had been upon hers with their tentative passion of renewed love. So, which was this, a second chance or the same old hell?

No. Not the same hell. This hell where Eric had come back unfeeling was worse.

She caught a fingernail not already bitten to the quick between her teeth. If this unfeeling man was real…

So was the body on the bluff and the very real possibility Eric was somehow involved with it. Sheriff Wickes would take him away. Lock him away forever. And, even if not, Lucille would learn he was alive and here…Lucille, who had the money and the power to take Eric away from her. Life had cruelly taken from her every person who'd ever loved her. Could it be any crueler?

She began to shake.

"You shiver," Eric said. "Shiver means cold."

He shrugged out of the jacket and swung it over her shoulders. The weight of its wool settling on her shoulders was real. The body heat it held, his heat, real. *Real.*

The first sob tore at her throat. The second ripped its way up from her gut. The third wrenched her heart from her chest.

She crumpled before him. He caught her in his arms and held her to his chest, her slight frame shivering uncontrollably in spite of the jacket he'd placed over her shoulders, all thoughts of Joe forgotten. He searched his memory for an explanation beyond coldness for such spasms. But it wasn't from his memory that he found an answer, not any recent memory anyway. What he knew in that moment as he held her seemed to come to him from deep in the cells of the body he wore.

He stroked her hair and shushed quietly in her ear. He rocked her against his body. Her tears soaked the front of his shirt. He touched his lips to the corner of her eye and tasted her tears. Salty. He'd expected that. But other properties, too. Properties not so easily identified, not so tangible. Properties that made him ache as he had when The Elite had decreed one-on-one mentorships obsolete—

when they'd forbidden him and Merlin further contact. The Elite had called *his* reaction anger and labeled *him* an anomaly for feeling the highly disruptive emotion.

When his anger faded to a deep sadness and his light dimmed dangerously low, The Elite had allowed him counsel with his old mentor. Merlin had explained grief, the element he tasted most strongly in Rebecca's tears, and urged, "You must hide your feelings."

When this mission came up, Merlin's argument that his ability to conquer his emotional excess convinced The Elite he made the perfect candidate for this mission. That he would enter the physical world understanding emotion and be able to resist whatever the physical world presented him.

The mission! Survival of the many.

He pulled back from Rebecca. "Tell me what you know of Joe."

"I'm falling apart. You've lost your memory. Why do you need to know about Joe?"

She asked too much. Dangerous to tell her why he'd come to her world—why he wore her dead husband's body. But he sensed what she knew of Joe would be of use to him.

"Joe is crucial to my...goal. How did you recognize his shape in me?"

She climbed out of his lap and beckoned him to follow her. She led him down the narrow stairs to the second floor, down the long hall and the wide stairs that curved its way to the first-floor entry hall. She led him across the black and white tile floor, past the grandfather clock in the corner, ticking away in cadence to the passing of their feet. She led him into the room where he had created a body that could function in this world, and stopped in front of the fireplace.

"Joe," she said, lifting her hand toward the painting above the fireplace.

A life-sized portrait of a man wearing the wool jacket he'd had on when Rebecca had entered the attic looked out at him. The man stood with legs braced apart, long legs, straight legs, legs braced apart as his had been when Rebecca had entered the attic. Behind the man in the painting, beyond a rusty metal railing, horizonless waves of the deep green of Lake Superior chopped at the air. Cold.

But not the man's face. He smiled down on them with warm brown eyes and a happiness that lifted every muscle in his weathered face. What possibly could have made this aging man so happy? This man who had to know he would someday die. Wasn't it better to live a contented life that would never end?

Contented.

Contented was not the same as happy.

He had always felt there was something missing in his life. Something that had made him restless. But he didn't know what it was until he'd looked into Joe Tierney's face and saw the happiness in the kind, painted eyes.

He felt its absence as a hunger in his own soul.

He stepped onto the hearth and reached for the gilt frame enclosing the painting of the happy Joe. He reached as though drawn by the man the artist had captured there…as though touching the painting itself might give him the answer to how Joe could've been so happy in his mortal life.

"Your grandfather," Rebecca said, hope coloring her voice. "Do you remember him now?"

What he remembered was why he was here. To complete a mission that would save hundreds of thousands of souls…and prove his mentor's training methods of merit.

He stepped down from the hearth. "I need the real Joe. Not a painting of him."

There was little color around her now, like there'd been when she'd collapsed in his arms in the attic.

Her eyes, their pupils huge and haunted, lifted toward a brass urn centered on the mantelpiece beneath the painting. "All that is left of Joe is in there. Joe's ashes."

He glanced from the brass container on the mantel to the one on the table next to the couch. It still lay on its side, its contents spilled across the tabletop. He understood what was inside the brass containers, understood how he'd managed to clone the body of the wrong man. Given he had no way to re-energize in this world, he could not clone another.

Still, he took the urn of Joe's ashes from the mantel.

"Lucille's very particular about how that's handled," Rebecca said, stepping to his side.

He gripped the lid and her eyes widened. "You can't open that!"

He wrenched the sealed lid from the urn before she could stop him and sank his fingers into its ashy contents. Maybe he could find the memory he needed just by touching the man's remains.

"Joe," he murmured.

"Joe," she whispered. "He died twenty years ago when you were fifteen… after Sonny nearly drowned. Remember us talking about Sonny's accident earlier?"

He nodded and sank his fingers deeper into Joe's ashes.

"The two of you were playing a game of chicken. The first one to turn back toward the dock would be a chicken. Neither of you would quit. Do you remember?"

He searched all that remained of Joe—searched his ashes for a memory in their DNA…though not the memory she asked him for.

"When Sonny went under—when you couldn't find him, you called for help. Remember?"

He found little among the ash. A word here, an image there. Fragmented pieces of a life cut short. Nothing as complete as the memory that had come to him from the DNA residue on Eric's clothing. From Eric's fresher DNA he'd remembered a woman's touch…Rebecca's touch.

"Joe ran down from the house and dove into the lake," she prompted

He shook away the memory of her touch. He couldn't let her physical enticements distract him again. He forced himself to concentrate. Still, he could pull no memories from the ash and fragmented bone even faintly as strong as what he'd glimpsed from the residue in Joe's jacket.

"He got you to shore first. You were exhausted, on the verge of going under yourself. Then he went back for Sonny. You said Joe stayed under so long you thought Superior had taken him, too. But then he surfaced with Sonny. You told me Sonny was limp as a rag doll when Joe hauled him onto the dock, but that Joe revived him. Remember?"

Why couldn't she be quiet?

"Joe died three days later. Do you remember that?"

She stood within reach, her shoulders hunched, her arms wrapped tightly around herself, and chewing on a fingernail. He found himself tempted to wrap her up in his own arms, to stroke her narrow back. Her kind were indeed temptresses.

He growled and yanked his hand from Joe's ashes. Surprise blanched across her face and she dropped her hand from her mouth. He shoved the urn into her arms, declaring, "You waste my time, Woman. Do not interrupt me again with your foolishness again."

"Foolishness?" She shouted after him as he stormed out of the parlor. "You were the one who asked how I mistook you for Joe. You said you needed to know because it was crucial to your goal."

As she listened to his feet hammer up the steps, she added in a deflated voice, "Isn't your goal to remember?"

Defeat dragged at her shoulders. Carefully, she replaced the lid of the urn. Peering up at the painted Joe, she whispered, "I'm sorry, Joe. I thought it might help him remember. I thought telling him about how you died might jar loose some memory."

She stepped up onto the hearth and placed the urn carefully on the mantel. She peered up into the painting once more.

"Forgive me, Joe."

He smiled back at her with that ever-present benevolent smile of his. She felt forgiven. If only those in the real world would forgive her as easily. If only there were someone in this world who made her feel as safe as Joe Tierney did when he looked down on her from his place above the fireplace.

Joe, to whom she had turned her first night at The Bluffs, her honeymoon night…after Eric had fallen asleep. They had made wonderful, glorious love twice. They had fallen asleep in each other's arms. But she'd awakened in the wee hours of the night feeling alone and frightened…even with Eric at her side. She'd been afraid she could still lose him even though they were married. She hadn't wanted to wake Eric with her silly fears.

Somehow, she'd found her way into the parlor, to Joe's portrait. Or maybe she'd sought out the portrait because Eric had told her so many good things about the man in it—because, the first time Eric had shown her Joe's portrait, she'd seen Joe's kindness in every brushstroke of his self-portrait.

"Joe," she breathed up at him. "How do I make him remember?"

She peered into Joe's eyes. Those kind, hazel eyes. They seemed to tell her she would have to figure out the key herself. Was she up to the challenge?

Chapter Eight

He'd put Joe's jacket back on. But all he'd gotten from it was the sensation of a ship's deck rising and falling beneath his feet, the feel of the cold spray of water lashing up off the hull, and an appreciation for the scent of clean, cold air as its original wearer peered across the expanse of Lake Superior as the sun rose. All that space and one shimmering ball of yellow. He could understand why this would be a strong memory of Joe's.

He also now understood why Joe painted the shelf in the kitchen that held the cookbooks sunshine yellow. But nothing in such memories brought him any closer to finding The Capsule. Not so much as a hint of where the element was hidden.

He scanned the attic for the hundredth time. Or was it the thousandth time? He'd lost track. His kind would laugh at him…if they had a sense of humor.

His gaze settled on the nearest dormered window overlooking the lake. Beyond, the lake had turned a leaden gray beneath an ashen sky. Night approached. He'd been here nearly twenty-four hours and was no closer to completing his mission than he'd been the moment he'd cloned himself into an antiquated body.

He scanned the boxes and trunks yet to be searched. Finding the clue to where what he sought was hidden was just the first step. Like his mentor, he believed such a valuable object would not be hidden within reach of any physical being. Once he found the *clue,* he would then need to decipher it in order to locate The Capsule.

He rubbed weary eyes and stretched cramped muscles. A most bothersome growling came from his stomach. Hunger again? These bodies were limiting. No wonder his sort had evolved away from need of them.

Rebecca dug the battered metal colander out from its cubbyhole under the sink, straightened and stared out the darkening window over the sink. On the stove, the spaghetti sauce had thickened and was ready to serve. She'd gone up to the attic only once since the blow-up in the sitting room. She'd asked him to come down to the kitchen and eat something. He'd commanded her to leave. Not wishing another confrontation, she complied. She was weary of Eric not remembering her, yet afraid he was beginning to remember the greedy wife she'd been. She had always wanted more of him because, however much time and attention he gave her, it was never enough.

Maybe she didn't deserve for him to remember her. Maybe he didn't belong with her. Maybe she should call Lucille.

She eyed her cell phone in the corner of the kitchen counter…next to that damnable special delivery envelope. The woman couldn't even let her have a few final days to say good-bye to her husband in peace.

Rebecca threw the colander at the envelope. How could a man like Joe have loved so spiteful a woman?

Kind, tenderhearted Joe—that's how everyone who'd known him referred to him. The folks of Copper Ridge still talked fondly of him, even though he was an outsider. The only outsider she'd ever heard them talk about as though he were one of them. She wished they'd accept her that way.

Not that the folks of Copper Ridge weren't nice to her. They were, for the most part. But she was still an outsider. Something she would've been whomever she had married.

Though with Eric, a boy raised by a man everyone had loved, she might've eventually fit in with these quiet country folk…if she'd been brave enough to face down the one fear that kept her from letting them settle in at Copper Ridge. In this one way, *his* lack of memory worked in her favor. She hoped he wouldn't remember Alice first.

The stove timer buzzed. Rebecca sighed, retrieved the colander, and set it in the sink. At least she had Eric's body to keep healthy.

She lifted the spaghetti pot from the stove and dumped the noodles into the colander. Steam fogged the window above the sink, graying the last fading pinks of the sunset. By the time she dumped the spaghetti into the sauce-filled bowl, the windows were black with night.

"Keep his body healthy," she murmured as she set a tray for a husband who refused to come downstairs to eat…a husband she'd been told was dead. She could do at least this much for him.

No. There was more she could do to help him remember. Maybe one painting couldn't jog his memory, but what about photographs?

"If Mohammed won't come to the mountain, the mountain comes to Mohammed," sang a voice that sounded of forced cheerfulness from the stairwell. Rebecca rose from the stairs, carrying a tray. He hadn't even heard her open the door at the base of the steps this time. His senses were dulling as they had earlier when he'd needed refueling.

But the scent of whatever was on the tray she carried made his mouth water. Such failings these physical bodies had, and this woman seemed intent on exposing him to every one of them. He frowned at her.

"It's a saying," she explained on a shaky voice as she approached. "It just means that, since you won't come downstairs to eat, I've brought the food to you."

He grunted and returned his attention to the box between his knees. She toed a stack of books off a box at his elbow. He forced himself not to react to the thumps of the tomes hitting the floor, not to sniff at the heavy, tangy aroma of tomatoes, garlic, and oregano assaulting his nose. He forced himself not to lean into the brush of her elbow against his shoulder as she placed the tray on the box.

He continued rifling through the papers in the box between his legs.

"I don't suppose it would help to remind you what happened this morning when you didn't eat," she said, straightening between him and the single bare electrical bulb lighting his work area.

He paused and gave her a sidelong look. "I do not feel dizzy, my vision is clear, and you are blocking my light."

"Oh," she said, her lips making a small oval, those lips that had tasted too delicious.

She stepped away.

He blinked.

"Finding what you need?" she asked, biting at a fingernail.

He squinted at the printed material in his hands.

"Your blood sugar is dropping," she said. "That's why you're having trouble focusing."

He grunted without looking up at her. His fingers fumbled with the uneven pile. An envelope labeled Bank of Michigan popped out of his grip, spewing small, uniform slips of paper across the floor.

She squatted to help him gather up the slips of paper, their heads nearly knocking as he bent at the same time. She chuckled and looked up at him.

He did not smile, though he had found her chuckle a pleasing sound. But he was not here for his own pleasure.

Her fingers stilled amidst the dust and scattered scraps of papers, and her laughter died. Her eyes turned sad. "Unless you're looking for something financial, you're not likely to find what you're searching for among the cancelled checks."

His fingers flexed around the slips of paper as he searched his memory lobes for a definition of *check* beyond that of a mark. He should not be thinking this slowly.

He frowned and shook his head in wonderment of these antiquated bodies. How had her species survived as long as they had? She apparently mistook his shaking head as a refusal of her help.

"Let me at least help you keep from passing out." She nudged the tray of food closer to him.

"I will eat when I need to," he retorted, refusing to even look at the enticingly scented food.

"You need to eat *before* you get dizzy or your vision blurs."

He waved her away, breathing through his mouth so he would not smell the tempting food.

"Waiting too long drains your body to a point where you could pass out before…refueling can replenish you."

She was right…at least about food. He lifted the plate from the dinner tray, grabbed a handful of spaghetti and stuffed it in his mouth.

She shouldn't have been surprised when he didn't use the fork. This was a man who hadn't known how to dress himself this morning or known not to eat mothball flakes. She opened her mouth to explain about eating utensils. No. Lessons on eating etiquette could wait until another meal. Right now, she needed to remind him he could trust her to help him.

"Slow down and taste it," she urged. "Remember how much you liked peanut butter when you first tasted it this morning? And the apple this afternoon? You liked that, too."

So much had happened since finding him in the night, since waking to him reading books in the library.

No. Not reading. He'd been…scanning the pages of the books in the library… and retaining their contents. What kind of brain damage makes a man forget how to eat and dress, but makes him some sort of savant when it came to reading?

"Already know what spaghetti tastes like," he said before cramming another fistful of pasta into his mouth.

"You remember spaghetti?" she asked tentatively.

He nodded, chewing, speaking around his mouthful of food. "From Joe's jacket."

She eyed the jacket tugging across his shoulders with his every movement. "From Joe's jacket? How do you know what spaghetti tastes like from Joe's jacket?"

He swallowed and reached for more spaghetti. "Memory in DNA."

"Eric, honey, remembering something from DNA is impossible."

He snorted as though she'd said something ridiculous when he was the one believing the ridiculous.

"Human beings can't decipher DNA without some very complicated equipment. You got that memory from your past," she said. *"You* remember spaghetti because…you remember it. It was a favorite food of yours."

He looked up at her, fingers poised at his mouth with the last scoop of spaghetti. He was looking at her as though she were the brain-damaged one, the delusional one. Clearly, he believed what he said, this man, eating spaghetti with his fingers, tomato sauce dripping down his chin.

She snagged the napkin off the dinner tray and held it out to him. "Wipe your chin with this…and your hands."

He accepted the paper cloth and scrubbed awkwardly at his fingers, in the end licking his fingers clean.

"More efficient," he said.

"But not very thorough." She took the napkin from him and dabbed at his chin. "Drink your milk. It's good for you."

Her hands smelled of garlic, tomatoes, and some sort of cleanser. Soap. She had a gentle touch. *Nurturing.* The word popped into his brain. She had done much to help him today…in spite of her distracting nature.

Nature. Perhaps that's all there was to her ability to distract him. A lesson from basic ancient studies came to him. The lesson had noted that physical beings were governed by the codes of nature. Survival. Comfort. The need for other beings of their kind. Only Merlin still taught anthropology, a subject deemed antiquated in a society no longer dependent on the physical.

He drank the milk as she requested, his lingering thoughts about the sociability of her kind cut short by a more immediate thought. He wasn't so sure he liked milk. Too late now.

And getting later.

He glanced at the dark dormer window. He had only seven nights in which to complete his job. Transporting a physical object limited him to orbital paths, and that's when the next path would be open to him…or anyone…for another fifty years. And, by then, his kind could be wiped out.

"There's a cupcake on the tray for you, too," she said. "I put them on the grocery order because you liked them."

The woman talked of food when there was the survival of an entire society dependent on him. He scowled at her. "Like I liked licorice?"

She shrugged, took the cupcake off his tray, and settled on a box opposite him. "Maybe you don't like cupcakes anymore."

The wrapper crinkled as she peeled it off the dark brown object with white loops embossed in the smooth substance coating its top. His stomach didn't growl. But this new aroma…sweet, rich, chocolaty. Though he wasn't sure why he thought of the word "chocolaty". He didn't know what *chocolaty* was. It was probably part of some memory fragment in the cells of the body he wore.

She took a bite of the little cake. He licked his lips and tried not to think about how the sweet crumb clinging to the corner of Rebecca's lips and her mouth might taste together. He scowled. "Leave."

She shook her head, licking the crumb into her mouth. "I can help you."

He snorted. "You distract me."

She fingered a creamy white substance from the center of the cupcake and licked it from her finger. He snatched the remainder of the cupcake from her and crammed it into his mouth, damning himself for allowing the distraction.

The rich flavor of chocolate filled his mouth, the sweetness of the white loops in the stiff frosting aroused sensors at the back of his throat, and the thick white cream coated his tongue.

"I can help you learn about Joe," she said, bringing him back to his purpose.

He quickly chewed and swallowed when he wanted to savor the flavors and demanded, "How?"

"Pictures," she said, bounding off through the storage under the eaves. She dragged a box out of the shadows and into the circle of light from the single bulb. Dropping to her knees, she motioned him down beside her.

He frowned. "The painting of Joe did not give me his memories."

"Photographs taken over the years might reveal the story you search for."

She might've been wrong about Joe's painting being of help to his mission, but she'd been right about far more things today. He could give photographs a try.

He squatted and pulled one of the books from the box. It wasn't like the books downstairs in the library or the others boxed in the attic. These books contained squares of shiny black and white images. People. Pages of them.

He brushed his fingers across the slick paper, surprised by the feelings zipping up his finger from the glossy images. But none felt familiar.

"Which is Joe?" he asked.

She leaned close and looked at the open book he cradled in his hands. "These are from before Joe. Lucille's parents and grandparents."

She poked through the books until she found one covered in pale leather. "Let's start with an album from later years."

"Album," he repeated as she opened the book over the top of the box.

"Photo albums contain photographs," she said. "Pictures."

The pictures in this album were rectangular in shape and colored. She flipped pages until she came to one of a man with sandy hued hair, his arm around the shoulders of a boy with dark hair. The boy was using both hands to hold up a fish whose tail trailed onto the ground. She tapped the photo.

"You were eight here. You'd just caught your first Northern. It wasn't long after your parents…died."

He touched the photo, ran a fingertip back and forth across the boy's face. He felt the boy's pride…and a happiness that he couldn't quite understand in one who'd so recently experienced a loved one's death. Rebecca wanted to die over the loss of her Eric. He'd rebelled when The Elite separated him and Merlin. Were these versions of grief?

He shook off the distracting thought and tapped the boy's chest. "Joe?"

"No. That's Eric. That's you." Color shuddered off The Woman kneeling next to him. She watched him expectantly.

Apparently, he did not respond as she hoped.

He tapped the other image in the picture. "Joe?"

She nodded and he ran his fingertips across the image of the man. Pride for the boy. Nothing more.

There were more photos of Joe and the boy, and some with a woman who had dark hair like the boy. She clung to Joe's arm and her mouth smiled. But her eyes were haunted by loss. He touched her image and immediately pulled his hand back. More than loss haunted this woman. She was afraid, deeply afraid.

"That's Lucille," The Woman Rebecca said. "Your grandmother."

"Joe's wife," he said, studying the woman, wondering what about her had so captivated Joe.

"That's right," Rebecca continued. "Joe's wife. Do you remember her?"

He recalled the sentimental letters that he'd read that Joe had written to her. Another distraction. Nothing more. He shook his head and flipped to another page, and another and another. A loose photo slipped from between pages. He picked it up and looked at it.

"Do you recognize yourself?" Rebecca asked, a hopeful tinge pulsing through her aura.

Joe and the dark-haired boy were older in this photo and joined by a boy the same size as Eric but with carrot-colored hair.

"That was the last photo taken of the three of you before Sonny's accident," Rebecca said, her voice low and a little unsteady. "D-Do you remember the accident?"

He shook his head.

"Your grandmother tore up the original after Joe died. You found the negative and had two copies made. One for you and one for Sonny. You hid your copy among the pages of your scouting book because you figured your grandmother would never look there. You were right. She wasn't much of a scout fan. All that boy stuff, she used to say. She was still saying that after I came along. She said it any time you went off golfing, or playing tennis…any time you called Ben Jarvey to set up a fishing charter here."

He studied the way Joe hugged the two boys to his sides, his smile. It was the expression of a happy man. Even though he had suffered the same loss his wife had, the death of Eric's parents…the death of his child. And he smiled, though he would soon die himself.

"Do you remember?" she asked in her small, thin voice.

He remembered, but not what she asked him to remember. He was remembering the shock that rippled through his world when the first of his kind died. Only a handful were old enough to recall the finality of death. Then a second life energy failed and the populace were horror stricken. There was no rationale for these deaths. No way to reason a way around them. By the third, all-out panic broke loose. They had an epidemic. A world of beings who'd risen above physical ailments, who'd found immortality, were now dying.

He needed Joe's help. He needed to find a way to communicate with a dead man to save a world.

"I need Joe's memory," he said.

"You mean Eric. You are Eric," said the woman who so badly wanted him to remember someone he wasn't.

He shook his head. "I need Joe's—" He struggled to find a way to explain to her what he needed without bringing up the DNA issue again. "—words," he finally settled on. "Books containing his words."

The colors of her aura dimmed and her shoulders sagged. "Do you know what a journal is?"

"A record of transactions," he recited.

"Or a record of experiences and reflections," she said.

What she said was among the definitions.

"Joe kept a journal," she said.

He eyed her with greater interest. "What do you know of Joe's journals?"

"I know where they are."

"Show me," he demanded, rising.

She headed for the stairway and he followed. She called the room they entered on the second floor the master. Lucille's and Joe's bedroom.

She led him to a small desk in front of a window. "This was Joe's desk. You told me Joe liked it here because of the view it offered of the lake while he wrote in his journal; and because Lucille never complained if he set his cocoa on it without a coaster or tapped his pipe against its leg. Do you remember?"

Of course, he didn't remember it. He wasn't here to remember such nonsense.

He'd have told her that except he'd have had to explain something her kind couldn't comprehend and he hadn't the time to waste on explanations.

He touched the worn wood top of the desk. Instantly, he felt a strong connection to Joe. "Where are his journals?"

She opened a deep drawer, revealing several leather-bound books, spine up. He lifted one out. Emotions hit him like icy waves. Strong emotions. Snippets of memories. Too fast, too many for even his high-powered brain to give order to. It was enough to tell him Joe Tierney poured his soul into the journals he wrote at this desk. The journals had to hold the key to the answer he sought.

She switched on the desk lamp as he opened the journal.

"I used to sneak in here when you were out on your fishing charters with Ben Jarvey and read Joe's journals. It made me feel closer to you. I also got to know your grandfather this way."

"Why did you want to know him?" he asked even though it shouldn't matter to him.

"Because you said he was the single, most influential person in your life and I wanted to know the man who made you who you are."

"Was not what Eric told you enough?"

She gave a little shrug, her voice when she spoke small and thin, her aura dim. "Apparently not."

Chapter Nine

"Woman. Woman."

The word invaded her dreams, dreams of running along a beach with Eric laughing next to her. Dreams of her wrapped around him as he moved inside her. Dreams of him promising to never leave her.

"Rebecca," the voice said, Eric's voice strained and tight.

But that couldn't be. Eric was dead.

Wrong. He had amnesia.

She woke with a start. The ceiling above her was familiar, but the bedding wrapped around her was not the quilt she and Eric had picked out for their bed. She'd fallen asleep on Lucille's bed and Eric was shaking her.

She sat bolt upright. "Did you remember something? Did something in Joe's journals jog a memory?"

"My stomach does not feel good," he said, grimacing.

She blinked at him, his face pale and his brow beaded with sweat. The room was too cool for him to be sweating. She scrambled off the bed, barely untangling herself from Lucille's bedspread when he doubled over.

"Eric?" She slung an arm around his shoulders and braced him against her side. "Take small breaths." She demonstrated with a few pants.

Whatever pain had gripped him, it was passing. She felt it as his muscles eased and his breathing evened out. She helped him down onto the edge of the bed.

"Did you eat anything other than what I've given you?"

He shook his head.

"Are you sure? Nothing to drink other than what I've given you, either?"

"Noth—"

He doubled over, his body going rigid.

She rubbed his back, chanting, "Small breaths."

This spasm passed more quickly.

"How long have you been in pain?"

"A while. But it was not so bad until now."

She felt his forehead. "You don't have a temperature, but you are clammy. Maybe something to calm your stomach will take care of it."

She guided him from the bedroom into the bathroom. "Let's get you an antacid."

She barely got the commode lid down when his knees buckled. She staggered under his weight as she settled him on the seat. "Are you sure you put nothing in your mouth other than the food and drink I gave you?"

He looked up at her through pained eyes and held up his finger.

"Your finger should be okay," she said.

"Tongue, too?" he managed to croak out.

"Your tongue belongs in your mouth."

She retrieved a bottle of pink liquid, shook it, opened it, and handed it to him. "Drink some of this."

He took a healthy swig. She rubbed his back, feeling his tension. Fresh beads of sweat popped out on his forehead.

"I might have to take you to the hospital," she said, struggling to contain her own panic. If some doctor searched out his medical records from a Chicago-based data bank, they'd find out he was supposed to be dead. They'd notify the sheriff and all hell would break loose.

"No leave," he uttered through gritted teeth. "I must complete my mission."

Mission? He'd said he would kill anyone who tried to take him away from the house. Not that he was in any shape to stop her.

"I don't want to take you to the hospital, either. But I don't know what's wrong with you. Maybe you swallowed some of those mothball flakes and the poison is just now affecting you."

"No eat mothball flakes," he growled.

"Maybe it's some sort of block…age." The last half of the word trailed from her mouth as she eyed the bathroom door behind him, wondering… "When did you last go to the bathroom?"

"Got pill in bathroom," he croaked out, "and two glasses of water."

She groaned with realization. "This pain, is it cramping?"

"Involuntary spasmodic contraction of a muscle," he recited through gritted teeth.

She pulled him to his feet, flipped up the commode cover, unfastened his pants and dropped them. "Sit."

"Why?"

"Just sit and bear down." She handed him a roll of toilet paper. "Use this when you're done. I'll wait in the hall."

Several minutes later, he came out of the bathroom.

"You're looking a lot better," she said.

"I am feeling much better," he said, heading for the master bedroom, though his gait was none too steady. "Depositing of waste from these bodies is a most messy business."

She peeked inside the bathroom. Oh yeah. Messy business. She flushed the toilet.

He stumbled against a wall. She sprinted after him, catching him by the arm. "You've been up nearly twenty-four hours. You're overly tired. You need sleep."

"Need to search."

"Not only does this body need food and drink and to empty itself of waste products, it needs rest to replenish itself. If you don't sleep, you will collapse. Then how good will you be to your *mission*?"

"Your logic makes sense. How long will I have to sleep to renew this body?"

"Eight hours is recommended."

He frowned at her.

"Even a few will help," she amended, hoping it was enough to persuade him.

"I will sleep a few hours, then."

She helped him into the bed at the far end of the hall where they had lain so many nights together…where they had made love for endless hours. His eyes were closed before she had his shoes off.

She drew the quilt over his shoulders and stood at the side of the bed, watching him sleep curled up on his side like he always did. With his lips slightly parted and shaggy hair feathering his brow, he looked boyish…vulnerable, even. Not at all the image of a man who could kill another…or choke a woman unconscious.

She closed her eyes in an attempt to shut out those thoughts she didn't want to face. It was brain damage, that's all. Society couldn't—wouldn't—hold him accountable, would it?

She knew the answer, and it wasn't the answer she wanted.

She moved to the far side of the bed, slipped off her shoes, and climbed in beside Eric. His heat was like a magnet to her sad soul. She eased up against his back, careful not to disturb him, and slipped an arm over him. He did not stir, and she fell into blissful slumber pressed against the back of the husband she'd thought she would never hold again.

He stretched, easing the stiffness from his muscles. He felt rested…and warm and safe. Must be the cocoon of bedding tucked around him and the warm sunlight slanting through the lace curtains covering the balcony's French doors.

Bedding? Sunlight?

He sat bolt upright, fighting off the covers and squinted into the sunlight. Bright. Very bright. Translation, it was far later than he'd intended to sleep, than he'd told Rebecca to let him sleep.

"Damn her!" The curse slipped from him without thought, a phrase from deep within the memory of his DNA.

He cursed again at the randomness with which memories came back to him as he bounded from the bed and into the hall. The floorboards were cool beneath his bare feet. He hadn't removed his shoes. She must have.

A memory zipped through him as he dashed toward the back stairs, a memory of her fingers around his ankle as she slid off the shoes, of him wiggling his toes in the cool night air before he slid between the bedsheets. She had slipped in behind him, a warm body against his weary back, a comforting arm settling over him. Seductive. So very seductive, the physical aspect of her world. Damn her and her ability to distract him.

Damn himself for succumbing.

As he neared the bathroom, he heard water running. He put his ear to the door. He heard more than running water. He heard humming, a woman's voice. *Her* voice.

A low growl vibrated up his throat and he shoved the bathroom door open.

In two strides, he reached the tub and tore aside the milky shower curtain. Instantly, her arms crisscrossed her body. But she'd covered herself too late. He'd already memorized every naked millimeter of exposed skin beneath her startled aura.

Lost to his sort were the words with which to describe the tender hues of skin. Long lost were the undulating landscapes to which her tapering ankles, rounding calves, and flaring hips could be compared. Yet, without ever seeing a fully naked female form, even in single dimension imagery, he perceived her to be all gentle curves and soft slopes.

Intuitive knowledge dictated he touch those slopes and curves. And he wanted to follow those base instincts.

He wanted to touch the pebbly terrain circling the tip of the breast peeking out from under her folded arm.

He stepped over the rim of the tub.

She backed away from him, her heels stubbing against the sloping porcelain side of the tub. The spray of the shower hammered the space between them, pelted the front of his shirt and the legs of his trousers as that base need he had no experience with drove him forward. The sting of the hot water made him pause, providing him with a window of rationality.

But the steam roiling up around him zapped the oxygen from the air and the moisture from his throat. His brain became incapable of retrieving anything beyond core needs. He peered into her wide, sea-green eyes. Those cool eyes could quench the thirst burning through him. She could save him from the clotting vapor suffocating him.

She'd rescued him before.

Or was it her heat he needed now, a heat more scalding than the steam closing them in together? Weakness, to want what he couldn't have, warned a fragment of reason.

Except, he could have her. Here. Now.

If he was willing to force her. He had the power. He had the means.

He had the need, and the water drummed down over him, rhythmic and pulsating. The impact of each liquid spearhead drove deeper the point of that one base drive known to all mankind.

He cupped his hands around Rebecca's water-drenched face. The surprise and fear that had filled her eyes when he'd ripped aside the curtain disappeared, curiosity and something else he didn't quite comprehend replacing it.

He stroked the pad of his thumb along her full lower lip and her lips parted. He trailed his fingertips across her cheek, and she tipped her face into his touch. He fingered a dark, damp curl from the corner of her eye and she unfolded her arms from her chest.

He ventured further, trailing his fingers from her temple, along her jaw, and down her throat to the ridge of her collarbone. Her skin was incredibly soft and slick. He cupped the crests of her shoulders, their curve a perfect fit to his palms.

He touched the backs of his knuckles to the inside curve of one breast. She drew a sharp breath, causing that breast to rise against his fingers. He slid his fingers lower, the breath shuddering out of her.

He fit his hands to her narrow waist, spread his fingers across the small of her back, and rubbed the flaring points of her hipbones with his thumbs.

Her head fell back and her lips shaped a gasp.

He touched his tongue to the arc of her throat, catching the rivulets of water cascading off the strands of hair clinging to her neck and shoulder. Her groan vibrated beneath his lips and echoed along his own vocal cords.

Her fingers caught the bottom of his sodden shirt and peeled it up his flanks and off over his head. As she pushed his slacks and shorts off his hips and down his legs, he memorized the trail of her hands down his naked limbs. She flicked her tongue against him and his knees buckled, almost sending him into a heap with his pants in the bottom of the tub.

He caught himself against the wall of the enclosure and, snagging her by the upper arm, hauled her up between him and the tiles. He pressed his nakedness against the length of hers. Some unspoken message prompted him to bury his face in the curve of her shoulder to her neck, to nibble and nip at the tender flesh there.

She cried out and hooked one leg over his hip, raising and opening herself to him. He throbbed against the nest of her curls. If there remained a last vestige of reason inside his head, it died in that instant of contact. Every ounce of oxygen-rich blood spiraled to that one point of flesh that marked him as a man.

She hiked herself higher and he felt her welcoming slickness. Instinctively, his hips thrust forward. Easily, she slipped against the peak of his manhood.

Exquisite splendor, thin membrane molding perfectly over nerve-rich flesh. He drew his muscles together for the instinctual plunge that would drive him fully into her.

With a guttural cry, her legs tightened around him, urging him toward the same end.

But through the din of drumming water and rushing blood, her wail echoed in his ears, one word composed of two discordant syllables that screeched sharp against a fragile ego.

"Eric!"

It shouldn't matter that she called out another man's name at that moment. It shouldn't matter if she called out any name. The act they were about to perform was one born of basic instinct, an animal instinct, a pleasurable sensation born of the need to insure the future of the species. Need. Pure and simple.

Yet, her calling out another man's name shimmied a cold trail along pathways that had milliseconds ago swelled with desire. He wanted to complete what he never had before, or likely ever would again, the joining of two bodies and the release of animal needs. Why did the vocalization of a name hold him back?

Why did it make him press her back against the tiles away from him when she squirmed to take him inside her?

Because the species he needed to insure the future of wasn't hers. Because, no matter how much he wanted to satisfy the hunger of the alien body he inhabited, he needed more so to prove himself worthy to his kind.

Because he wanted something more than the experience of the flesh, and, as long as she called him by another's name, that wouldn't—couldn't—happen.

"Don't stop," she panted out, struggling to hang onto his shoulders, squirming for penetration.

"Why?" he growled, pressing her shoulders hard to the wall. "So you can delay me further?"

Rebecca stopped squirming, the pressure of his hands on her shoulders, his sharp words, his snarl bringing her back to the reality of the man who'd stepped fully clothed into her shower. Eric wasn't the man he'd once been. He wasn't even the man he'd been moments ago when he'd touched her with his old passion, when he'd stroked her lips, brushed the hair out of her eyes, and nuzzled her throat the way she loved.

She shook her head in answer to his question. "I didn't make you come in here, Eric. You climbed into the shower with me."

"You cast me unconscious. You removed my shoes."

"I made you comfortable when you fell asleep."

His eyes narrowed at her. "You made me sleep too long."

The tile wall grew hard and uncomfortable against her spine. He'd frightened her when he'd torn open the shower curtain. He'd looked so angry. And he frightened her now that the anger had returned to his eyes.

"I-I let you sleep as long as you needed," she sputtered out.

"You waste my time," he all but howled.

She flinched and slid her legs from his hips, her feet coming down on his sodden clothes in the bottom of the tub. Stepping into a running shower fully clothed didn't make sense…unless the man was hungry with lust. Unless he'd remembered that he loved her.

But he hadn't.

"Don't you feel rested?" she ventured of the man who'd lost Eric's memories.

His chin came up between them. Bingo. Reason still worked with *this* Eric.

"I feel…"

"Sharper? Re-energized?" she supplied.

"Yes."

"You needed the rest, Eric. You needed to sleep in order to think more clearly."

His eyes narrowed on her. "Again, you do what is necessary for the well-being of this body."

"Everything I do is for your well-being, Eric."

He gave her a head to toe glance. "You do not lie. I see the truth about you."

"I would never do anything to hurt you. I love you."

He scowled and stepped back from her, the shower spray a wall between them. "Love is a useless emotion."

"Love is all there is," she returned in a small voice that was nearly drowned out by the rushing water.

His lips pulled across his teeth. "Foolish emotion."

She shook her head.

He glanced around the confines of the shower. "What is this you do to your body?"

The reminder of how badly brain damaged he was squeezed at her heart and she explained sadly, "This is showering."

He raised his palm into the spray and let the water spatter through his fingers. "Why do you do showering?"

"I shower to clean my body."

He snorted and dropped his hand from the shower spray. "This body must be cleaned as well as fed and rested?"

"Cleaning keeps the body healthy."

"Healthy?"

She stepped through the shower spray, picked up one of his hands, and held it up in front of his face. "See the grit under the nails? The dark stuff. That's dirt, and it's full of germs that could make you sick."

He pulled his hand free of hers and held it close to his face, frowning as he examined his fingers. "Dirt. Germs." He pointed to a red residue in the creases of his knuckles. "Is this also dirt and germs?"

"It's dried spaghetti sauce."

"Ah. An edible."

He moved his fist toward his mouth. She caught his hand and shook her head. "Never eat—" She was going to say food that's been sitting out for more than a few hours when she realized all the exceptions to that rule she'd have to list, like raw fruits and vegetables, crackers, cookies, and on and on. "Never eat spaghetti sauce that's been dried in the creases of your fingers. You need to wash your hands."

He nodded and sighed. "You must teach me how to clean this body."

Her heart thumped a hopeful rhythm. He needed her, and that was all that mattered to her at that moment.

"First, you wet your body…as you already have, then lather up with soap." She motioned toward the bar of soap melting in the corner of the tub where she'd dropped it when he'd startled her.

He picked it up, held it in his fist, frowning. "Slippery."

"Yes," she agreed, holding a washcloth out to him. "Very slippery."

He looked quizzically at the cloth.

"I'll show you," she offered, taking the soap from him and lathering up the washcloth. She hesitated briefly before scrubbing the soapy cloth across his chest.

"See how it's done?" she said, smiling when he didn't jerk away from her touch. She should let him wash himself. He needed to learn how to clean himself. But she couldn't stop touching him, not now that he allowed it.

"Close your eyes while I wash your face or the soap will sting your eyes."

He did as he was told without argument. Finally.

"You need a shave," she said, when the washcloth snagged on his stubbled chin.

"To remove the beard with a razor," he recited.

"Yes. I'll show you how later," she said, cupping his chin and lifting his face into the spray.

He sputtered and pulled back. "You drown me, woman."

"I'm rinsing off the soap."

He blinked, rubbed at his eyes, and nodded.

"Raise your arms so I can get your pits. They're important to clean."

"Healthy?"

"More polite. Makes you smell more pleasant."

"Mmmm."

"You used to like to lather up your entire body before rinsing," she said, clinging to happy memories as she soaped him up, willing him to remember them, too. "You called it soaking your body, like when you take your car to a car wash and the automated sprayer covers the car with soap and soaks your car."

"You must wash your transports as well?"

She laughed and nodded, refusing to let his odd speech and memory loss drive away her good mood. Not at this moment when they stood naked together in a warm shower, her tending his body because he needed her.

She circled him, soaping his back, his flanks, his buttocks. No tan lines. A fact she couldn't ignore no matter how hard she tried.

A man who'd not been out in the sun for nine months could have lost his tan lines. A satisfactory answer that prompted more difficult questions.

Where had he been all these months? Who'd been taking care of him?

Lucille? The grandmother who wanted him to herself as much as Rebecca?

Rebecca shook away the negative thought. She wanted to stay in the moment where Eric needed her and he was completely hers.

She moved around him, soaping a hip and the mat of hair low on his chest and the furry trail down his stomach toward where his sex hung in semi-arousal. It would take little to bring him back to full arousal and, given how much more receptive to her he was now than when he'd stormed into the bathroom, she suspected he'd be much more willing to complete the act. And maybe, just maybe, making love to his wife would bring back his memory of her.

Maybe it would bring him fully back to her.

She knelt before him. Reality glared at her. An unscarred abdomen. Where was his appendectomy scar? She'd ignored its absence when she'd dressed him—told herself she hadn't noticed its absence then, given she'd been fixated on the return of a dead husband.

But there was no more ignoring the glaring fact of his body's inaccuracies.

Skin grafts, she feebly argued. But why bother hiding a scar on a man whose wife had already been convinced he was dead? And there was that nagging question of how a body wandering naked through a stormy night bore no weathering. Even the soles of his feet had been unblemished, clean.

He reached down, took her by the upper arms and guided her to her feet. "Something is wrong?"

She looked him in the eye. "What happened to your appendectomy scar, Eric?"

He didn't blink in confusion. He looked at her as though he found her question…normal. But he didn't answer her. Instead, he took the soap and washcloth from her hands, stating, "I can finish cleaning myself."

"Be sure to rinse completely when you're done," she murmured, stepping out of the shower and away from him as though he were a stranger.

A stranger who looked identical to her husband…except for the absence of tan lines and a scar. He stood there in the spray, looking at her with those knowing eyes until she drew the shower curtain closed between them.

He knew he was supposed to have a scar low on his abdomen. She'd seen it in his eyes.

Chapter Ten

The dash of yellow that had flared above her head when she'd asked him about the scar told him she was beginning to use more of her head and less of her emotions. In his world, that would be a good thing.

But they weren't in his world. They were in hers and, in hers, he found himself troubled that she was growing more rational. Not a logical reaction… unless he found her rationality threatening.

He rinsed himself as she'd instructed and slid aside the shower curtain. She stood in the middle of the bathroom, a towel wrapped around her head and another around her torso. Though she faced him she didn't look him in the eye.

She reached past him and turned off the water, then handed him a towel, instructing him how to "pat" himself dry and "tuck" the towel around his waist. When he'd finished, she motioned him out of the tub.

The air in the small room was laden with moisture. "Steam," she called it, still not looking him in the eye. She didn't need to. The colors of her aura told him she was beginning to realize he wasn't who she wanted him to be.

"Condensed gas in the air," he stated.

She nodded, turning toward the sink and murmuring, "You need to shave. This is a razor," she said, holding up a contraption constructed of plastic and metal. "And this is shaving gel." She held up a can labeled "Aloe enriched."

"African plant from the lily family," he stated.

"Huh?" She blinked at him.

"Aloe. A plant from which drug and fiber are harvested to soothe skin. Also used to make a laxative." He frowned at her. "Is my face constipated?"

The corners of her mouth twitched and she bit her bottom lip as she shook her head. She handed him the can. "Read the directions."

"Is my face wet?" he asked when he'd finished scanning the directions.

She patted his cheeks lightly with her fingertips. "It's still wet enough."

"It says I need to take a small amount on my fingers and work gently into my face." He tipped the can to and fro. "How do I get a small amount from this?"

She instructed him where to put his fingers and how to press the button on the top of the can. He pressed the button.

"Let it go," she yelped as mounds of green gel snaked from the can, over his fingers, and into the sink.

"That is more than a little?" he said.

"That it is," she muttered, taking the can from him. "Use what you have in your hand."

He worked the gel into his face as the directions on the can instructed. When he smeared the lather up the side of his nose, Rebecca stopped him.

"Put it only where you have a beard."

He tested the difference between the skin on his nose and the skin along his jaw. His nose was smooth, his jaw prickly. He looked at Rebecca's jaw. It looked smooth. He touched her jaw, her cheek, leaving dots of lather on her smooth skin.

"Where is your beard?" he asked.

She looked at him with wounded eyes. "Women don't have beards. Just men do."

"And I must shave my beard?"

She shrugged and put the can in the cabinet above the sink. "You don't have to shave. But most men do."

"Why?"

"Fashion, I suppose," she said, looking away.

Why the avoidance? Only minutes ago, this woman had gazed at him with eyes full of emotion. She'd responded to his touches in the shower with passion. She'd opened herself to him.

He frowned, and his gaze fell on her breasts now covered with the tightly tucked towel. Did she cover herself because she'd begun to realize he wasn't her Eric? If so, she should also cover the slope of her neck to her shoulders. This he had found as enticing as the soft curves of her breasts. With her hair gathered up in a towel on top of her head, that slope was well exposed. That lovely, gentle slope was red.

With his fingertips, he touched the patch of red marring her pale skin. She flinched and he withdrew his fingers. She brushed hers over the space where his had touched.

"Why is your skin red?" he asked.

"It's a little chafed."

"Made sore from rubbing. What did it rub?"

Her gaze ricocheted from his chin to the floor. "Your beard stubble."

"Ah. This is why men shave their beards." He placed his palm over the chafed area of her neck. It took little energy to restore her skin. Far less this time than it had the bruises on her throat that his choking her had caused. Certainly, he could afford to use up such a small amount of energy.

For a moment, she swayed into his touch and gazed up at him with the same passion with which she'd gazed at him in the shower. He found he liked her looking at him that way. Then her vision cleared and she pulled back from him.

"You'd better shave before the shaving cream dries out." She started to hand him the razor, but hesitated. "I better do this the first time…so you can see how it's done."

She turned the sink faucet on and held the thick end of the razor under the stream for a moment, explaining what she was doing. Then she drew the razor from the bottom of his ear to the edge of his jaw. There was a scraping sound followed by her relieved sigh. She repeated the act from cheek to jaw several times, moving a razor's width with each stroke, rinsing the razor every few strokes…standing there between him and the sink. So close, he could feel the heat off her thighs against his. So close, her elbow bumped against his chest every time she twisted around to rinse the razor. So very close, the colors of her aura mingled with his and filled the steamy room with a soft glow.

She paused. Did she see the brightening colors, too? Did she feel the heat pulling them toward each other?

"Go like this," she said, contorting her mouth in a way that stretched her upper lip.

He mimicked her, and she made a short razor cut from his nose to his lip, then paused again. She lowered the razor.

"You really should see how this is done." She slid out from between him and the sink and wiped the mirror above the sink with a small towel.

A man stared back at him, the same man he'd seen in her eyes just before she'd fed him peanut butter, though this time he had white foam on half his face. He reached out. The man reached out at the same instant and their fingers met, but all he felt was a smooth glassy surface.

"It's a mirror," she said from his elbow. "That's your reflection."

"Eric's reflection," he corrected.

"Yeah," she murmured.

"Is he appealing to look upon by your standards?"

"Yes, he's very handsome."

"Well-proportioned in appearance," he stated, recalling the definition for handsome. He lowered his hand from the mirror and looked at Rebecca. "You have a well-proportioned appearance."

A rosy hue colored her aura and climbed her throat. He touched her face and found it quite warm, far warmer than the chafed patch on her neck had been. "Do I chafe you?"

She shook her head. "I'm blushing."

"To redden in the face from modesty or embarrassment. Do I make you feel uncomfortable?"

She peered up at him, her eyes sad.

"I do not want to make you…uncomfortable," he said, not sure why he cared about her comfort level.

Her mouth flexed a wistful smile. "You don't make me uncomfortable. It's just been a long time since anyone called me…*well-proportioned in appearance.*

She handed him the razor. "You'd better finish shaving. The soap is drying."

She turned beside him, their reflections staring out at them from the mirror as she instructed, "Make the face I showed you."

He stretched his lip over his teeth.

"Good. Now use the razor like I showed you."

He drew the razor over his skin, effectively clearing a path of soap. He smiled at his accomplishment.

"Good aim," she said, "but you need to use the blade side of the razor."

She turned the razor around in his hand. He slid the razor up his throat and felt a stinging sensation. He drew back and a thin line of blood seeped from his skin.

"You nicked yourself," she said, stepping around to his unshaven side. "Let's start with a less tricky area, like your cheek."

"Don't want to *nick* my cheek."

"You need to learn how to do this."

"I do not need to shave. You said so."

"You can't go around with half your face shaved. You have to finish the job… at least for today."

He scowled.

She took his hand in hers and guided it from ear to jaw. "See. Light pressure."

A couple more swipes and she let go of his hand. He managed two more swipes before nicking himself again. When it came to shaving the underside of his jaw, he balked again.

"Too close to my throat. Cut throat and die."

"You can't cut yourself bad enough to die with a razor blade."

He considered what she said. She had guided him well up to this point. She had chased away the dizziness with peanut butter. She had protected him against the police and warned him about poison with what had nearly been her last breath…when she'd thought he was Eric.

He eyed her aura. No false lime green.

He finished shaving with but a few more minor nicks. He didn't like their sting at all and placed his palm over his throat, healing the nicks there.

He was working on the cut on his chin when Rebecca gave his throat a closer look. "What happened to the nicks on your neck?"

She touched her own throat. Was she remembering how he'd healed her bruises after choking her?

She pulled his hand away from his chin and examined it. "How did you do that?"

Had he revealed too much to The Woman who now eyed the towel he'd tucked around his waist where it covered no scar?

She looked up, stared him in the eyes. "You nicked your neck and your chin. I didn't imagine that...did I?"

He said nothing, instinct warning him to remain silent, an old instinct that had to do with self-preservation. Logical and appropriate. An entire society depended on his mission's success. Better she not know the truth. Better he not let her see again that space where there should've been a scar.

"I will dress myself," he said, dragging his sodden slacks from the tub.

"You aren't wearing those, not unless you have some way of instantly drying them." She looked at him as though she expected him to actually dry them.

He shook his head and released the sodden slacks to her. She tossed them over the shower rod, instructing, "Wash the rest of the soap off your face and dry off. I'll go lay out fresh clothes for you in our—the bedroom."

By the time he got to the bedroom, she already had her shorts on and was dropping a t-shirt over her head. His were nowhere in sight.

"I need my clothes," he said from the bedroom entrance.

She spun toward him, droplets of water scattering from her hair. "That was fast of you."

She pulled open drawers, grabbing out of them articles of clothing. "They're only knock around clothes, but they're all that's...dry."

She handed him a dark t-shirt and faded jeans. Then she was gone, scooting past him out the door, her bare feet padding down the steps.

Something had changed with this woman who had dressed him and washed him, this woman who had stood naked before him, who'd opened her body to him.

Wrong. She'd opened herself to Eric. Her Eric.

But he wasn't Eric.

And she was beginning to realize that. Which raised the question of whether or not she would still feed him, clean him...protect him once she knew for certain he wasn't her Eric. He needed to know if he was still safe with her...and from her. And the sooner he knew, the faster he could get back to Joe's journals.

She gazed into Joe's gentle, painted eyes, searching for an answer to how Eric could've healed those shaving nicks. Could some phenomenon caused by the accident have altered his state to the point that he'd become a healer? Is that how he survived the plane crash? How he repaired shaving nicks and eliminated an old scar?

Or had she imagined those cuts? Maybe there'd been no nicks in the first place. Maybe the residual soap had obscured them enough that she'd only thought he'd healed them. Healing wounds with the touch of a hand was impossible.

She touched her throat, recalling how warm her neck had felt when he'd cupped his palm over it…after choking her unconscious. Her throat had felt bruised until he touched her again.

What kind of man could heal injuries?

Even if the shaving nicks were a figment of her imagination, what about his reaction to the missing scar? Or was that, too, no more than her imagination?

What about his not remembering food and clothing? Does such a selective amnesia exist?

Joe smiled his enigmatic smile, the hazel eyes peering into hers suggested she already knew the answer. But she didn't want to face the truth now any more than she had nine months ago.

She felt *him* enter the room, a quiet stirring of the air.

"You introduced me to Joe's portrait on our honeymoon," she said, desperate to prove the man in Eric's clothes was Eric. "Remember?"

She faced him where he'd stopped just inside the parlor doorway and searched his face for a fragment of memory. There was none in his smooth brow or his cold eyes.

A nervous smile tugged at her lips. "Did you know that I used to come in here and talk to him? That I came to him for advice…and reassurance?"

Not a flicker of reaction.

"Right," she murmured. "Not even Eric knew about those visits."

The smile she'd forced across her mouth pulled at her cheeks, heavy, leadenly heavy. She let it slip away and her voice, when she spoke, came out barely more than a whisper. "Just tell me you're Eric."

He moved to the end table beside the couch where the urn yet lay on its side, its ashes spilling out. She'd been told those ashes were Eric's.

He scooped up a palm full of the ashes and held them out to her. "This is Eric."

She shook her head, her throat growing tight. "No. You're Eric."

He strode closer, ash-filled hand extended in front of him.

She backed away from those ashes—away from him, still shaking her head, still insisting, "You just don't remember."

Her heel bumped hard against the hearth and she stumbled back against the fireplace. He stopped in front of her, that damned ash-filled hand still stretched out at her.

"There is nothing for me to remember," he said.

"No," she choked out, steadying herself against the cold stones.

"Your Eric is dead," he said in his dispassionate voice.

"No," she howled, slapping his hand and sending the ashes flying. "You didn't die. Those ashes belong to someone else. This whole thing's a hoax. Your grandmother took advantage of an opportunity, that crash, to hide you away from me. Or maybe she even staged the whole thing, feeding you drugs to make you forget."

He dropped his hands to his sides, remnants of ashes falling from his fingers and the cold, unrelenting eyes refusing to release her as he stated, "I do not have his scar."

"Cosmetic surgery. Skin grafts."

He shook his head, one small, sad shake. "Your Eric is dead."

She clamped her hands over her ears and bolted from the room, running from a truth she had known all along in her heart. He wasn't Eric.

He'd given her the truth, and it caused her to run away from him. Though he somewhat understood her actions.

When the great energies of his world began dying off, it had started amongst the oldest. His Merlin, being one of the most ancient, provided him motivation beyond the respect of The Elite for succeeding at his mission.

He'd lost his friend once already when he'd been denied Merlin's tutoring. Suffered greatly for it. To lose him forever would be beyond bearable.

Not that he'd be allowed the luxury of assimilating his loss. Grief, in his world, was a non-useful, non-essential emotion, an emotion that wrought illogical reactions.

But she was allowed grief...this woman of an antiquated, physical world. Though she needed to be watched...because of those illogical reactions. She might well be truly dangerous to him now that he'd made her see he was not *her* Eric—that Eric was dead.

He moved into the hall. The door to the deck was open. He stepped outside. The deck was empty, but he heard the slap of bare feet against wooden steps.

From the gazebo, he watched her descend the stairs to the dock almost at a run. When she reached the end of the dock, she fell to her knees and buried her face in her hands.

When contact with Merlin had been denied him, he'd wanted to howl his rage. He'd wanted to lash out. Fortunately, he'd had no vocal chords with which to howl or hands with which to strike. Such an outburst would have cast him into the lowest levels of his world—would have cost him this chance to prove Merlin's teachings had merit. For this, as well as Merlin's life, he needed to be the one to retrieve the element that would save the energy forces of his world—his people's lives.

Just as Rebecca might need to act upon her newfound knowledge. She might use it against him. That last was why he must monitor her.

He brought Joe's journals to the gazebo where he reread them and reread them until day eased into evening. He called down to her that he needed food. But she remained at the end of the dock, her knees drawn up against her chest and her arms hugged around them.

So he watched her from the kitchen window as he ate cornflakes from the box the way she had the morning after his arrival. Later, he watched her from the library window as he searched Joe's journals yet again for something more than the daily notations of weather, his comments on life, and his thoughts about the grandson with whom he shared his life…Eric.

It made him realize, of all who'd schooled him, only Merlin had considered their time together special.

How long she'd sat hunched with bare arms wrapped around bare legs on the soggy dock Rebecca didn't know. She'd long since stopped feeling the chilly slap of the air against her exposed skin. What made Rebecca shiver was the icy emptiness inside her chest.

Eric had promised. Right up there on the balcony of the corner room on the second floor overlooking this very dock, their room where they'd slept and loved and planned their future together. Eric had promised to never leave her. Over and over, she'd made him promise—made him promise every year on the anniversary of their honeymoon…except this last…because he had left.

The damnable evidence was in an over-turned urn on a table in the parlor. The damnable man without Eric's scar holding out to her Eric's ashes wouldn't let her ignore reality any longer.

Whatever he was, a long-lost twin, a relative with an uncanny likeness to Eric, a stranger altered by a surgeon's blade, he wasn't Eric.

He wasn't Eric.

The ache of loss tore at her throat and burrowed into her chest. Even the thin-lipped Lucille couldn't have been so cruel as to alter some man's appearance to fit Eric's just to drive her crazy. And for what purpose, to drive her away from the Bluffs? She'd already agreed to give up ownership of the only place she and Eric had ever called home…though they'd never lived there full-time. That had been the result of the deal he'd made with his grandmother…the trade-off. The house he loved for his services as CEO of the Tierney Foundation. Unfortunately, his obligations to The Foundation prevented them from making The Bluffs their fulltime home.

And the fact Eric's first love still resided in Copper Ridge.

Rebecca winced, knowing she had been a willing participant in his grandmother's deal. At the time, she'd thought it might ingratiate her to Lucille. But it hadn't.

And now, The Bluffs which Lucille had sworn she hated, she wanted back… wanted to take away from Rebecca the place where she and Eric had been happiest. Maybe Lucille could be that cruel.

The heavy overcast pressed down on the leaden lake reaching out before her, that vast, cold lake that never gave up its dead. Yet, in the days when Eric was here with her, the waves crashing against the bluff infused her with energy. Now, without him, those cold waves only sucked at her soul.

"You win, Lucille," she cried out.

Stiffly, she unfolded herself and stood, the autumn air cool across the backs of her knees. Beneath her feet, the damp boards creaked. Pine and the mustiness of decaying leaves scented the air. She licked her lips and tasted the metallic tang of the ore rich rock upon which Copper Ridge and The Bluffs had been built. For a moment, Rebecca wondered if imminent death always sharpened a person's senses. She wondered if it had sharpened Eric's.

Maybe she would be the one to win in the end, not Lucille. If this played out the way she intended, she'd be the one with Eric.

She gathered herself up on the edge of the dock, took one last long breath of air, and dove head first into Lake Superior.

Chapter Eleven

He closed the journal from the last year of Joe's life. He'd studied this stack of journals again and again, and still he'd found no clue that would help him find The Capsule. He tossed the book back on the desk with the others. He fingered their spines. They encompassed the years Joe's grandson had lived with him, telling of their nightly star gazing, of their frequent explorations into the area's old mine shafts and caves, and of a shared love for a vast lake. Those journals gave him insight into the relationship between a boy and his father figure…insight into something he'd come close to with Merlin.

What he needed, though, wasn't in these journals. What he needed, he suspected, would have been noted in Joe's earlier years, his first years here, the years long before Eric became part of his life.

He opened the oldest of the journals from the desk drawer to its first page. It started with temperature readings, barometric pressure, and wind velocity as each new day's entry began. This one was dated a few months before Eric came to live with him and his Lucille, before Joe had to write of losing a son. His entries had been full of observations of everyday life up until that point. They turned introspective for a while after that, talking about the ache of his grief or his rage against death.

Those weren't the entries *he* needed to accomplish his mission, though—to prevent the dying out of a superior race. If only Joe had kept journals back then. *If?*

He examined the spines of the journals, each labeled with a year. Joe Tierney was too meticulous a record keeper not to have kept records of his every day in this place. There had to be journals dating back to his earliest days on the bluff.

Rebecca hadn't given him all of them.

He rose from the desk, strode down the hall, and out onto the deck. The evening air slapped at his face, damp and cool. The scent of pine filled his nostrils. The sound of lapping water touched his ears. Too many sensations in this world. Too many distractions…like the woman who touched too much.

He scanned the dock below where she'd huddled all afternoon and evening. She wasn't there now.

He scanned the steep stairway climbing from the dock. He peered through the shadowed gazebo. He searched the deck and the side yard and forest that crowded in on the yard before turning his attention back to the dock.

Had it not been for her white t-shirt, he might not have seen her gliding through the dark water away from the dock. Such a strange thing to do, swim off at night in a lake that rarely warmed above the mid-sixties—that, even in summer, threatened hypothermia. Hadn't she told him that was how Sonny had drowned?

He watched her slicing her way through the black water, driving herself away from the land. No hint of slowing. No hint of turning back. If she continued swimming away from the land as she was, she was going to drown.

Alarm blasted through him, and he bolted through the gazebo, careened down the steep stairs, and dove into the lake.

The shock of the cold water punched the breath from him. The instant his head broke surface, he sucked at the air. Hypothermia could take his body as well, he realized belatedly. He should drag himself up on the dock and let her go. It was a solution to his concern that she'd expose him.

But that same elusive *something* that had driven him down the steps and across the dock into the water wouldn't allow him to let her go…something beyond logic. It drove him after her, muscle memory taking over the body he wore, making his arms reach, streamlining his form, slicing him through the dark water after the pale shirt.

He caught her by the leg.

She screamed and went under.

He released her leg, grabbed her arm, and hauled her up.

"Let me go," she gurgled, swinging her free arm at him.

But her movement was uncoordinated and he easily avoided the blow, flipped her onto her back, hooked her head in the crook of his arm, and began one-arm swimming them back toward land, a position that seemed dictated by latent memory.

She struggled weakly at his grip, her words slurred. Something about dying.

Which was exactly what they were both going to do if he didn't get them out of the cold water soon. And soon was the best his brain could calculate. His body temperature was dropping, his muscles hurt something fierce, and his limbs felt like lead.

He looked toward up the face of the bluff—looked toward where the house should be. In the night-darkened silhouette of landfall ahead, he saw not so much as a glimmer of light from a window.

He felt the currents now, pulling at them, and understood what was happening. He swam toward the black wall of land, hoping whatever shore they hit wouldn't be sheer bluff. He'd never get them both up its rock face.

He swam them into the shadow of the jutting bluff, fighting the drag of the tide, battling the recoil of the waves as they crashed against the bluff and rolled back on themselves. His unprotected toes stubbed against submerged boulders. But boulders meant shallower water and shallow water meant shoreline.

He swam until the wall of rock loomed before them, until the waves battered them against protruding rocks and his toes found the pebbly bottom. He dragged them out of the water and onto the narrow strip of shoreline.

The wind sliced over their wet bodies. He shivered. She did not. She was unconscious and her pulse was faint.

He glanced about the darkness for some sign of shelter, but discerned nothing but the smell of recent death. Something beyond the decay of washed up seaweed and dead fish. Something reminiscent of…human.

The overcast thinned for a moment, and a shaft of moonlight slid across the strip of shore where they huddled, with its stones polished by the daily ebb and flow of the tides, and up the wind-battered bluff face. Part way up the bluff, the moonlight found a void, a black hole in the stone wall.

Caves were for exploring, hiding, and sheltering in. He'd read of those options in a book on spelunking, the fictional *Tom Sawyer,* and in Joe's journals. They would be safe from the elements…if that black void was a cave.

He tossed Rebecca over his shoulder and climbed the jagged face of the bluff, once more allowing muscle memory to guide him. He let his hands decide which pieces of stone to grip and his toes which crevices to dig into. The edges of the stone were sharp against his shoeless toes. Where had his shoes gone?

He scanned his memory as his fingers and toes searched the stone wall. The shoes, he recalled, had popped from his feet when he'd hit the water.

A sharp edge of stone sliced into his skin. He wished he still had his loafers, though climbing a rock wall did not sound like a job for anything called loafers.

By the time they reached the black hole in the bluff face, his fingers were bloody, his nails torn, and his feet cut. But he'd gotten them well above the waterline of high tide. How deep the cave was and how much shelter it would provide was yet to be determined.

He crawled into the indentation, dragging Rebecca along with him. He could see nothing. Even Rebecca's aura was too dim to light the space. But she shivered. That was a good sign, though how he knew that he didn't know. Maybe from a book or Eric's DNA.

A blast of wind cut through the fissure. He felt its chill clear to his bones. His body heat wouldn't fend off hypothermia for them both much longer… unless he was willing to expend a great deal of his limited energy. He'd already foolishly wasted some on healing his shaving nicks…and her bruised throat.

Rebecca's teeth chattered. They needed better shelter.

He felt along the stone floor, feeling his way deeper into the black hole. He crawled forward until he struck his head on rock.

A quick calculation of energy reserves and time remaining in this physical state and he held up his hand, concentrating his energy into the center of his palm. The light energy gathering there filled the indentation with a soft glow. The void was shallow, but there was a narrow hole at its back big enough for a couple grown humans to crawl into.

He stuck his illuminated hand into that hole and discovered it climbed deeper into the bluff. There were no sharp edges in here, just ribs polished smooth by eons of tunneling water.

He rolled onto his back, repositioned Rebecca on top of him and, using his elbows and heels, shimmied his way along the stone channel. He could've stopped anywhere along that upward sloping tunnel. They were out of the reach of the autumn night air whipping across the great cold lake against the bluff. But, something urged him deeper, some memory that didn't belong to him.

When the tunnel opened into a chamber, he knew where he was, though the ceiling of the chamber wasn't quite as high as he remembered it being. But the firewood was stacked against the back wall just as he remembered, and the sleeping bags still tucked behind a stone outcropping where they'd always been kept.

He rolled Rebecca onto the floor and arranged the kindling and logs within the fire pit of stones as the owner of the memory had been taught. Holding his hand palm down over the wood, he focused more of his energy on the wood that had been drying for two decades. It quickly ignited, filling the cave with a warm glow.

She sat up, her eyes slits in the firelight. "What are you doing?"

"Warming us up," he answered, shaking the dust out of the sleeping bags and spreading them out by the fire. They smelled musty and tufts of insulation poked from holes chewed by rodents. But they would soften the stone floor.

She sighed, her eyes drifting shut. "W-We need to get out of these wet clothes."

"Another reason…my sort…evolved away from…physical bodies," he said between clacking teeth as he peeled off her clothes and tucked her into the joined bags, then removed his own and slid in behind her.

Heat melded their naked flesh together in spite of their chilled skin. A strange sensation. Pleasant and disturbing at the same time. He gazed down on her, watching, pondering the wisdom of such contact, especially when the flames danced enticingly in the damp ringlets framing her face. But her lips still bore a bluish tinge.

"You will catch your death," he said, recalling what she had said to him his first day with her. "I understand now."

He settled in against her back and pulled her closer. He hugged her until she stopped shivering. He hugged her until her skin warmed. And he hugged her as he dozed with her in his arms until…

He woke to cooling air and an empty space where she had been lying. He sat up and found her squatted by a low fire, a golden profile of soft curves and gentle slopes.

"What are you doing?" he asked.

"Adding wood to the fire. It was almost out." Her voice was thick and her words slurred. She was not yet fully recovered.

"Come back where you will be warm," he said. "I'll tend the fire."

"It's done," she said, sliding into the sleeping bags he'd zipped together—sliding in beside him.

"You will catch your death." He repeated the phrase because it was the truth and because he didn't know how else to express his concern for her well-being.

She sighed wearily. "I wanted to catch my death. You shouldn't have come after me."

He raised himself on one elbow and peered down on her softly lit profile. "You wanted to die? That is why you swam out in the lake?"

A tear seeped from beneath the dark lashes feathered across her fire-lit cheek and she answered in a voice that was little more than a whisper. "Yes."

"Why would you want to die?"

"Because I don't want to live without Eric."

She didn't say *can't,* like her life-support was connected in some way to his. She'd said she didn't *want* to live.

"I do not understand why the loss of a breeding mate would make you choose death over life."

"Then you've never been in love," she murmured.

He'd come from a place where love matches were banned and loving attachments ridiculed, a place of higher thinking where no one wished to die for any reason, least of all for something as impractical as love. "Love is a useless emotion."

"Love is everything," she said in a thin voice, peering up at him from beneath heavy lids. "What are you? Some long hidden away twin of Eric's? A bad seed that Lucille kept locked away?"

He looked through her wounded aura, at the teardrops caught in her eyelashes. She would be better off were she not burdened with her dependency on love… or any emotions. Perhaps the truth could free her.

He answered her question with a quiet, "I am not a twin."

"Some long lost relative who happens to look just like Eric, then?"

Gently, he fingered a curl back from her cheek. "I am not his relative."

She blinked sluggishly up at him. "Then why do you look so much like Eric?"

"Because what you see is made from him."

"*Made* from him?" she asked, her eyelids drooping.

"From his ashes. I cloned this body from his ashes."

She yawned, her words slurred. "Not possible. We've only cloned animals. Never humans."

"It *is* possible. Though not from as small an amount of DNA as those from my world can. A benefit of higher thinking without the distraction of emotion."

She blinked as though it took great effort to keep her eyes open. "And where is your world?"

"In a galaxy far from yours."

"Hmph." The sound escaped her lips on a weary breath as her eyes drifted shut one last time.

She had taken the truth about him better than he'd expected her sort would. Perhaps her kind were not as irrational as his kind thought they were. Perhaps their kind were not so different after all, and there was hope for them…her.

With a fingertip, he traced the soft slope of her cheek, the gentle curve of her jaw, and the silky contour of her lips…those beautiful ripe lips that had tasted of peanut butter and passion. He touched his lips to hers, tasted them with the tip of his tongue.

Perhaps, after he obtained The Capsule and before he had to leave, he could sample those lips again. What harm could there be in partaking of a little *research.* Maybe he could even sample the whole woman, a woman who would welcome him as the man he was.

Rebecca woke sore and disoriented. She blinked at the stone ceiling above her and the fire in the center of the stone floor with its streamer of smoke drifting toward a rusty dark crevice in the far wall. Cool air wafted over her back. She found the source of the breeze in a dimple of a tunnel opposite the crevice. The walls between were cast warm gold by the firelight and marked with the etchings of a man and a boy doing boyish things. She'd read of this place in Joe's journals. Eric had told her of it. But he had never brought her here…to his and Joe's cave.

Had she succeeded after all? Had she died and ended up in Eric's heavenly sanctuary on Earth? Had Eric at last let her completely into his world?

She sat up, the sleeping bag slipping from her naked shoulder, stirring its scent around her. Apprehension snaked into her elation. Did heaven include a sleeping bag that smelled of vermin? Did death leave you on a stone floor?

Dream or reality? Life or death?

Then *he* unfolded from the crevice. Eric…smiling.

She rose from the sleeping bag, allowing it to pool around her feet. "Eric?"

The smile faded from his mouth and the brightness in his eyes dimmed. "I have found an easier way out for us."

"An easier way out…for us?" Did that mean she'd done her time in purgatory? Was he taking her to their heaven? Or their hell? Did it matter? Whatever happened, they'd be together in it.

He snagged her clothes off the rocks by the fire and handed them to her without looking at her. "Get dressed."

Eagerly, she dropped the tee over her head and pulled it down over her torso.

"We need to get back to the house," he said as she tugged her shorts up over her hips.

Hope flared through her. Maybe the past nine months had been nothing more than a nightmare after all. Maybe Eric had never died. Maybe they were still together and still alive, both of them.

"When you say house, you mean The Bluffs, right?"

"Hurry," he snapped. "I have only four more nights before my mission must be completed."

Mission? The word stilled her fingers in mid-zip.

She raised them to her throat. She didn't want to remember why. Just as she didn't want to hear the word *mission.* Those details were from her nightmare.

He smothered the fire and the cave went black, save for a white glow that lit the path to the tunnel.

"Where'd you get a flashlight?" she asked, not sure how she knew he shouldn't have had one.

"Flashlight," he recited in that troubling cadence she'd come to know since entering this nightmare. "Illumination device operated by battery. I do not have a flashlight." He faced her and lifted his hand palm up to her. The center of his palm glowed bright white.

She stumbled backwards from him, remembering that he'd told her Eric was dead before she'd fled to the dock and the one damning word he'd spoken in the night as she'd drifted into exhausted slumber. *Clone.*

He stretched his hand out to her as though all she needed was a closer look. "It is but a concentration of energy."

She shook her head and took another step back away from him. "What the hell are you?"

"I am what I told you I was last night. I am your Eric's clone. This way," he commanded, motioning her into the crevice.

She shook her head, backing further, tripping past the rocks surrounding the fire pit. "No."

"Last night," he stated, "you listened as I told you who I was and where I came from. It did not distress you. Do you not remember?"

Fragments of memory slammed into her. Impossible things. Things she thought she'd dreamed. She kept shaking her head, kept backing away until she felt the stone wall at her back.

"We can discuss it later," he said, holding his hand out to her, that hand with the impossibly glowing palm. "Now, we must get to the house. We must find the rest of Joe's journals."

"Impossible," she murmured, staring at that glowing palm, inching along the wall toward the tunnel.

"You do not have to be afraid of me, Rebecca," he said, taking a step toward her.

Her fingers found the break in the wall behind her. She turned and dove into the opening, scrambled on her hands and knees down the narrow hole toward the hint of reflected light. Daylight? An exit? She hoped.

Her hope was rewarded this time. She burst from the tunnel belly down into blinding sunlight and damp air, almost too late realizing how very much air there was at the mouth of the tunnel and how little ledge. She looked down on the dark green waves of Lake Superior crashing over a boulder-strewn shoreline.

"That is one way down from the cave," the man who claimed to be Eric's clone said from behind her.

She scrambled onto her backside and pressed herself against the stone wall at the end of the ledge.

He squatted in the tunnel entrance, watching her. "If you survive the descent," he continued, "you'll still need to find a way to climb to the top of the bluff, and climbing is hard on the body."

He held up dirty, bruised, and scraped hands…except the center of that one palm where she'd seen the impossible.

"I thought you could heal things," she challenged, remembering the shaving nicks she'd convinced herself she'd only imagined.

He lowered his hands. "I concentrated on warding off the hypothermia."

"Yeah. Right."

He folded his fingers together. A glow visible between his fingers, even in the bright morning light. When he opened them, the bruises and abrasions were gone.

"I didn't imagine you healing your shaving nicks, did I?"

He shook his head.

"And my throat…after you choked me?"

He nodded.

A humorless laugh snorted from her. "And you really are a clone…unless I'm still in my nightmare."

He shook his head again. "No nightmare. Real."

She eyed him, looking for some telltale clue that he wasn't human but saw none. "What are you inside there, some little green man?"

"No little green man. Pure energy."

"Energy?"

"You would see me as light."

"Like the light in your hand?"

He nodded.

"So, you don't have a body."

"My people have evolved beyond the need for bodies."

"Evolved, huh?"

She hugged an arm across her stomach and lifted a chewed fingertip toward her mouth. But, the moment her fingertip touched her lower lip, she remembered what his lips had felt like brushing against hers. Eric's lips.

"You kissed me," she accused.

"That was a mistake."

"You kissed me."

"You were tempting. Touch is tempting. In my world, we do not know touch."

"I can't imagine a world without touch," she said, looking down at the water churning among the deadly rocks.

"Imagine a world of great intellect," he said.

"It sounds cold and unemotional," she said, squinting through the stars of sunlight reflecting off Superior's choppy, dark waters. She didn't know what to feel.

"Come with me, Woman."

"Tide's coming in," she murmured, wondering if death might still be preferable.

"Rebecca."

He sounded so much like Eric. She closed her eyes, wishing away the last nine months. Wishing it all to have been a bad dream or a colossal mistake.

"Let me take you home, Rebecca."

She opened her eyes. He'd extended his hand toward her…Eric's hand. She looked into the pale blue eyes, their corners creased with concern…as Eric's so often been. Ironic, that he should remind her most of Eric at the moment when she truly knew he wasn't the man she'd loved.

Yet, she took his hand and let him guide her back into the tunnel, back to the chamber where Eric had learned life lessons from Joe Tierney. She followed him and his glowing hand as he led her through the upward sloping, ever narrowing tunnel away from that place where a boy and a man had played at being boys.

She hadn't realized she was crying until he hauled her out of the narrow gap between moss-shrouded stones and onto the forest floor. There, in the damp depression deep in the forest, he captured one of her tears on a fingertip and brought it to his lips. Eric used to kiss away her tears.

And hold her.

And love her.

He tasted her tear, tasted the grief in its chemical blend…and other hormonally charged elements he didn't fully recognize. But he also tasted the hint of anger in its composition. He recognized it, not from the DNA of the body he wore, but because of his own experience with anger. It went beyond his being denied Merlin's mentorship. He'd spent the better part of his life suppressing an emotion that was all but banned in his society in the hopes of fitting in. Though, back then, he didn't know what he was angry about.

He studied her where she stood atop the rock, caught among the rays of sunlight filtering down through the evergreens. Even coated in dust and tangled with leaves, her burnished tresses captured the shafts of sunlight and made them dance in time to her movement. She was a beautiful creature who did not value life. Such a waste.

He stepped around the base of the stone outcrop, the mossy forest floor a spongy cushion beneath his feet, the autumn leaves rustling overhead, and the sunlight…bright with the light of life. He had to admit she was not the only thing of beauty in this world.

"I do not understand why you would want to give up all this over one lost life," he said.

She looked down at him, her voice when she spoke, tight and hard. "All this?" She swept her hand through the air. "You mean all this *physical* stuff?"

He nodded.

She snorted. "I thought you and your kind *evolved* beyond the need for the physical."

He climbed onto the stone beside her and lifted his face into the shafting sunlight that had made its way through the hardwoods and towering pines, lifting his face into its warmth. "You were right about my world being cold. There I would not be able to feel the sun on my face. Do you not value that?"

She shook her head.

He pointed at a yellow-leafed Poplar and a cluster of red-leafed Sumac. "Look at all the colors your world allows." He inhaled deeply. "Smell your air. It is rich with fragrance."

He took her by the shoulders and turned her into the breeze. "Listen to the wind in the pines. Your world sings."

Her shoulders didn't move beneath his hands, she didn't lift her face to the light, and she only barely sniffed the air before she responded. "Without love, you smell only the decay, you hear only the emptiness, you feel only the chill, and color is…just color. You should've let me die."

She ducked out from under his hands and started up the hill, her feet slipping on the pine needle strewn slope, her fingers scrabbling for underbrush.

"No wonder your kind are doomed to die off," he called after her. "You do not value life."

She spun at him and dug in her heels. "You're a fine one to talk about valuing life, coming to this world without knowing how to survive here. You would've eaten poison, if I hadn't stopped you. Then you tried to kill me for saving you."

"I thought you were attacking me and that you were expendable."

"I've proved not to be expendable to you, haven't I? But, to me, Eric was *not* expendable." She climbed the hill, moving farther away from him. "Eric cannot be replaced, so don't even try to take his place."

"I never intended to take his place."

She faltered ever so slightly in her climb.

"I meant only to borrow a body. Unfortunately, I erroneously borrowed the wrong one."

She spun at him, all but howling, "Your *borrowing* Eric's body was wrong for me, too. Why did you have to swim out after me?"

"I did not *have to.*"

"But you did."

That was true. He had gone after her, compelled by something other than reason. Something his kind would not condone.

"Why did you save me?" she demanded.

Because irrational need drove me after you.

Because I want to know what it is to be wanted as you want your Eric.

"Because you are still of use to me."

She was of use to him.

Rebecca stared at the yellow police tape inches from her face. She'd climbed the steep slope almost to the top of the bluff with that *you are of use to me* phrase buzzing in her ears. One more step, two at the most, and she'd be on top of the bluff…where a man had been chased or thrown to his death.

The police tape snapped in the wind atop the bluff, reminding her that the *man* climbing the slope behind her might well have killed one person who'd gotten in his way already. He'd almost killed her.

But she was alive now because she was of use to him. How was that for irony?

A lifetime of struggling to make herself at least needed, if not wanted in this foster home or that one, trying to find a place to fit in—a place she could call home. She'd come close at The Bluffs with Eric…who had never needed her enough.

But now he was dead, his grandmother wanted her out of her life and away from The Bluffs, and the only being who wanted her in any way was an alien clone.

An *alien.* Could she really believe what he told her—what she'd seen?

Did it matter?

She hoisted herself onto the rocky outcrop and stepped over the yellow tape. She stepped to the edge of the bluff above the narrow ledge entrance to Eric's cave and looked down. Below, the waves slapped against the rocks, swirled, and eddied. Dizzying. She could still end it all. She swayed.

But the wind off the lake careened up the bluff and slammed her back. Too bad she hadn't the energy left to fight for death.

She turned in the direction of the house and trudged off across the bluff, too numb to think or feel…or fear. She traipsed across stone worn smooth by the wind and polished slick by watershed. She trod through the woods stretching between bald rock and the bluff house. She strode from the woods, across the yard, and onto the deck. She said nothing. Neither did the alien in Eric's skin until she reached for the kitchen door.

"I need Joe's older journals," he said as he caught up to her.

Her hand froze on the doorknob. She hadn't hesitated to give him Joe's later journals because she'd thought they would help Eric remember his past…when she still thought he was Eric. But this…man…wasn't Eric and she wondered if she should show the cloned alien, who had choked her unconscious and might well have murdered a man, anything more at all.

She turned between him and the door, and looked him in his Eric-blue eyes. "Why do you need Joe's old journals?"

"People in my world have begun to die. The Elite, the leaders of my world believe it is from an air-born virus brought back from the physical world. To recreate the antidote, we need a rare element. There is only one known piece of this element remaining and it was hidden in your world. I've come to retrieve it, and I believe the clue to its location is in Joe's journals."

He'd answered so immediately, so directly it made her believe he spoke the truth…or had well-rehearsed his lie.

"And you need to find this antidote within the next four days."

"Yes. At midnight four nights from now," he explained. "Orbital paths that will enable me to transport a physical object will line up."

She faced him, arms folded over her chest. "What will the removal of this *object* do to the future of my world?"

"Nothing. It has no bearing on your world."

"Yet it is here. Why?"

He hesitated ever so briefly before answering. "It was brought here by an explorer of my kind. Returning visitors needed it to inoculate themselves upon reentry into our world."

"There are other visitors here?" she asked.

He sighed. "The Visitor Program was terminated some time ago when exploration into the physical world was deemed meritless."

"What happened to the remaining supplies of this inoculation stuff?"

"The Elite ordered all sources of the element destroyed to discourage further exploration."

She huffed. "Not too smart for an advanced society."

His chin came up defensively, though concession laced his tone. "It was a mistake. Will you help me rectify that mistake?"

She studied him a moment, pondering whether or not a world that had *evolved* beyond love should be saved. Then again, look what the quest for love had done to her.

She turned away from him and reached for the doorknob. "I'll think about it."

His hand closed over hers, keeping her from opening the door, and his breath whispered against her ear, he stood so close. "I do not need you to find the journals. I can find them on my own now that I know what I am looking for."

She stood there between him and the door, her hand trapped in mid-turn. "Then what do you need me for?"

"Perhaps I don't."

She shook off his hand, opened the door, and charged into the kitchen. He followed, heading straight for the stairs.

"You should eat something before you pass out from low blood sugar," she called after him.

He paused, one foot on a step, his hand on the railing, and looked at her. "Why do you care if I pass out?"

She opened her mouth to respond. But no words formed that made sense, not when he was no longer Eric.

She closed her mouth and shook her head. "I guess I don't care."

But she did. The fact nagged her through her shower. It nagged her as she pulled fresh jeans and a t-shirt from the dresser for herself and stared into Eric's empty drawers.

It nagged her as she picked at the peanut butter and jelly sandwich she'd made for herself. She'd thought she'd had enough peanut butter and jelly to last a lifetime…until Eric had come back to her and found a passion in peanut butter.

But he wasn't Eric.

Except in body.

She couldn't stop worrying about that body poking around the attic in its dirty, rumpled clothes. She couldn't stop worrying that he might have swallowed enough lake water to make him sick.

And she couldn't stop worrying that he needed to eat.

Why *did* she care?

Her hand slid across her abdomen, an involuntary action that suggested an answer…a stunning, insane answer.

She bolted up the steps to the second floor, barely slowing as she took the turn to the attic steps. She stopped when she reached the top of the stairs. He was bent over a trunk, tossing out its contents.

"You won't find Joe's journals in there."

He straightened from the trunk, his hair tousled, his clothes rumpled, his eyes wary. "I found no others in his desk."

He watched her through those intoxicating, Eric-like eyes as she made her way through a maze of opened trunks, emptied boxes, and pulled out dresser drawers, their contents strewn across the floor. Not her doing, this mess. She'd always been meticulous about restoring them to their original order. An expert interloper, she knew to cover her tracks. Knew to never give those whose lives she encroached upon—whose pasts and presents she borrowed—reason to send her away.

She stopped in front of him, looked him in the eye, and thumped him on the chest. "What happens to this body when you leave?"

"It dies."

Her heart stuttered a beat, though it was the answer she'd expected. But she'd had to make sure before she proposed the outrageous.

"Give me what I want, and I'll show you where the rest of Joe's journals are."

"I told you, I don't need your help." He turned to the next box.

"Yes, you do. You're wasting time searching here and you haven't the time to waste."

He tore the lid from the box, seeming to ignore her. But his mouth tightened.

"By your own calculations," she pressed, "you have to leave four nights from now and you haven't even found the clue to where to find what you came to retrieve."

He lifted out a shoebox and tossed it aside, old bank receipts spilling across the floor. Apparently, he'd learned enough to know Joe's journals wouldn't fit in such small boxes.

"What if the journals don't tell you where to look?"

"They'll tell me," he muttered.

She stepped close to his side as he rummaged through the remaining contents of the box. "What if your object is hidden someplace not readily accessible? What if you need time to get to it?"

His hands stilled, his ear cocked toward her.

"I can help you by getting those journals for you right now."

He straightened, and looked her in the eye. "What makes you think I can't force the information out of you?"

"What can you threaten me with, death?" she said, meeting his gaze without blinking. "You know I'd rather die."

"There are worse things than death," he said.

"I know. I'm living it now."

His eyes narrowed. "My people communicate telepathically. What makes you think I can't get inside your head and probe your mind?"

She hadn't thought about any of that before. But she did now and took a gamble. "Because, if you could do that, you'd have done it by now."

The corner of one eye twitched. Bingo. She'd guessed right. He couldn't get inside her head, at least not without invitation. Time to make him the offer.

"You can't *take* the information from me, but I will trade it."

His head tipped an interested angle. "Trade?"

"You give me what I want and I'll give you what you want."

"You want me to kill you?"

"Or give me a reason to live."

His eyebrows hitched higher onto his forehead. "What can I give you that would make you want to live?"

"Eric's baby."

Chapter Twelve

What she wanted required that he copulate with her. The idea sent the blood flying through his veins…yet made the muscles at the hinges of his jaw clench. "What makes you think I would agree to leave a child in your world?"

"A few hours ago, you said my world was warm and full of texture and color. You said it smelled good." She jutted her little chin at him. "We have peanut butter."

He grunted. "You are an emotional species bound by antiquated instincts."

"Why should you care? It's Eric's DNA I'm asking you to give me."

Eric's DNA. All along, it had been Eric's DNA she'd fed and cleaned. Eric's DNA she'd saved from eating poison. Eric's DNA she'd protected. Not his.

She lifted her chin another degree. "You need the information I have if you are to save your world."

"The end justifies the means," he said, not sure why her rationale bothered him. After all, it had been her thinking he was Eric that had prompted her to save him and take care of him. Whatever her motive—her end, it had served him. If copulating with her expedited his getting Joe's journals, that would serve his end and, in the process, he'd experience something none in his world had ever returned to tell of.

There was a warning in that reasoning. But he seemed unable to hear it above the hammering of blood in his ears, unable to see it in the green eyes gazing up at him, those thirst-quenching eyes. Such hope they held.

And need.

He had never known what it was to be needed until he'd volunteered for this mission. Before then, he'd been the one in need—in need of Merlin's teaching, in need of an expertise that would make him valuable to his world—in need of being needed. He was needed now.

Her aura shimmered uncertainly and her shoulders pulled in on her as she bit at a hangnail and he smelled her blood. She was so needy, so in need of him.

He drew her fingers from her mouth, closed his hand around them, and concentrated his energy there.

"Why do you bother?" she asked, her voice a thin whisper.

"Because it pains you."

"The pain of losing Eric is unbearable. Fix that."

"I can't bring him back to you, even if I wanted to."

"But you can give me a piece of him."

He released her fingers. "No more hurt."

Rebecca looked at her fingertips and found their cracks closed and the redness gone. Eric had never scolded her for her nail biting. Unlike his grandmother, his approach had been supportive, supportive enough that she'd often gone long stretches without biting her nails to the quick. Eric had always been able to make her feel better. But he'd never been able to heal her.

But this alien could.

She pressed unsteady fingers into the hollow between her breasts, the threadbare fabric of her t-shirt stretching across her thudding heart. Eric's dust-smudged fingers flexed in the air between them.

No, not Eric's fingers. Those fingers with less than perfectly manicured nails weren't Eric's. Not that Eric minded getting a little dirt beneath his nails now and then. Corporate leader notwithstanding, he never apologized for a callus or two.

But he was ever mindful of keeping those nails clean. Just as Rebecca was ever aware of the chewed down state of her own. No space there for the common dirt his grandmother equated with her to collect.

Jetty strands of Eric's hair brushed the collar of his blue shirt. *Baby*-blue. Not quite the shade of Eric's eyes. Yet, she couldn't make herself look away from him.

Nor did he look away, this creature wearing the DNA of her dead husband, who was virtually no different from the husband with whom she'd made love in this very house.

She ached to press her body to his. She ached to stroke his coal-colored hair and press her mouth to his Adonis-like lips. She ached to climb his rock-hard terrain, open herself to him and take him inside her.

Eric, that is. Not this man. But he was Eric. Or was Eric now him?

Confusion spun through Rebecca, stirring up the moats of her conflicting thoughts and emotions. Like the explorations of an alien clone who had disturbed the layers of dust draping four generations of storage in an attic.

Alien?

Clone?

She had to be crazy.

Besides, she didn't even know if he could function in that capacity.

Wrong. She knew. *Everything* appeared functional when he'd shed his clothes in the shower and pressed his naked body to hers. He possessed the ability to do what she asked of him.

But, would it be a betrayal to Eric to make love to this man who was Eric only in body? Was it betrayal to know she'd willingly receive the fruits of this male's body?

Not if she accepted the body as Eric's. And it was Eric's flesh down to its last atom…if she believed this strange man was indeed Eric's clone.

And she did. She needed to…or die.

She swayed toward the man standing in Eric's skin, his heat a gauzy web reaching out to her. He could heal her, all of her. He could leave with her a piece of her beloved Eric, this creature from another world.

"Please," she murmured.

He touched her cheek, her sweet, soft cheek. She closed her eyes and pressed the side of her face into his palm. Her bright, silky curls slipped across the back of his hand.

She was so very tempting to him. Her with the blues of her spirit surging about her, banishing the dying grays of her aura, an aura now spiked with orange vitality, red passion, healing green. Hues those of his world could only sense. Hues he didn't know existed.

Colors *he* restored to her with his touch.

This is what it was to have someone need you—want you. This musky scent rising from her. Her aching moan. Her throbbing pulse. The hum of an electrical charge that built in her body and jumped to his. Her body called to his.

An alarm tingled up the back of his neck. But, one look into her soft, sea foam green eyes and it was muffled. Then she stroked her fingertip across his lower lip, a touch so light it made him want to beg for more.

Her hand brushed his cheek. Her knuckles skimmed his ear. Her fingers wove through the hair at the nape of his neck.

In some part of his brain, alarms sounded. But the antiquated body governed by primal instinct would not heed the warning, not when she was pulling his face toward hers.

Her lips parted an instant before they touched his. The tip of her tongue slipped along the seam between his lips. She tasted of peanut butter and something else sweet and cool. She tasted of longing, of need, of lust.

The creature he'd become in this physical form reacted. He parted his lips and accepted her tongue. She tickled the roof of his mouth, titillated the carnal core of a creature made extinct in his world.

Timeless instinct dictated he take possession of her, that he commit to memory that which was now his. He took her into his arms, his hands mapping the points of her shoulder blades, the curve of her spine, and the flare of her hips. His palm cupped her behind and he pressed her close, pressed that hot delta of hers against his throbbing need. He needed to link with her.

He groaned into the cavity of her mouth.

She tore at the fastenings on the front of his pants and dragged him down onto a pile of old quilts with her.

"Eric," she murmured against his mouth.

A chill shot through him, cooling the blood flying toward that one point in his body that would take him someplace he'd never dreamed possible. He only wanted to couple with the woman. He only wanted to experience the pleasure of the flesh…and expedite the locating of Joe's journals. It shouldn't matter that she spoke another's name.

But it did.

It was enough to allow him to hear the alarms clanging inside his head, louder and sharper than the siren song of the woman's body. There was a reason why none in his world could boast of having sampled the carnal flesh. Those that had tasted the forbidden never returned. They had stayed in the physical world. They had remained mortal flesh and died as a result.

He pulled away from her, leaving her reaching for him, crying out, "What's wrong?"

"I will not be trapped."

"I'm not trying to trap you," she said steadying herself.

"You are a trap, you with the pleasures of the flesh."

"No. I just want Eric's baby. You will be free to leave. I want you to leave."

He jerked back as though she'd physically struck him. But it was her words that had struck the blow. They hit him square in his hungry soul—in that hungry spot where he wanted to know what it was like to be so badly needed by someone that she would rather die than live on without him.

"Please," she cried out, her fingers closing on his wrist.

A shock wave of soul-wrenching ache jolted up his arm from her fingers, the ache of loss and longing, of loneliness and despair. Feelings all too familiar to him. Even the self-recrimination he heard inside his head seemed familiar, though it was so gender specific this reproach had to be hers.

"Why do you call yourself whore?" he asked.

Rebecca let go of his wrist and staggered back against a chimney, scraping her elbows on the rough bricks. She wanted to shake her head against that label, to deny it.

When Eric had introduced her to his grandmother as his intended bride, Lucille had accused her of trapping him. Lucille had called her a whore. As did the last woman who'd fostered her the night she'd caught her husband trying to crawl into Rebecca's bed. Given that she was about to open herself to a stranger the way she had only to Eric, it must be true.

Even if he'd genetically replicated Eric's body. Eric wasn't just a body. Yet, that was precisely what her grief and need had reduced him to. What she'd reduced this creature to…this man who'd come here to save his world.

"I'm sorry," she whispered, her eyes lowered. "I shouldn't have asked you to… You have more important things to do than…"

She stepped out from between him and the chimney. She couldn't face him— had to get away from him.

"You need to get out of those musty clothes," she murmured as she made her way toward the stairway. "You should take a hot shower."

"But…"

"I'll get the journals while you shower," she said, weaving her way away from him.

"And then you expect me to impregnate you?"

She stopped at the top of the stairway but did not look back. "No. I don't deserve Eric's child. I realize that now. You have something important to do. You have people to save."

He'd followed her down to the second floor. He'd wanted to chase the reproachful thoughts from her head. Even now, after showering and wrapping himself in a towel, knowing what his first priority must be, he still felt the need to comfort her.

He found her in Joe's and Lucille's bedroom. She stood in front of an open drawer of a tall chest of drawers, stroking a black t-shirt she cradled in her arm.

"It's one of Joe's," she said, looking up at him, offering it to him. "The shirts you wore of Eric's are both dirty. This one of Joe's should fit you."

He took the shirt from her.

She closed the dresser drawer, her fingers lingering on the brass drawer pulls. She raised shimmering eyes at him. "Lucille kept all Joe's things in place after he died."

He didn't understand why that mattered to her. But then, he didn't understand why he cared about her pain.

She glanced at the shirt dangling from his fist. "I've laid out an old pair of Eric's jeans on the bed in our—my room for you to wear...and set out your deck shoes."

"I need special shoes for walking on the deck?"

She shook her head. "It's just a term for rubber soled shoes."

"Loafers you don't loaf in and deck shoes not specific to decks. You have a complicated language for your objects."

A sad smile pulled across her lips. "Yeah. We're weird that way. Comes with living in a physical world."

"Of course."

"Joe's older journals," she said, opening the cedar chest at the foot of the bed. "They're in there, on the bottom. I found them during one of our visits here when Eric asked me to get a quilt from the chest. I was only interested in the more current ones in his desk—the ones that covered the time Eric lived with him and Lucille."

She met his gaze. "It was Eric I wanted to know about."

"I understand."

"Eric that I wanted you to remember because I thought you were him."

She had a good heart. He saw that in her aura. He saw, too, that her heart hurt, had seen the dark spike above it in the attic when she'd attempted to seduce him. "Who called you a whore?"

Rebecca blanched. "How can you know about that?"

"I heard it here," he said, tapping the side of her head.

She shrank away from him, breaking contact. "I thought you couldn't read my mind."

"I can, if invited to."

"Up in the attic, I didn't invite— I wasn't telling you— I wouldn't have said—"

"That word?"

She took another step back from him. "How did you know I was thinking it?"

"In this world, do you not call out when you are in need of help?"

"We yell *help*, not..." She let the statement fade, still unable to say that one shameful word.

"Sometimes, strong distress gets transmitted to all within range to help."

"Help?" She eyed the man who had let her retreat from him without following, wondering how this man of logic—this man who'd nearly choked her to death, could now display such compassion. Suspicious of his shift in perspective, she asked, "What makes you think I need your help over a word?"

"Because words that label one hurt."

"And you know this because?"

Pain flickered in his Eric-blue eyes. "I have my own labels; labels that, in my world, are as distasteful to me as whore is to you."

She winced. Maybe he did understand, yet she challenged, "Your *advanced* society sounds like it's no better than mine."

"In some ways, it is not."

She tilted a dubious chin at him. "If they malign you, why then do you serve them?"

"For the same reason you allow the labeling of two rigid old women to affect you. You want them to see they are wrong. You want their approval."

She started to protest. But he was right. She did want those who'd labeled her a whore to see they were wrong. She even wanted Lucille's approval. She now saw she wasn't the only one in the room seeking approval.

"Wanting approval is emotionally driven, correct?" she asked.

"Yes."

"That you want the approval of those of your world, doesn't that make you emotionally driven?"

"That I have latent emotions is my failing."

"Who made you feel inferior because you had feelings?"

"No one had to *make* me feel inferior. I am."

"By whose definition?"

"The Elite decreed it long ago in our mission statement; that the goal of all beings is to strive toward perfection and emotion obstructs pure logic."

"And pure logic is perfection?"

"Yes."

"If your kind *needs* to strive for perfection, does that not imply you have egos? Doesn't an ego imply self-awareness and would that not be emotion driven?"

He sucked in a breath. "We are evolving."

"Your kind are dying."

His head jerked back as though she'd struck a blow.

She took a step toward him. "You seek the approval from a society predicated on pure logic yet is still driven to rank its beings by degrees of imperfection. Ranking people implies a need to make one's self more important than another. Such a need is emotionally driven."

His brows knitted together.

"Your Elite are not perfect."

The furrows in his brow deepened. Here was a man who had come from an advanced society, who had evolved beyond the need for a body, who could heal bruised and torn flesh yet found himself lacking...just as she did herself. She had spent her life trying to be the perfect child, the perfect woman, the perfect wife. For the first time, the impossibility of perfection struck her.

Her logic had echoed his own questions, questions he'd never dared explore for fear of...

Of what? Finding out his world was flawed? That they were wrong to deny emotions—wrong in doing away with one-on-one student/mentor alignments? Logically, he understood. Had his and Merlin's relationship been founded on destruction, their bonding was dangerous. But it had been purely about learning, student from mentor.

Wrong. They'd had an emotional bond. Something he recognized when he'd read Joe's writings about his relationship with Eric. There was a similarity in how Merlin spoke to him and how Joe wrote about Eric. He missed that connection.

Still, an entire world needed his help and he had no time to dwell on his own longings.

The evidence filled the library at mid-day when Rebecca brought him a sandwich and milk. Her aura, her expression, the tone of her voice slapped against him like the turbulent waters of Lake Superior against its rocky shore. He couldn't afford the distraction of all her emotions.

She appeared in the library doorway, pausing there until he glanced up from the journal spread open on the desk, before asking, "Have you read them all?"

He nodded, too frustrated about his lack of progress to care what her emotional energy did to him. "I'm certain the key must be in the first journal, though."

"Why?" she asked, settling a shoulder against the doorframe.

"The year coincides with when The Capsule would've had to be hidden."

"Is there something in there that seems like a clue to you?"

He shook his head. "Nothing obvious, and I'd expect the clue to be more recognizable to my kind." He thumped a knuckle against the journal. "But I sense it has to be here."

"Sense it? You? The man of logic?"

He shrugged and flipped through the pages of the journal. "Maybe there's use to instinct after all."

"Admitted the perfect being from the perfect world," she said.

He looked up at her, saw the playful slant of her lips. He couldn't resist the upward pull of his own lips as he returned, "I thought we agreed neither of our worlds was perfect."

Her smile faded. "Maybe it's not in the journals."

He shook his head. "Putting the clue in the journals makes the most sense."

"You've pointed out that we humans aren't always as logical as your people."

"Joe was logical."

She straightened from the doorframe. "What makes you so sure?"

She was growing more logical. Asking more logical questions, questions he wasn't sure she needed to know the whole truth of. He settled for half the truth. "Joe was meticulous in his record keeping."

She nodded. "Maybe it'll come to you if you take a break, rest—"

"I have no time for resting." He tapped the journal page open before him. "Maybe if I knew why these words are capitalized."

She moved to his side, leaned over his shoulder, and read the entry he pointed out.

"The Fishhawk is a boat," she said.

"A boat?"

"It's the name of a boat." She tapped the tip of her index finger against the entry. "See how it says *The* Fishhawk. *The* in front of a capitalized word usually denotes the name of something."

"Usually, but not always?"

"Sometimes it's capitalized because it's at the beginning of a sentence. Sometimes out of poetic license."

"There are several words in these journals capitalized in the middle. Are these what you call *poetic license?"*

"Doubtful. Let me see them."

He slid out of the desk chair and motioned her into it. Leaning over her, he flipped through pages, pointing out the words in question. Peg*A*sus. U*R*sa Major. Aquil*A*.

"These are constellations," she said of the words with the oddly placed capitalizations. "And there's nothing poetic about putting caps within their names."

"But some do not have capitals within their names." He said. "Like here. Draco and Cassi*O*peia. The capital appears only in the second constellation. And here." He pointed out Androme*D*a and Cepheus. "The abnormality appears in the first name but not the second. And in Lyra, Serpe*N*s, and Hercules, it appears in the middle name only."

She peered up at him. "A code perhaps?"

"Logical."

"Read off the capitalized letters within the constellations," she said sliding the journal towards him and pulling out a sheet of paper.

"N, O, R, D, and two As," he recited and she wrote.

"Were they in any particular order?" she asked.

He named the letters in the order they appeared in the journal. "A, R, O, D, N, A."

"Arodna. Does that mean anything to you?" she asked.

"No," he answered, zeroing on a notation near the front of the book.

She glanced up at him. "Are those the letters from front to back?"

"No. Back to front."

"If I flip them around, they spell ANDORA," she said. "That's a country in Southern Europe…though it would be misspelled. Could you be looking for a country?"

He shook his head. "It would not be far from here."

"It could be a ship, too, I suppose."

"A*P*tomia," he said, flipping to the back of the journal and tapping the notation.

"I don't recognize that constellation," she said.

"You wouldn't. It's from my world."

"How would Joe know of a constellation from your world?"

Another direct question. He frowned. Considered how to answer—how much to reveal. If he left a child in her womb—in this world, it could likely carry his DNA as well as hers and her Eric's. There were things he should reveal to her.

He raised an eyebrow at her. "I am not the first Visitor to your world. Was that not implied when I explained about the inoculations?"

"Yeah," she said, puzzling out what that meant. "Joe knew one of you, too?"

He should answer her. But he had a duty to the beings of his world.

The needs of the many.

Now was not the time for revelations that would distract Rebecca from the job at hand.

He tapped the name of the foreign-to-this-world constellation, stating, "The capitalized letter is P. That is the first letter in the name. P-A-N-D-O-R-A."

"Pandora," she said in a tight voice.

"Is that bad?"

"We have a myth here about a woman named Pandora who released all the evils of the world from a box she'd been warned not to open." Her eyes widened at him. "Just what is it I'm helping you find?"

"Immortality," he said.

"Nine months too late for Eric," she muttered, sagging into the back of the chair.

"Perhaps I put that too simply," he said in a tight voice, knowing whose immortality Rebecca wished for, remembering how it felt to have those sea-green eyes gaze wondrously at him when she'd thought he was Eric.

A powerful lure, to be everything to another being. A dangerous temptation, an attraction that places the needs of one above the many. It made him want to know the kind of bond that, when lost, made one want to surrender life.

That was exactly what had happened to those who went exploring from his world and never returned. They had chosen to surrender their lives. He could not. A world of beings depending on him to save him.

He paced to the far side of the desk and faced her. "Consider an advanced society. Pure energy. Pure intellect. Our great thinkers ponder the mysteries of the universe. We debate the reasons for cultures going extinct. We have learned to avoid the mistakes others have made. We have earned the right to immortality."

"Are you so sure your culture hasn't outlived its usefulness?"

He gaped at her, to raise such a question went beyond forbidden.

"Maybe your kind have come full circle in its evolution," she added, leaning forward and bracing her elbows on the desk. "Maybe it is your culture's time to become extinct."

He shook his head against the hypothesis she proposed, even though it suggested a reason his people's energy had started to die off. "We are not meant to go extinct. We are perfect."

"They don't consider you perfect. You said so yourself."

And there was the logic. If *all* his kind were perfect, how could he have been corrupted by seeking knowledge? Was that not the purpose of his species? All he'd done was ask questions.

The wrong ones, apparently. Perhaps The Elite wasn't as open to all knowledge as he'd been led to believe. Perhaps they had evolved into self-serving agents focused on proving their own theories. That Merlin, one of the oldest and once most revered among them, had been pushed aside because of his unrestricted teachings evidenced that.

"They consider bodies of no use," she said. "Yet they send you here where you need a body to do their bidding."

"It is a means to an end," he said almost absently, taking in her reasoning.

"Ah yes. You're to retrieve an antidote, a *tangible* object that will ensure the continuation of a species who have decreed bodies useless, yet a body is what you need to accomplish your task."

"I am beginning to see bodies are not useless. But, they are cumbersome and demanding of care."

A melancholy smile carved at the corners of her lips. "Bothersome enough to *evolve* beyond?"

"We evolved away from the physical for many reasons," he answered quickly, before he condemned all his kind for eons of flawed thinking.

"And you believe yourself better off for it?"

"I'm more efficient without a body," he said, clinging to a lifetime of beliefs— to the fact that his perfect Merlin had given up his body.

"You can return to your world and never miss *peanut butter*?"

He drew a deep breath, knowing he would never forget peanut butter…or her. And there was the most dangerous flaw of her world. "In my world, we would never become so attached to anything that we would rather die than live on without it."

"Attachments don't make you want to die," she said, her voice low, thin. "Having someone taken from you that you love—someone who was your entire purpose—that's what makes you want to give up on life. But, given death is unnatural to your kind, you've never lost anyone to compare my grief to."

Remembering how it felt when he was denied Merlin's mentorship, his chest tightened. "I have had my losses."

Her eyes widened. "Someone you loved?"

"We do not love."

"Love isn't about bodily function. Why wouldn't you have love in your society?"

"Such attachments are dangerous. Bonding in smaller groups weakens the greater mass, creates confusion."

"When you suffered these…losses, did you grieve them?"

"Grief is distracting."

"Did it not leave a hollow feeling inside you?"

He recalled his anger when access to Merlin was denied him…and what had come after. He gave a small nod.

"That's grief," she said.

He shook his head. "You grieve and it makes you want to die. I do not want to die."

She rose from her seat. "Because you still have a purpose. You need to retrieve something that will save your species." Her eyelids slipped low over her eyes. "I have no reason to live on."

"Is that why you want Eric's baby?"

She circled the desk to him. "I want Eric's baby so I can have a part of him with me again."

"So you will have a reason to go on with life. So your life will have a purpose."

Merlin had urged him to find purpose when he'd been stuck in anger and grief. Purpose was at the root of why he'd volunteered for this mission, because he needed to prove his mentor hadn't been wrong in sharing knowledge beyond the accepted criteria.

Purpose. Now that he fully understood his motivation, he could understand her need for something to live for.

Chapter Thirteen

What he said about why she wanted Eric's baby crystalized what Rebecca had known all along. In life, she'd had no purpose beyond serving Eric's needs. That's why, in death, she still clung to him, unable to leave his ashes in his childhood home with those of his grandfather. She'd even said it herself when bargaining with the wearer of Eric's DNA for Eric's baby, not because she wanted a baby, but because she wanted a piece of Eric.

He looked at her with infinite compassion and fingered a lock of hair off her cheek. "If I accomplish my mission ahead of schedule, I will give you your purpose, Rebecca. I will impregnate you with your Eric's baby. This I promise."

From the darkness of her subconscious, a thought scratched its way into the light. Was that why Lucille had clung to Eric after his parents' death and her beloved Joe's death? Would Eric's child assuage her grief?

Or, would she too become possessive and bitter like Lucille?

Studying the earnestness in the eyes of the man who'd traveled across galaxies to save his world, she was certain of one thing. Whatever the outcome, she had purpose for the next few days, though not the one she'd thought she'd needed.

"We need to find out what The Pandora is," she said.

He flipped to a page in one of the shipwreck books on the desk. "Could it be this ship?"

She read the passage he pointed to. "She's deep. Too deep to be attractive to the weekend diver. Nothing valuable in her cargo that would interest the professionals, either." She tapped the last line in the paragraph giving the ship's general location. "She's not the most stable wreck. She's on the edge of a trench. Part of her has already broken off and fallen into it. A dangerous dive for even the most skilled."

"That would make The Pandora a good place to hide something you do not want easily found," he said.

"What if The Capsule is in the section that's slipped into that trench?"

"This is not a problem," he said.

She studied him. So normal, so human looking. Yet, so capable of non-human things. She'd almost forgotten what he was capable of, this man who believed the end justified the means.

She touched his arm. "You're not going to commandeer some mini-sub or diving bell to retrieve your object, are you?" *And kill more people in the process.*

He looked her in the eye, a sadness in his that reached into her heart and made her regret doubting him. "I do not need to forcibly take control of your machines to accomplish my mission. I have other options available to me."

"Of course you do," she returned, wanting to believe him…needing to believe he would not easily take a life.

He thumped the volume on shipwrecks in front of them. "How do we find this Pandora?"

She read, noting, "It doesn't say exactly where along the trench it sunk. We're going to have to search Lake Superior archives at a maritime museum for that information, or maybe through the Coast Guard." She frowned. "Better if we avoid the Coast Guard. They're like police."

He grunted agreement.

"If only I had Eric's laptop," she said.

"Laptop?"

"Computer. Do you know what a computer is?"

"An antiquated mode of information gathering via the Internet."

"Close enough."

"Where do we find a computer?"

"The local library amounts to little more than a couple rooms of books in a private residence. I doubt they'll be hooked up, but I can call them and find out. My cell phone is in the kitchen."

She was about to step into the hall when *Eric* said, "Sonny."

"What about Sonny?" she asked, turning back to him, finding him looking out the library window.

She followed the trajectory of his gaze. There, outside on the deck, nose pressed to the glass, stood Sonny.

What was he doing here? It could have just as easily been Sheriff Wickes who'd snuck up on them and seen the alien wearing Eric's DNA. Gooseflesh prickled up her arms as she raised her hand and spread her fingers in a half-hearted greeting. At least Sonny had already met this Eric.

Sonny lifted his face from the window and nodded toward the deck-side door. Rebecca hurried into the hall entry, intent on turning Sonny away. But Sonny hadn't come alone. Visible beyond the windowed door was the stout figure of Sonny's mother. Flora smiled through the glass at her. There would be no turning Flora away.

Rebecca opened the door and greeted her guests through a forced smile. "Flora. Sonny."

"Guess you didn't hear us knocking at the back door," Flora said, stepping into the hall, a foil covered plate in hand. "Knowing you two were in town, I had to make one of my homemade apple strudels for you."

"Apple strudel," the alien said, joining them—taking the plate from Flora, holding it to his nose, and sniffing. "Apple good. Juicy. Sweet." He looked at Rebecca. "What is strudel?"

"A pastry," she said. "Sweet."

Flora folded Rebecca in her cushioned arms, murmuring in her ear, "Sonny told me Eric had an accident."

Caught in Flora's motherly embrace, Rebecca wanted to confess everything. She wanted to tell Flora about the plane crash. She wanted to talk about the emptiness of widowhood with a woman who knew that loneliness.

Rebecca wanted to weep away the grief no one else had bothered to understand.

But to tell Flora the whole truth about Eric meant explaining that the man standing in front of her bearing the likeness of a dead man was an alien clone. Given that alien would accomplish his mission at any cost, such a revelation could turn bad for Flora and Sonny.

Sniffing back her tears, Rebecca disengaged herself and motioned everyone into the parlor. Too late to turn Flora and Sonny away. At least her *Eric* seemed more interested in sampling apple strudel than murdering an old woman and a simple-minded man whose visit interrupted his mission.

She followed the trio into the parlor. Sonny circled the room like a prizefighter dancing out of reach of his opponent while Flora turned on Eric and took the plate of strudel from him.

"Let's put that down so I can give you a hug."

Hug...for the alien who didn't like to be touched?

Flora had him in one of her cushy embraces before Rebecca could react. *Eric* towered above Flora's silver-haired head, arms akimbo, his eyes asking Rebecca's instruction. She hugged her arms across her stomach. Gingerly, he crossed his arms around Flora's shoulders.

Flora gave Eric's ribs a little pinch as she released him. "Nothing wrong with you that a little pastry can't fix." Her eyes shimmered with unshed tears in Rebecca's direction. "Would you get a knife to slice the strudel with, dear?"

Rebecca nodded and hurried through the house to the kitchen. She didn't like leaving Flora and Sonny alone with her alien. What if he said something incriminating? What if he found their questions threatening?

Rebecca closed her fingers around the first handle they touched in the knife drawer and rushed back toward the parlor. From the hall she heard a shrill, "You're going to break your neck."

Rebecca bolted into the parlor, pulse pounding.

"That's what your grandmother always said when she'd catch you climbing my apple tree," Flora finished in her natural voice.

"No broken neck," Eric's clone recited from the couch where he sat, an arm draping the back of the couch behind Flora's head. "Just one broken arm."

Rebecca stopped breathing. How could he know that the real Eric had once fallen from the Lindstrom's apple tree and broken his arm? For one dazzling moment, that part of her still clinging to the impossible wondered if this whole alien business wasn't some colossal creation of an amnesiac's blank mind. That Eric might yet be Eric.

Flora wagged a chubby finger at Eric. "Lucille would've liked to have chewed my head off over that accident."

"Joe considered the event a passage of boyhood," Eric's clone responded.

Passage of boyhood.

Rebecca had seen that inscribed some place. Where?

In one of Joe's journals.

"Hey Becks, you plannin' on fighting us for the first slice of Ma's strudel?"

Rebecca gaped at Sonny who was bobbing from foot to foot at the far end of the couch…where Eric's urn still lay on its side, his ashes spilled across the tabletop. But it was the way Sonny's bright eyes flicked from her face to the vicinity of her breasts that snagged her attention. She glanced down and saw she held the biggest knife the Tierney kitchen boasted in a death grip.

She forced a chuckle and mentally nudged herself forward toward the tea table where the strudel waited. "You asked for a knife and I deliver."

Before she could relinquish the utensil to Flora's capable hands, though, Sonny made one of his hundred and eighty degree turns onto another topic.

"That was Arnie Johnson they found dead at the bottom of your bluff."

The knife clattered against the marble tabletop.

Flora shook her head. "Poor man. Been drowning himself in the bottle ever since the mines shut down. Which is why I never liked you hanging out with him." She shook a finger at Sonny, then folded her hands back in her lap and sighed, the strudel forgotten. "Looks like Arnie finally did himself in for good this time."

Rebecca rubbed sweaty palms together. "Have they come up with a cause of death yet? Could he have drowned and washed up on the shore at the bottom of the bluff?"

"Superior don't never give up her dead," Sonny said, trailing a fingertip through the ash spilled on the end table. Then he grinned at her. "Don't cha know?"

Oh, she knew all right. Glacially deep Lake Superior was too cold for the usual gaseous transformations that brought a body to the surface to take place.

"Appears he fell," Flora offered.

"Or was pushed," Sonny interjected.

Eric's clone drew his arm from the back of the couch and leaned forward, forearms braced on his knees. He looked ready to spring to his feet.

Flora lifted her face toward her son. "That could have been you, young man. You were out mighty late that night, chasing your funny lights in the sky. I better never hear you've been scampering about them bluffs in the dark."

Sonny's eyes pinned *Eric*. "Arnie had bruises on his neck."

Though his face remained impassive, Eric's clone's fingers tightened into fists.

"I heard the collar of his shirt was burned off," Sonny elaborated.

The clone's eyes narrowed at Sonny.

"Probably got struck by lightning," Flora said.

"Lightning," Rebecca repeated, her fingers straying to her throat, remembering what it felt like to have the life squeezed from her.

"He coulda been murdered," Sonny chirped. "Yeah. Maybe he saw something he shouldn't have."

Eric locked eyes with Sonny. Rebecca didn't like the interest he was taking in Flora's son.

"Keep talking like that young man," Flora said in her best mother-is-laying-down-the-law voice, "and I'll take your computer away from you. All that cyber-sleuthing business is giving you ideas."

"Not my computer, Ma," Sonny groaned, breaking eye contact with *Eric*.

"You're all I have left." Flora's voice cracked.

Sonny snorted. "Can't keep me from chasing down UFOs."

Flora threw her hands into the air. *Eric* fingered the handle of the knife on the coffee table. Rebecca chewed a nail.

Sonny circled the couch, stopping directly in front of her and Eric. "You guys see them weird lights up here the night before they found Arnie?"

Flora moaned. *Eric* picked up the knife she'd brought to cut the pastry with… that big, sharp knife.

Rebecca swallowed hard. "It was storming that night, Sonny," she said, glancing between the man of another world and the man with the mind of a boy. "There was nothing but lightning to see."

"No lightning," Sonny said, rocking on the balls of his feet. "This was a ball of light."

Eric raised the knife. Rebecca stepped forward, about to throw herself between Eric and Sonny. If only he'd look at her, read the plea in her eyes... read her mind.

Don't hurt them. Please don't hurt them.

"Didn't you see the lights darting around the sky that night, Eric?" Sonny asked, his focus fixed on the man in Eric's body.

Eric's clone brought the long, steel blade down on Flora's strudel. Again and again, he cut into the flaky crust, drawing everyone's attention. When he was finished severing the entire pastry into irregular pieces, he selected a large piece for himself and bit into it.

"Mmmm. Strudel good," he said as he smacked, though he hadn't released the knife and his knuckles were white around the handle.

Flora gave Rebecca a sympathetic look.

"You always noticed everything, Eric," Sonny said, his voice ominously suggestive.

Eric swallowed what he'd been chewing and looked up at Sonny. "I haven't exactly been myself lately."

Chapter Fourteen

Rebecca waved good-bye to Sonny and Flora from the kitchen doorway. She couldn't shake the feeling that Sonny and Eric had been baiting each other…which of course was ridiculous. Sonny hadn't the mental capacity to spar with a being from an advanced culture.

Sonny backed his truck out of the driveway. Flora and Sonny were safely on their way. They'd barely turned toward town when *Eric* brushed past her.

"Where are you going?" she called.

"I need to take care of a security issue," he said, vaulting the porch railing into the side yard.

She glanced between her alien, who sprinted across the yard through the harsh rays of a setting sun toward the woods, and the plume of dust spewing up off Sonny's truck tires as he sped off down the road…Sonny, who'd pushed for answers to incriminating questions.

The road wound through the woods as it descended the bluff into Copper Ridge, some places looping close to the face of the bluff. Did her alien rush off because he meant to intercept Sonny and Flora at one of those loops in the road?

"Eric, wait," she called, turning toward where the yard met the woods. But he was nowhere in sight.

Just gone…into the woods…through which the road down to Copper Ridge and Flora's general store wound.

I need to take care of a security issue.

She didn't want to think what that *security issue* might entail. Neither could she let whatever *it* was happen. Not if it endangered Flora and Sonny.

She sprinted down the porch steps, across the yard, and into the woods. The towering pines cut what remained of daylight in half. She squinted, adjusting her eyes, stepping into a hole and stumbling. She glimpsed him as he crested a rise the next hollow over.

She hurried after him, slipping down a slope on the pine needle strewn forest floor and scrabbling her way up the far side. What did she think she could do if she caught up to him—if his intent was to silence Sonny? He was faster, stronger, and far more motivated than her.

Wrong. He may be stronger and faster, but he was no more motivated to save his world than she was to save Sonny and Flora.

She ran through the pines, the long shadows reaching through the forest like cell bars. Out on the lake, the sun was setting fast. It would soon be dark and she wouldn't be able to see.

She charged on, struggling to keep him in sight—to keep up. A bright light momentarily blinded her. The harsh rays of sunlight slicing into the woods between the tall tree trunks? She heard more than saw the movement between her and the road. Him? An animal? Her imagination?

She bolted toward it, racing away from the glare of the setting sun. The forest floor dipped and she tripped, landing hard on her stomach.

The sky turned purple and orange. Sunset. The forest would blacken into night in minutes and he was nowhere in sight.

Maybe she was overreacting. Maybe a dead man below their bluff was coincidence. Maybe the security issue he'd run off to take care of had nothing to do with Sonny and Flora.

The end justifies the means. I am authorized to eliminate anyone who tries to stop me.

A scream cut through the darkening woods. A guttural sound so tortured, Rebecca couldn't identify whether it was human or animal. But, with an aching certainty, she knew something had just died and she feared her alien *Eric* had something to do with that heart-rending death-wail.

Rebecca paced the perimeter of the small balcony outside hers and Eric's bedroom, the damp air chilly against her bare limbs. The cold wasn't the reason she hugged her arms tight about herself, though. She'd failed. At *what*, she wasn't completely certain.

Hours had passed since Eric's clone had disappeared across the bluff where the police ribbon flapped in the wind. What kept him away most of the night where one man had already been found dead? Was he hiding two more bodies?

She whispered into the air stirring up off the lake. "Please let me be wrong."

She could be. No one but Sonny had suggested murder. Though Sheriff

Wickes had implied there was something unnatural about the position of the dead man's body at the bottom of the bluff. Still, he hadn't come back with more questions, and the fact the police had all but abandoned the crime scene suggested they'd written the incident off as an accident. Her paranoia was simply working overtime creating a worst-case scenario, right?

She cocked an ear toward the dark woods. She listened for the pad of rubber-soled shoes across stone, the crack of a twig…another scream. Crickets chirped. An owl hooted. But there were no human sounds.

He might've simply taken the name of that ship they'd deciphered from Joe's journals, retrieved his *capsule*, and gone off with it.

Loss gripped her stomach. Fresh loss twisted up through her heart and into her throat. He'd promised to give her Eric's baby. And if he was gone, she'd lost that last chance.

Her selfishness horrified her. He'd nearly choked her to death. He could've killed Arnie. He might have killed Sonny and Flora tonight and she was agonizing over what his leaving would cost her. How could she be so selfish?

Or maybe he had harmed no one. Maybe he was on his way back to her now. Maybe…

She peered into the blackness of the forest, searching, listening for the answer.

Neither a flutter of a single feather nor so much as the whisper of a lone leaf upon the breeze answered her. Like any creature fearing danger, she waited, paralyzed with apprehension, every nerve ending on alert. She'd never known abject fear could be so soundless.

Rebecca staggered, catching herself against the flaking rail of the balcony. God help her, she was more terrified that Eric's clone wouldn't return at all than she was that he'd return with blood on his hands.

He watched her from the shadows at the edge of the yard, her white t-shirt more a beacon in the darkness than any light emanating from the house's windows. What was there about this woman's need that called to him?

Maybe it was the familiarity of it, now that he understood his own need. Or maybe it was the fact she needed him. Maybe this was the reason he kept thinking of Joe Tierney's sentimental writings about this world, which locked him in a cumbersome body. But this business of love…

Love had made the exotic Rebecca unable to move beyond the past. Love made her cling to a man dead and gone.

A man whose DNA he wore, which would enable him to experience a woman in the carnal sense. A man whose name spoken on her impassioned breath had stopped him dead when he'd nearly mated with Rebecca in the shower. It shouldn't matter to him what she called him. Next time, it wouldn't. It couldn't.

Moonlight shimmered among Rebecca's rich tresses and reflected off her heavenly face. Before coming here, he hadn't known moonlight was cool. He hadn't known the flesh of a woman's body was warm. All the empty eons of his life he'd thought he'd sought the light when what he'd yearned for had been the warmth.

What warmth felt like was something Merlin hadn't been able to telecommunicate to him…Merlin, who was the only ancient to have known the physical world before bodies had become obsolete. Merlin had known what it was to touch another body.

And, via mind blending, Merlin had allowed him access to all his memories from eons past. Merlin had shown him the physical world. Even though The Elite had since decreed such memory-sharing dangerous, his having shared the physical memories of an ancient had been the most compelling argument in favor of sending him here to retrieve The Capsule. He must prove himself worthy. He must prove Merlin was right to have passed on the memories of the old ways—of the physical days. That those memories were important to their evolution to know what they gave up.

He must prove such knowledge, even though it made his kind vulnerable to the seductions of the physical world, would not corrupt. He would show The Elite he had resisted the temptation, even after sampling all it offered, and still chosen to return to pure energy form.

Rebecca's face tipped through the moonbeams and she looked directly at him. Though she couldn't possibly see him. He hadn't moved and, with his black hair and dark clothing, he could be no more than another shadow among the trees.

Yet, hers was no happenstance glance. No furtive, searching look. She knew he was there. He saw it in how her shoulders snapped back and by the shudder of her aura. He smelled her musky awareness on the night breeze. He felt it in the yearning reaching from her heart. Merlin had met a Rebecca of his own and he'd not resisted. He'd allowed himself complete contact. He'd risked grounding himself body and soul…and still moved on to pure energy form. Like his mentor, he would resist the temptation to stay in the physical.

Not that it would be difficult to leave Rebecca. Love did not enter the equation for her. She did not expect him to stay. She'd said so.

He strode toward the house, keeping to the shadows. He would sample her, but he would expose nothing of himself to the woman whose face was split between the cool illumination of the moon and the warm light wedging across the small balcony from the open French doors.

He would take what he wanted and she would get what she wanted, her husband's DNA passed on to another life. She would get what she wanted and he would experience what he desired. That's all, right?

He paused, wondering if that was truly all she wanted.

Then she lifted one hand from the balcony rail and spread her fingers toward him. Her reach lured him like a siren song.

He bolted out of the shadows and into the light spilling from the kitchen windows. Two at a time, he climbed the rear stairs to the second floor. His long strides ate up the distance to the bedroom. Three more and he was on the balcony behind her.

She stood in the same spot where she'd been when she'd looked his way. But she looked out at the lake now, that lonely stretch of cold, dark water. The setting moon marked the point at which black sky met black water and seemed to reach across the deceptively calm surface toward them. Had she even reached out to him? Or had his overwhelming desire to touch her face half in moonlight and half in electric light overpowered reason?

He shifted his weight from his toes to his heels. The floorboards beneath him creaked. She tipped her profile in his direction, lifted her face halfway into the warm glow from the room behind him.

He went to her and cupped her cheeks in his palms, tangling his fingertips in the curls at her temples. He'd expected warmth and coolness to be divided by the shading of the illumination. He hadn't expected the surface of both sides of her face to be cool, hadn't expected their underlying heat to be equal.

Nor had he expected tears scented with both relief and fear.

She fingered the rip along the shoulder seam of his shirt. She took his hands in hers, her thumbs tracing his torn fingernails. Anguish flared from her and gurgled in her throat.

"What have you done?"

Her fear blasted through him, painfully raw. What she feared ripped through him as clearly as he'd heard the whore word in her mind in the attic. It hurt that she would think of him as a heartless killer. But he couldn't blame her. He'd choked her unconscious and told her he would do whatever was necessary to complete his goal. No lie.

"I have located a safe place to hide The Capsule until I leave."

"Does that mean…"

He couldn't bear for her to speak what she thought—couldn't bear to address how her doubt pained him; and he cut her off with, "I need Sonny's computer."

Did that mean he hadn't killed Flora and Sonny, or that he had, therefore accomplishing two goals: eliminating two people who could expose him and freeing up Sonny's computer? She'd heard that death wail. But he'd said only that he'd found a place to hide The Capsule once he obtained it. Might she have heard nothing more than a wild animal catching its nightly meal?

The doubts—the questions churned through Rebecca as she drove them into

Copper Ridge, its old houses and aged storefronts rising from the predawn fog to their left like veiled ghosts. To their right, the vast waters of Lake Superior slipped under the fog and among the rocky shore with a deceptive calm.

Yet for all her fears, here she was helping him, driving him into Copper Ridge, to Flora's general store, her home, and Sonny's computer. Why? For the DNA he possessed, DNA he could pass onto a child?

Or to save the rest of the good folk of Copper Ridge from becoming victims? *Really?*

Did she truly think he'd wipe out the entire populace of Copper Ridge to get what he wanted?

The end justifies the means.

Oncoming headlights illuminated the fog and she slowed. The car coming at them eased from the mist, the bank of roof-mounted lights an unsettling omen. All she had to do to stop the sheriff's car was flash her lights at him or veer across the road in front of him. Then she could tell Sheriff Wickes she had a killer in her car.

Her fingers moved to the lever that controlled the lights. The sheriff's car rolled past, her hand frozen in place. Slowly, she rolled forward along Copper Ridge's narrow main street, watching in the rearview mirror as the sheriff's taillights faded off up the bluff road, where one man for certain had already died, and ended at the only house atop the ridge, The Bluffs. What question did Sheriff Wickes have for her that he needed answered before dawn? Or maybe another body…or two had been found.

The decision not to alert the sheriff pinched at her stomach and tore at her heart as she steered the Jeep through the miasma at the base of the bluff. She didn't deserve Eric's baby, not at the price of innocent lives. But she clearly wasn't strong enough to deny herself Eric's baby. She was beginning to understand why Lucille had done all she had to keep Eric to herself. Rebecca swallowed hard against the realization of just how alike she and Lucille were.

Her fingers tightened on the steering wheel and she wheeled the Jeep off the main street, past the parking area alongside Flora's general store, and around back to the living quarters. She turned off the headlights, killed the engine, and stared up at the pale-yellow light shining from a window of the second floor living quarters. Did that mean Flora and Sonny were alive?

She glanced to either side of the Jeep. No sign of Sonny's truck. A bad sign. But she hadn't seen it anywhere along the bluff road into town, either. That was hopeful.

The man who looked like her Eric trailed a fingertip across her cheek. "Do not weep."

She swiped away his hand and opened the Jeep door. "Let's get this over with."

They climbed the outside stairs toward the Lindstrom's back door. Not so much as the groan of a straining timber emanated from the building. She prayed it was the muffling fog making the living space seem silent, empty.

The damage in her world was done. She could only help him stop the deaths in his world and maybe prevent more deaths at his hand in hers.

She stopped on the landing at the top of the stairs, no movement visible beyond the curtained window with its yellow light.

He pressed in behind her, crowding her toward the cross-buck door, his heart tapping against her spine, a solid, unruffled rhythm. Of course, he wasn't rattled. For him, anything he did was justified.

He reached past her for the doorknob. Because he didn't know a person didn't just walk into another person's home? Or because he knew there would be no one home?

She shivered, caught his hand in hers, and drew it across her stomach. Holding her breath, she knocked on Flora's door.

Almost immediately, the door swung open and Flora stepped into the opening.

Rebecca's knees buckled. His arm tightened around her waist, holding her up.

"What a pleasant surprise," Flora said, stepping back and motioning them into the warmth of her kitchen. "Just in time for some hot sticky buns. I just took a pan out of the oven."

"Eric would like to use Sonny's computer," Rebecca said, managing to gain her footing and hold onto him, keeping him from Flora's reach. The less contact, the less chance of bodily harm to anyone.

Still, he slipped free and followed his nose to the pan of cooling buns on the countertop beside the stove. He poked one, and Flora slapped his hand good-naturedly, scolding, "You boys have no manners when it comes to my baked goods."

Just in case her alien misread Flora's swat for a threatening gesture, Rebecca snagged him by the arm and ushered him away from Flora.

"Sticky buns good," he said around the syrupy finger he sucked on.

"Sit, sit," Flora urged, motioning them to her kitchen table. "Who would like coffee?"

"Eric's in a hurry," Rebecca said, driven by an urgency to get what they needed off the computer and leave before something went wrong. "I suppose Sonny is still asleep."

Flora grunted. "Every time there's a bright light, he's off chasing UFOs. Coming back from your place last evening, when the woods lit up, I thought he was going to leave me stranded on the road."

Flora had seen the light, too.

"Guess he couldn't wait to get back up the bluff to check it out," Flora went on. "That boy was bouncing around this house hours ago. Woke me up. That's why I've got sticky buns out of the oven at this early hour. You sure you wouldn't like to sit a spell and have a bun?"

"We just need to—"

"Sticky buns good," alien Eric repeated, reaching for one.

Rebecca's fingers tightened on his arm, holding him back. He found her peering up at him intently as she enunciated carefully, "I really think we should get what we need off the computer and get out of Flora's way."

"Heavens, you two aren't in my way."

He felt Rebecca's urgency in her grip, saw it in her eyes and the colors pulsing around her, and heard it in her voice as she spoke to Flora. "You'll be opening up the store soon."

Flora waved her off. "Not for a good hour or so. Besides, it's not like folks here don't know to come around to the back if I'm late opening up."

"I *am* limited by time," he said.

Flora looked from Rebecca to him and back to Rebecca, compassion shading her aura as she chuckled. "Boys. They are an impatient lot." She waved toward the hallway across the adjoining living room. "Eric knows which are Sonny's rooms. I'll pack up some sticky buns for you to take home."

Eric knew which room, but he didn't. When they got to the far side of the living room, he looked to Rebecca for direction.

"I don't know, either," she whispered.

Peering over her shoulder toward the kitchen, no doubt making sure Flora's back was turned, she cracked open the first door on the right. The four-posted bed was covered with a floral printed quilt and the windows covered in lacy curtains.

"Flora's," Rebecca said, closing the door quietly.

The first door on the left was a bathroom and the second a shelved space Rebecca called a linen closet. The second on the right had a wall papered in faded pictures of airplanes and a plaid cover on the bed.

"Sonny's room," Rebecca said, "but I don't see a computer."

"Rooms," he recited, recalling Flora's exact wording. "Sonny's room*s*."

In tandem, they turned to the door across the hall. The hall light wedged in across the bare floor as they opened the door. No ambient light from a window open to the false dawn invaded this room. Rebecca reached inside and flicked on the overhead light.

"Bingo," she said, hauling him across the room to the crowded computer desk that sat next to a window whose glass had been papered in foil.

He took in the entire space with a glance. Stacks of books on UFOs and alien abduction piled on the floor. Fuzzy photos on glossy magazine paper were tacked to the walls. Plastic models of flying saucers and space shuttles, stations, and ships dangled from the ceiling on fishing line.

Rebecca sat down in front of the computer and turned it on. A light flickered on the tower as the unit whirred to life. His kind had used such antiquated machines long before he was created...before his kind had learned to store all information in their own memory banks.

"Do you want to do the search?" she asked.

He bent over her shoulder and eyed the brightly colored screen with its multitude of icons. Much as he'd like to explore what, in his world, would be considered an artifact, speedy recovery of The Capsule was more important.

He shook his head.

She closed her hand over a small oval object which she slid across a pad imprinted with the image of a green creature with an oversized cranium and large slanted eyes. At the same time, a tiny saucer-shaped craft slid across the screen to one of the icons. A click and another screen popped up. She typed a series of words that made no sense to him into a box and clicked again.

"Search engine," she said as another page opened.

"A tedious process," he said.

"I haven't even put in the search for *The Pandora*, yet."

He grunted and straightened. "Much better to have all the information in your head."

"If everything you needed to know was inside your head," she said, "you wouldn't be here searching for information on some sunken ship."

"You have a valid point," he conceded.

Her aura shimmered with a pleased hue. She had taken his logic, his concession as praise. Odd, how making her feel good gave him pleasure.

Better than the fragmented aura she'd given off when he'd come back from the woods. And when the sheriff had driven by them this morning, her conflicting colors had alarmed him. What did he expect? She feared he'd killed the Lindstroms. When he'd read her fears on the balcony, he hadn't liked Rebecca thinking he would have killed Flora, with all her nurturing light.

But he could not let her feelings get in the way of his success. Emotion clouded reason and often put individual life above the benefit of the collective whole. Look at how she would rather die than live without her mate. Most illogical.

Yet he wanted her to feel that strongly about him.

He grimaced and stepped away from her. He wasted his time debating personal wants. He had one ultimate purpose, to retrieve the element sealed in The Capsule. That would make right everything truly important.

"I found it," Rebecca said.

A chart of Lake Superior's bottom filled the computer screen in front of her. At least what sonar, the occasional man-made mini sub, and remote cameras had been able to explore was noted on the navigational map. There was a lot of Superior that remained a mystery to the human species.

The alien wearing Eric's DNA leaned over her shoulder.

"It's the area where *The Pandora* went down," she said. "All we need to do is zero in on the precise location—"

He reached around her and took command of the mouse, speeding through pages as fast as the dial-up connection would allow. His arm bumped against hers, his breath whispered across her temple, and his hand, braced to the back of the chair, made Rebecca want to sink back into the circle of his arms.

She leaned back and breathed in the essence of the man wearing her husband's DNA. He smelled a little piney still from last night, and tangy with Eric's aftershave. She could almost feel the roughness of his beard-shadowed cheek. Just a fraction of an inch from touching that face that looked identical to Eric's. This was the reason she hadn't been able to turn him over to Sheriff Wickes as he'd driven past them on the street. Because he looked like Eric. Because seeing him hauled off would be like watching Eric being taken away in handcuffs...or wrapped up in a straightjacket or whatever else they would use on him.

Or maybe she'd be the one they put in a straightjacket.

She squeezed her eyes shut against her shame. She'd been prepared to help him, to make love with him even after she thought he'd killed Flora and Sonny. She was weak and selfish and didn't deserve the comfort of his heat.

She slid out of the chair, letting him take her place at the computer desk. She stood to one side of the bank of computer equipment, hugging her arms around herself. Her focus must be to keep him from harming anyone else.

Assuming he had caused Arnie's death. Sheriff Wickes' questions—what he'd said about the position of the body at the bottom of the bluff—suggested something amiss. Sheriff Wickes, who'd driven his cruiser up the bluff this morning. If not because Flora and Sonny were missing after visiting The Bluffs, then why? That death-wail she'd heard?

Rebecca shook off the thought. She didn't want to speculate on what sent Wickes to The Bluffs. It had to be enough to know her alien hadn't murdered Flora and Sonny, that she'd been wrong to think he had.

She reached for his shoulder, felt his heat, the woven imprint of his knit shirt just barely brushing her fingertips when a floorboard creaked behind her. She spun around like a thief caught stealing.

One shoulder leaned into the woodwork, Sonny smiled at her from the doorway, a smile that didn't reach his eyes. "Ma said you guys were back here."

Eric rose from the desk chair, commanding, "Print this."

He turned toward Sonny.

She hesitated, torn between doing as ordered and putting herself between him and Sonny. She compromised by staying on her feet as she punched buttons on the computer keyboard, on the alert should she need to protect Sonny. Distracted, she clicked off the screen that was to be printed. She muttered a curse.

"What?" he asked.

"I closed the window."

"Window?" From the corner of her eye, she saw him glance toward the room's covered window.

"Your page on the computer," she amended.

He reached around her for the keyboard. She waved him away. "I can get it back."

"What'cha looking for?" Sonny asked.

"The location of a shipwreck," *Eric* said before she could give Sonny a more vague answer. The less amateur sleuth Sonny knew, the better.

Rebecca clicked on the history icon and a list of recently opened pages popped up on the screen. Which one was the page she wanted? The abbreviated postings all looked the same to her. With a silent oath, she clicked on the one she thought it might be.

The page that opened wasn't about shipwrecks. It was for *The Chicago Tribune* archives. When she recognized which archives were shown on the screen, her blood ran cold and a deafening drumming rose in her ears that made Sonny sound like he was talking from the end of a long tunnel.

Blocking the screen with her body, she hit print, then somehow pulled up the page her alien needed and punched the print command again. With both files loaded into the print buffer, she closed the incriminating windows. But something warned her to delete the history for the pages she and *Eric* had visited.

She stepped in front of the printer beside *Eric*, likewise blocking it from Sonny's view.

Sonny had straightened from the doorjamb and was talking animatedly. "It's the hottest computer game around. Wanna play?"

"We must go when my chart is printed," the alien said, his tone far less amiable than when he'd spoken to Flora. But then, he didn't have Flora's sticky buns distracting him and he had the location of his shipwreck practically in hand.

"It's a really cool game," Sonny pressed, skirting her and *Eric* for the computer.

He turned after Sonny. She caught him by the wrist, their eyes meeting as Sonny bent over the keyboard.

Zip, Zip, zip, went the old printer behind her.

He glanced at the printer behind them, then back at her, his eyes seeming to say he understood.

Rebecca leaned a hip against the desk between the computer and the printer as Sonny clicked on a mushroom cloud-shaped icon.

"It's got all these aliens zapping each other. You gotta blow 'em up before they blow up Earth."

Rebecca nodded for Sonny's sake. But all she was hearing was the zip of the printer. All she saw was *Eric* frowning as he studied Sonny. She willed the printer to finish its job.

A window of stars and galaxies popped open, catching Rebecca's eye. A saucer-shaped craft whizzed across the screen. Sonny hammered the mouse button, sending tracer-like streaks of light after the craft. When they connected, the craft exploded into a fiery ball that sent debris into space.

Zip, zip, zip, printed the lines across the paper.

"It's a neat game," Sonny enthused, punching buttons.

The printer ratcheted the first sheet clear of the printing mechanism. Rebecca snatched the paper from the printer, folded it, and jammed it into her pocket as a second sheet ratcheted into position. Eric's clone didn't so much as blink in her direction.

"Aliens battling to the death," Sonny said, twisting in his chair at them. "Ya wanna try it?"

Zip, zip, zip went the printer as it printed out the location of *The Pandora*.

Eric's eyes narrowed further at Sonny. Rebecca looped her arm through his, her voice raspy in her dry throat. "We've got things to do."

"Not even one game?" Sonny pleaded, rising from his chair and motioning Eric into it.

Zip. Kerflunk. Kerflunk.

Rebecca grabbed the paper from the printer and tugged *Eric* toward the doorway. "We need to go."

"Come again," Sonny called, stepping into the hall after them.

She waved at Sonny without looking back at him—without slowing. All she could think was that she needed to get somewhere safe, where she could pull out that first page she'd printed and read that document someone before them had pulled up on Sonny's computer...Eric's obituary notice.

Chapter Fifteen

Rebecca stopped the Jeep at the end of the alley out of sight of the Lindstrom's, pulled the first paper from her pocket she'd printed off Sonny's computer, and unfolded it. The morning sun had burned off the fog and now cut sharply through the driver's side window and across the inked words on the paper in her hand. Its words hadn't changed. They still reported Eric's death.

Why had Sonny searched out a copy of Eric's obituary from a Chicago newspaper? Why had he even thought to inquire about such a thing? Because Eric acted like a very odd Eric? Sonny, of all people, should understand about brain damage. Of all people, Sonny should've accepted her explanation of Eric's lapses.

But he hadn't, as evidenced by that notice she'd found in his history file.

Which meant—

"We need a boat," *Eric* said from the passenger seat.

"Sonny knows Eric is dead. He's seen Eric's obituary notice."

He folded the printout containing the coordinates of *The Pandora* and looked at the paper in her hand.

"Yes," he said, as though Eric's obituary notice was of no importance to him. "We need Ben Jarvey's boat."

Ben Jarvey, husband of Alice Jarvey, Eric's first love. A couple days ago, Alice Jarvey had been the last person she wanted Eric to see, for fear Eric would remember Alice before her. No chance of that now. Not with an Eric who wasn't Eric at all.

Still, it wasn't a good idea for the two of them to meet. Maybe there was another charter she could hire. But, finding and setting up an alternate boat and crew would delay things, and Sheriff Wickes could still be up on the bluff finding God only knew what.

And Sonny knew Eric was dead, Sonny who loved to gossip.

"Take me to Ben Jarvey's," he said, his tone low and commanding.

Rebecca glanced at her watch. Luck was with them. Post Mistress Alice Jarvey should be heading for work by now. That meant the only person they'd be dealing with would be Ben, who'd already seen Eric's clone. Better to deal with someone who'd already seen the false Eric than involve another who could later confirm he...or *she* had seen the man whose obituary notice appeared in a Chicago newspaper.

She crammed the obituary back into her pocket and wheeled the Jeep onto the main road toward the far end of town where the Jarveys lived.

Rebecca hadn't thought about Mandy, the only child born to Alice Jarvey...a child who bore Ben Jarvey's name but Eric Tierney's dark hair and pale eyes.

The child skipped ahead of them along the worn path leading to the Jarvey's front door. This whole thing was getting more complicated by the minute. A couple days ago, the paternity of Mandy Jarvey had been nearly as nettlesome an issue as Eric's death. Now, she realized, two worlds could be affected by what she did or did not do, and living in this one was Eric's daughter.

"During the off season, I keep Mandy," Ben was saying in response to Rebecca's questioning Mandy's presence, adding almost off-handedly, "so we can save money on sitters that way."

Rebecca had never before noticed how beaten raw by the harsh Superior winters the Jarvey house was...inside as well as out. But she noticed it now as Ben led them into the house that was barely more than a cottage.

Ben spread nautical maps across the kitchen table, and he and *Eric* bent over them.

Mandy tugged on Rebecca's arm. "My mommy made new curtains for my bedroom. Wanna see?"

Reluctant as Rebecca was to leave *Eric* alone with Ben, she went with the child. Where the rest of the house was furnished with faded, patched together hand-offs, Mandy's secondhand dresser had been painted with flowers, the headboard of her bed with fairies, and her sky-blue walls with birds, boats, and bumble bees.

"Aren't they bootiful," the little girl said, fingering an embroidered sunflower on one of the white cotton panels covering the window above her bed. "Mommy sewed them for me."

Alice Jarvey had embroidered all the decorative elements of the room into those curtain panels. "She put a lot of work into them. She must love you very much."

"Uh huh," the child answered with the kind of confidence a well-loved child possesses.

Tears burned at Rebecca's eyes. She'd never thought of Alice as a loving parent. She'd believed Alice had kept Mandy only as a link to Eric. She understood that kind of need.

Yet when Lucille had demanded a paternity test done on the child born six months after Ben's and Alice's hasty wedding, Alice had refused.

Maybe it was enough for Alice to know she had a piece of Eric. It would be for her. Lucille could shout from the rooftops of Copper Ridge that Alice refused a paternity test because the child wasn't Eric's. Rebecca suspected she understood why.

No Lucille to interfere—to take over Eric's child's life. She'd want the same should she have Eric's child. And Eric wasn't here to be denied…as he'd been with Mandy. Eric, who had known the moment he'd seen the child with thick, black hair and eyes the same bright blue as his that she came from him…just as Ben had always known.

Though neither man had ever spoken of it.

That's what Eric had told her when he'd explained why he'd not pursued paternity. Ben was a good man—a good father—and he loved Alice and wanted Mandy to be his. But Eric had always used Ben's charter services, even though there were bigger, fancier boats to be hired, and tipped him generously for his services.

Rebecca turned away from the child she wished was hers, tears scratching at the backs of her eyes. A painted mermaid with raven tresses and morning sky blue eyes sat upon a rock surrounded by water overseeing her fanciful world of fish, birds, and bees. Rebecca smiled and murmured, "Your mommy loves you very much to paint such magical pictures on your walls."

"Not Mommy," Mandy said. "Daddy painted the pictures."

Ben had been the one who'd painted the characters on the walls and furniture. Ben, who kissed his daughter's head when she squeezed in between him and the table where the charts of Lake Superior's bottom were spread. Ben, who gently admonished Mandy to wear her heavy jacket when she asked, "Can I show Rebecca the puppies outside?"

Ben, who gazed lovingly down on the daughter who was his only in name and heart.

Her child wouldn't have a father…because he'd died…because his donor would leave long before he or she was born.

Rebecca thought of how her own father had left her with strangers without explanation. She would not let her child suffer the unknown. Somehow, she would make sure her child knew about both his fathers.

His mind buzzed with details. The location of *The Pandora,* her depth, if she was still intact, or if some of her had broken off and fallen into the crevice alongside which she'd settled, how long a human body could sustain a deep dive in the frigid waters of Lake Superior…the tension spiking from Ben Jarvey's aura.

And that the child could see auras same as he could. He'd heard her whisper to her father when he bent to kiss her head, "It'll be okay, Daddy. He has nice colors."

She'd been referring to him. He also knew why she now told Rebecca she could have one of the puppies. The child could see that Rebecca's aura cried out for something to nurture.

"Papa says I can keep one," the child said.

"Which one have you picked?" Rebecca asked.

"That one." The child pointed out a pup surrounded in white light.

That one will not live long, he mind-spoke, directing the thought at the child, testing her.

"But she's special," the child retorted, looking up at him where he stood at the corner of the house.

"Very special," he agreed quietly, understanding something beyond the fact that the child could telecommunicate. Any child he gave Rebecca would not be solely hers and her Eric's. A part of him would be left here, too.

Two hours later, *The Amanda Jean* set on auto pilot, he ducked down the narrow stairs into the cabin below decks behind Ben Jarvey. From the back corner of the tiny built-in table where Rebecca and Mandy colored on a sheet of lined notebook paper, Rebecca looked up at him through hope-filled eyes.

For a moment, he forgot about the low ceiling pressing down on him and the odor of fish bait permeating the wood of the old boat. Her eyes spoke volumes to him. For an instant, he forgot what troubled him. But then he read the message in her eyes.

Soon, very soon, you will have what you need. Will you then give me what I want?

But what about what *he* wanted, he nearly shouted back at her, immediately shaken by his strong emotion. This was not good, not for a creature of reason.

"Might as well warm up. We got plenty of time yet before we get to the trench," Ben said, handing him a mug of coffee filled from an insulated pot anchored to the galley cabinet.

He closed his fingers around the hot cup and let the steam rising from it fill his nostrils. This world was filled with too many scents—too many senses, this world whose inhabitants had a limited life span. Could—should he leave a child behind that was partly his?

The boat dropped over a swell and he stumbled.

Ben snorted. "Just how long has it been since you've been out on a boat, Eric?"

"It's been a long time," Rebecca answered for him, tugging him down on the bench beside her.

The moment his thigh contacted hers, an ancient need tore through that part of him which was a throwback to a time before genetic engineering, an ancestral link to the almost prehistoric body he currently inhabited. In that instant, he didn't want to be on this boat with Ben Jarvey, plowing through waves toward a sunken ship. So much for his inborn powers of reasoning, for thousands of years of evolving.

The child glanced up at him from the back side of the table, curiosity scoring her wide brow. He hoped the people of this world would value her talents. He hoped they would value those any child from him would demonstrate...if he left one behind.

He frowned and took a swig of the coffee, scalding his tongue and registering its bitter taste. He coughed.

Rebecca patted him on the back.

"Am I supposed to like coffee?" he asked looking at Rebecca for answer, but she was staring at Ben, whose brow was puckered and his aura shimmered with question.

Rebecca shrugged at Ben. "Changing taste buds."

Ben eyed him furtively. "You used to like your coffee strong. Maybe you want something stronger to warm you up?"

"Not when he's about to make a dive," Rebecca said, a chastising note to her voice. She was looking out for him, taking care of him...the way she would his child.

He looked at Mandy, their matching eyes locking.

It'll be okay, came her thought into his head.

How can you know? he asked. *You are but a child. You yet need the care of your mother and...father.*

And there was the problem. If he mated with Rebecca—if he impregnated her, he would be responsible for another life form. He would want to stay with his child. But he couldn't...for the sake of a greater good.

The deck of the trawler tossed beneath Rebecca's feet. Beside her, *Eric* gripped the varnished rail of *The Amanda Jean,* his knuckles white. Maybe it was the high seas turning his face as gray as the clouds obliterating the mid-day sky, but she couldn't help sense there was something else that kept him from meeting her gaze.

She touched the back of his hand, his so very cold. She wanted to gather him in her arms and lend her heat to him. But, when she reached out to him, he turned away, shouting through the whipping wind, "We're slowing. Ben must have found something."

Unsteadily, he handed himself along the rail toward the wheelhouse. Given the curious way Ben watched him from the console, she knew he was wondering why the avid sport fisherman maneuvered like a first-time sailor.

She followed him onto the elevated wheelhouse where the sonar screen blipped over shadowy forms and measured depths, unable to shake the feeling there was something more than the culmination of his mission and a queasy stomach making him uneasy.

"Are we close?" *Eric* asked.

"Getting close," Ben answered.

Eric's gaze swept back and forth across the sonar screen, a deep crease scoring his brow. She eased in close to his side. He stiffened. She couldn't shake the chilling premonition that she was losing him.

A shadow crossed the screen. The blue eyes stopped scanning and focused on that shadow. He tapped the screen. "What is this?"

Ben eyed the image. "School of fish."

She slid her hand along the edge of the sonar equipment toward his. He curled his fingers away. Maybe it was because he was so close to finding his Capsule, because his mission was near completion and he'd soon be leaving.

Gone forever...like Eric.

He felt her uncertainty, saw it in the flickering shades of her anxiousness. It made him want to take her in his arms and reassure her. But there was nothing to reassure her about. He'd made the logical choice.

"That's her," Ben yelled, throwing the engines into reverse and thumping the sonar glass with a knuckle. "That's the upended keel of *The Pandora.*"

He'd missed the unnatural line of a hull caught by the sonar. That's what allowing himself to be distracted by Rebecca's need got him. And if he failed, the cost to his world would be unforgivable.

"Time to get into your gear," Ben said, anchoring the boat.

He let Rebecca help him into Eric's custom-made wetsuit, her capable hands tugging the rubberized suit up his legs and over his hips. Her palm slid up his bare chest as she eased the zipper up his torso. He wanted to cover her hand with his and promise everything would be okay.

But it wouldn't be. The part of *The Pandora* hung up on the edge of the trench was at the limits of what a human body could withstand. And, if The Capsule was in the part of the ship that had slipped into the trench, he would have to abandon Eric's flesh into the abyss of Superior's depths.

"Bye, bye," Mandy called from the cabin steps, the closest to the open deck her father had allowed her because of the choppy seas.

"She says good-bye as though you're going away forever," Rebecca said, tugging fretfully at the straps crossing his chest, her aura the colors of anxiety.

He stepped onto the diving platform without looking her in the eye. Rebecca's fingers, still hooked through the scuba straps, tightened, pulling him close. She brushed her lips across his and whispered into his ear, "Be careful down there."

He eased her fingers from his straps and pulled the diving mask down over his eyes, letting its thick, black rubber rim break the anxious hold of her sea-green eyes. He crammed the mouthpiece of the breathing apparatus between lips aching with the imprint of her brief kiss and stepped backward off the diving platform.

The first blast of frigid water soaking into the honeycombed rubber of the wet suit jolted through his body before the insulating layer of water the wet suit held around him warmed to body temperature. Likewise, the realization he'd touched Rebecca for the last time knifed through his heart. He could only hope her grief would pass as quickly. It must.

Forcing his head down, he dove, began his decent through the cold water. Water the same deep shade of green that rimmed the shimmering centers of Rebecca's eyes. He propelled himself into depths crystal clear as Rebecca's haunting irises. He sank into depths as dark as Rebecca's pleading pupils.

Be careful down there, she'd said.

He shook his head, attempting to clear his mind of the woman he could never have because she would become an obsession. Like Eric had become hers.

He paused in his descent and looked up.

Light funneled down to him through the darkening water. What if what he could have with Rebecca was more important than immortality—more important than proving his worth to a society of higher intellect?

"Nooo!" he howled around the clench of his teeth on the mouthpiece of his breathing apparatus, knowing he wasted precious air. There was more at stake here than his needs. The lead weight belt around his hips dragged him down toward a ship hidden somewhere in the looming darkness below. He had limited air, and a mission too important to too many to abandon for personal needs.

But, didn't he deserve one rhapsodic moment to carry him through eternity. Except he feared he would need—want—more than one moment of bliss in his life.

Or was the hundred and fifty feet of water compressing his blood vessels denying his brain the oxygen it needed to function coherently?

He hung in the lightlessness of the deep, in his own indecision yards above the massive shadow of *The Pandora's* hull. He shivered. His body temperature was dropping. Time was running out. What he needed and wanted was not worth risking the lives of an entire society. Just find The Capsule and retrieve it. That's what he was here to do.

Flicking on his battery-powered dive light, he strobed its beam across the hulking bow of *The Pandora*. Rotely, he followed the keel, scanning with powers beyond human comprehension for the tiny capsule without which he must not return. He searched until the battery-powered beam of light splayed into the nothingness of the gorge...where *The Pandora's* splintered-off stern had plummeted.

He hovered above the yawing emptiness. He felt like he was looking into his future, an everlasting, non-ending, empty future.

If he went into that trench, there would be no turning back, no changing his mind because he would have to leave his human body to dive that deep. He didn't want eternity without Rebecca. He knew that now.

But countless lives depended on him...Rebecca's included. Without a child to cling to, she might once again prefer death to life. If only she'd been secure in Eric's love before he'd died. If only he could reassure her life would get better.

If only he could give her everything she needed.

Maybe, if the rest of the wreckage had hung up somewhere short of the bottom of that trench, he could retrieve The Capsule and survive the dive. The human body could dive a hundred and ninety-five feet without a pressurized suit. He'd scanned that from diving manuals. He knew it from the memories in the DNA and the scuba suit he wore just as he knew Eric had loved Rebecca to his dying breath.

He looked into the yawing blackness below. He could still have his Rebecca and The Capsule if...

The dive would have to be fast for his human form to survive. Five minutes maximum.

He jackknifed into the abyss. He pumped his legs against the increasing weight of the water, driving himself deeper. The pressure squeezed the insulating pores of his wet suit together until there was no more space in which to hold a layer of body-warmed fluid. He shivered hard, his teeth chattering against the hard rubber mouthpiece, barely able to hold his wrist still long enough to read the illuminated face of his depth gauge. A hundred and eighty feet it read. Then a hundred and eighty-five, and still no sight of additional wreckage.

Give it up, cried a remnant of reason. Leave the body before it takes you down with it! It could. If the shell died around him, it would take him down with it.

At a hundred and ninety feet, his heartbeat slowed and his core temperature dropped so low he stopped shivering. Hypothermia dragged at his eyelids.

He wanted to sleep. He'd lost.

Chapter Sixteen

Rebecca didn't know much about reading sonar screens, not even simple ones like Ben's. But the alarm blanching across Ben's face told her everything she didn't want to know.

"What's wrong?" she asked.

He blinked from the screen to her and back again.

"What?" she demanded.

Ben pulled a breath through flattened lips. "He went into the trench."

Rebecca glanced at the diving deck at the stern of the boat where she'd last seen him, touched him. Where he'd avoided looking her in the eye after Mandy had called out her good-byes—good-byes that had sounded far too final.

Her blood ran cold as the water that had seeped through the toes of her sneakers when she'd stepped down onto the diving platform after him. The premonition she'd had as she'd hung onto the straps of his scuba gear had been too vague, too tangled with other worries for her to put into words then.

She looked down at the screen between her and Ben, at the tiny blip fading out of range. "How far can he dive and still be okay?"

"Damn fool," Ben muttered. "What the hell's so important about that wreck that he'd go into the trench after it?"

She could answer Ben's question, but she wouldn't. Just as she knew her alien understood the dangers of deep dives into frigid waters. He knew because she'd hammered the facts into him on their drive to the marina. He knew that to go too deep meant death.

The blood drained through her and she staggered back from the depth finder, her knees buckling. Ben caught her before she hit the deck.

She pointed at the sonar screen. "Keep an eye on him."

Rebecca watched Ben's eyes dart across the screen and knew he searched for a blip that had disappeared. Was she destined to again grieve a loss no woman should have to face even once?

"Magic man," squealed Mandy from the cabin steps.

Rebecca looked to where the child pointed and saw the black silhouette of a diver against the dark waves. Rebecca scrambled down the ladder from the wheelhouse and charged across the tossing deck to the dive platform, Ben on her heels. Oblivious to the chilling water washing across the grating, she dropped to her knees. Her alien managed to hook an arm around the flotation device Ben flung to him and hung on as Ben reeled him in. But, he lacked the energy to take the hand she offered him.

Ben snagged him by the straps of his gear and hauled him over the diving platform onto the boat deck. He stripped the scuba tank off his back. Rebecca pulled off his facemask and rubber headgear, cradled his shivering shoulders in her lap, and muttered, "You fool."

"He's gotta have the bends," Ben growled over her shoulder. "I'll start up the engines and radio ahead for a hyperbaric chamber."

"N-No!" This from *Eric* who'd pushed himself up onto one elbow. "C-can't leave n-now."

"But if you came up too fast—"

"N-not bends. J-just c-cold."

Ben caught Rebecca's eye. "He dove too deep. It's got him thinkin' funny."

Rebecca looked to the man in her arms. The clone gave a small shake of his head.

"Do what he says," she told Ben.

Ben frowned dubiously. "But—"

"Just do it," she snapped.

"Whatever you say. I'll go fire-up the cabin heater."

The minute Ben disappeared down the narrow hatch, Rebecca said, "I hope you got what you need."

His answer was in the sad smile he gave her.

She shook her head. "You're not going back down there."

"I must."

"Your body can't take any more."

"You mean Eric's body can't," he said quietly. "But mine can."

"No," she cried out.

"Too many lives depend on me."

She shook her head, refusing to give thought to what he was really telling her.

"You understand, Rebecca. I know you do. Your Eric gave me the memories."

Tears blurred her vision and her voice came out thick with emotion. "Then why did you even bother resurfacing?"

He touched her trembling lower lip with a shaking fingertip. "Because I need you to know that Eric loved you to his dying breath. I have that memory of his and I give it to you."

With that final, shocking fact, a bright light engulfed him, a light so bright she was forced to close her eyes. Like the night he'd shown up at The Bluffs, the light burned blood red through her eyelids and she knew he was leaving as he'd come.

"No," she wailed, clutching his limp body to her chest.

"No," she sobbed out when his head dropped in her lap. He couldn't leave her, not after practically confessing that he loved her.

"I will not let you go," she cried out, slapping his deathly pale cheeks. "Answer me, damn it!"

She couldn't, wouldn't lose him again.

With shaking hands, she laid him flat. With trembling fingers, she searched his throat for a pulse. She found none.

"ABC," she murmured, reciting the lesson from the first aid course she'd taken to fill her time, lessons she'd hoped she'd never be relied upon to use. She just wasn't the kind of person equipped to take command.

"A. Airway." She opened Eric's mouth and checked for any airway blockages.

"B. Breathing." She leaned close over his nose and mouth, listening and feeling for any breath. No breath.

She tilted his head back and lifted his chin and breathed into him. Twice she breathed for him. Twice she watched his chest rise and fall, but only with her breath...not on its own.

"Check carotid pulse," she muttered, searching his neck for the flutter of life that would tell her she didn't hold his life in her inept hands.

"No pulse," gurgled the words in her throat.

"Now what?" she desperately cried out.

"C," she frantically recited. "Check pulse? I did that. No pulse. C. C. Compression? God help me. Ben!"

But the howl of the wind swallowed her shout. She was only faintly aware of Mandy's calls of, "Daddy. Daddy."

"C. Compression," gulped Rebecca, her mind racing over her one-time lesson, remembering the warning that she could do more harm than good if she didn't know what she was doing...knowing only that a man's life was dependent upon her making his heart pump life sustaining blood into his brain.

"Let me do it right," she muttered through clenched teeth. "Bring him back to me and I'll be satisfied with whatever I get."

She positioned her fingers the measured distance down his sternum and pressed fifteen times. She remembered the lesson...even when panic screamed for her to hammer the life back into him.

Two more breaths, check for pulse, compressions. Then, during the third series of compressions came Ben's voice. "What the—"

"Do you know CPR?" Rebecca sobbed out.

Shouting for Mandy to stay put, Ben vaulted onto the deck. He dropped to his knees beside Eric's body opposite where Rebecca breathed into Eric's mouth. He unzipped the wetsuit, checked for a pulse, and performed a series of compressions while Rebecca caught her breath.

"I better radio for help," Ben said when they traded places again.

Rebecca nodded as she bent to breathe yet again into Eric's lungs.

"Don't leave me, damn it!" she panted as she pressed against his chest again and again. "Not again."

She didn't think about what she was saying in front of Ben and the child with her pointy little elbows braced against the top step and bright, round face braced in her chubby hands. Didn't stop to worry what it sounded like. The agony rasped from deep in her chest, up her throat, and across her tongue as she pleaded for him to come back.

"Magic fishy," Mandy called out from the wheelhouse and, on some peripheral level, Rebecca saw the five-foot Muskellunge fling itself over the diving platform onto the deck. She had neither the time nor the heart to spare any kamikaze fish. Not when she struggled for the life of a man who didn't value the flesh he'd created.

"Please not again." She wept, closing her eyes to what she feared was the inevitable even as she closed her mouth over the thin, blue lips.

Bright light burned through her eyelids. Was it wishful thinking or did those lips move against hers? She stopped breathing.

The mouth beneath hers tilted to one side. Those lips *definitely* moved against hers.

Stunned, Rebecca sat back on her heels. Through Eric's blue eyes, he looked back at her.

"I'd give you more of a kiss," he said on a husky breath, "but switching bodies takes a lot out of a man."

"Switching bodies?"

"Magic fishy," squealed Mandy as the deep-diving Musky slipped from the diving platform into the dark waters of the lake that never gave up its dead.

He'd won. He had The Capsule and his Rebecca.

Though he had no delusions why she'd breathed life into his empty shell up on the deck of Ben Jarvey's boat. He wore her Eric's DNA and she wanted his baby.

Yet he wasn't sorry he'd returned to her…and not just because he was free of the compressing cold of Lake Superior. He wasn't suffering the remorse of the deep now, either, snuggled into a blanket with Rebecca in front of the cabin's space heater. Only crushing fatigue kept him from stripping off Rebecca's clothes and giving her right here and now the seed she needed to create Eric's baby.

Crushing fatigue and Mandy's presence.

Mandy looked up from her coloring. "I'd go up on deck, but my daddy won't let me up there when it's rough or when he's going fast, and he's driving the boat real fast right now."

"It's not polite to eavesdrop on thoughts not intended for you," he said.

"Oh," Mandy said and went back to her coloring.

Rebecca glanced between the child and him. "You're communicating with her. How?"

"In the same way you and I communicated in the attic," he murmured. "Mind to mind."

Rebecca's eyebrows shot up. "But I was in distress when you heard my thoughts."

He hadn't the energy to explain the difference between reading her mind and mind-speaking with Mandy. "Children have more open minds."

She nodded, a faint smile lifting across her lips. "Just what thought was she eavesdropping on?"

He winked, the most energy he could expend at the moment. His muscles were spent. But, she'd caught his intent, judging by her smile and the mischievous twinkle in her eye.

"Maybe we should go back to Copper Ridge with Ben," she said, squatting in front of the bench built into the landing halfway up the stairs to The Bluffs where he slumped.

He shook his head. "I just need rest."

She glanced down at Ben, who stood on the lower deck of *The Amanda Jean*, a protective hand on Mandy's shoulder. He'd promised to wait until he saw that they got up to the house…in case *Eric* changed his "stubborn" mind about needing help.

"Remember what happened when your grandfather refused help after Sonny's drowning," Ben had said when *Eric* had ordered him to cancel his call for an ambulance to be waiting for them at Copper Ridge's marina.

"Joe died three days after rescuing Sonny," she said.

He raised his head and looked at her. "I just need rest."

She sighed. She had to believe in him. After all, given his insight, he should know, right?

He rose to his feet, still none too steady. She positioned him between herself and the railing and started up the last flight of steps to the house. By the time they reached the deck, he was leaning heavily on her. But they'd made it.

She waved Ben away and turned to the back door. Before her hand even touched the doorknob, the door opened.

Framed in the opening, her gray hair swept perfectly as ever off her face, her short, sinewy frame ramrod straight, stood Eric's grandmother.

For one suspended-in-time second, Rebecca considered running. As if the ice-blue eyes the woman shared with her grandson hadn't already seen the face of the man Rebecca propped upright with one shaky shoulder. Lucille Tierney would hunt them to the edges of the Earth if she thought her grandson had returned from the dead.

"Get him inside before he drops," Lucille snapped.

Rebecca obeyed, though not because it was what that autocratic old woman had ordered. She obeyed because the man leaning on her needed rest and the warmth the house offered.

Lucille's thick heels clacked against the tile floor as she followed them across the hall. "A hot bath will warm him."

"He needs to sit and catch his breath before he climbs another flight of steps," Rebecca countered, shouldering him into the parlor.

Lucille sniffed and headed for the fireplace. "I'll start a fire."

"Fine," Rebecca said, easing him down onto the couch.

He settled his head against the high couch back and closed his eyes. She caught herself raising a fingernail to her mouth and folded her arms across her chest instead. Now was no time to fall back on nervous habits. Not when she was going to have to explain to Lucille Tierney how her grandson could show up alive nine months after he'd died.

So, what the hell was she going to tell the woman? That he wasn't who she thought he was? That he was an imposter? That he was an alien clone come to save his world?

A fire blazing on the grate, Lucille rose from the hearth and faced them. Before either woman could utter a word, her alien spoke.

"You're the one he referred to in his journals as *his love,* aren't you?" he asked.

Lucille's chin dipped a fraction of an inch. "And you're another one of *them,* aren't you?"

"One of them?" echoed Rebecca. "What do you mean, *one of them?* "

"Doesn't she know?" Lucille asked the alien.

"She knows what I am," he said with barely the flutter of an eyelash.

Suddenly, Rebecca was the outsider again. She was the child barred from her dying mother's bedside. She was the kid being handed off from foster home to foster home…the woman too shy for friends…the wife of an executive without a pedigree. She was a stranger in Eric's childhood home facing two more people who shared a secret to which she wasn't privy.

She shifted toward the end table where her husband's urn should have been. Where Eric's ashes should still dust the table. Someone had cleaned up his ashes, and she knew exactly who that someone had been.

Rebecca spotted the urn on the mantel beside Joe's, all polished and gleaming. She looked at Lucille.

"You had no right to move Eric's ashes."

Lucille sniffed. "And you'd have left them to be scattered to the wind, I suppose."

Rebecca's hands balled into fists against her ribs. "He wanted his ashes scattered. Not closed up in some brass bottle."

Lucille's gaze slid to the man on the couch. "Good thing you didn't honor that request too quickly or you wouldn't have gotten him."

She turned to Eric's clone. "How does she know about your people?"

From beneath heavy lids, weary eyes peered up at her. "I told you, I wasn't the first."

"Who?" Rebecca demanded.

His gaze shifted past her. She followed the trajectory of his eyes to the portrait above the fireplace, Joe Tierney's portrait.

She faced Lucille. "Joe?"

Lucille gave a single nod.

"Joe gave up immortality for *you?*"

Lucille's chin came up and her lips thinned. "I wasn't always old and wrinkled. When I was your age, I too had smooth skin. I too had a glorious mane of hair. I had passion." Her ice-blue eyes narrowed. "They like passion."

Rebecca stumbled back against the arm of the couch, shaking her head.

Lucille's finely plucked eyebrows shot up onto her forehead. "Surely you've discovered that by now."

"We haven't— I wouldn't—"

Wouldn't what? Desecrate Eric's memory by making love to another man nine months after his death...unless that man was made of Eric's DNA and he could give her Eric's baby?

Lucille snorted. "You're a fool if you haven't made use of him."

"Made use of him?"

Lucille lifted a locket out from inside her blouse, opened it, and held it out for Rebecca to see. On one side was a picture of Joe, on the other, a lock of sandy brown hair.

"I met Joseph while I was away at school. He was studying for his masters in engineering. I was studying future husbands. We became an item, as they put it in those days. Then he broke his neck playing polo. Good thing he'd given me a lock of his hair in one of his besotted-by-love moments."

Rebecca blinked at Lucille, hearing what she was saying, knowing the man in that picture in the locket was Joseph Tierney, but not *the* Joe Tierney from whose genes Eric had come. It became clear to her now how Mandy had acquired her ability to telecommunicate. She was as much the great-granddaughter of the alien Joe as she was of the Joe who'd broken his neck. *She* carried both their DNA.

"So, you see, my dear, you and I are not so different."

Rebecca's chin came up, anger and shame slamming together. "I would never ask any man to give up immortality for me."

Lucille snapped the locket shut and nodded at the alien clone. "This Eric can give you babies, *our* Eric's babies."

"You talk like he and Eric are interchangeable."

Lucille's eyebrows edged upward. "Aren't they?"

Rebecca shook her head.

"The line can't end," Lucille stated. "It mustn't. This Eric can take on the other's identity."

"And give *us* babies. Is that all you used your alien for, to give you babies?"

A ghost of a smile tugged at the corners of Lucille's mouth. "He gave me *one* and from that one came Eric…whom you swore you loved."

"I did—do…" Rebecca's words trailed. She did love Eric, but it struck her that she might no longer need him in the way she had when she believed he'd come back to her. That she might have feelings for *this* Eric.

Rebecca gazed down on the man on the couch. His eyes were closed and his mouth formed a tight line. In any case, she had been about to do exactly what Lucille had done, use her lover's clone for her own end…a man whose name she hadn't even bothered to ask.

"Leave us," she said to Lucille.

"I'm sorry," she said. "I'm so sorry."

The moment the door closed behind Lucille Tierney, Rebecca's apology cut through the room and through him. He knew why she was sorry. He'd caught enough of her thoughts to understand her conflict.

She didn't want to do to him what she perceived Lucille Tierney had done to her lover's clone.

Even with his eyes closed, his fingers unerringly found her hand and he murmured, "Don't be sorry. I *chose* to come back to you."

"You shouldn't have," she croaked out. "I don't deserve your sacrifice."

"And my love?"

He felt her flinch. "I deserve your love even less. I would've used you as Lucille used her—"

He squeezed her hand. "When I jumped from human to fish body, I heard your pleas that I not leave. As I dove into the trench, I felt the urgency with which you worked to keep my human shell alive."

She shook her head. "You know why I kept Eric's body alive. You know there was nothing selfless in what I did."

He tugged her down on the couch beside him. "You care for me more than you're willing to admit."

"How can you know that?"

He laid his head on her shoulder, so weary. "I was able to hear your thoughts, your words, and feel your efforts—your emotions."

She stroked his brow. "You're tired. We'll discuss this when you're rested."

He snuggled into the warmth of her body.

"And you're cold. You need to get out of these damp clothes," she said.

He nodded. "Help me off with them."

She tugged off his jacket. He shivered. She rubbed his arms, warming them.

He peered up at her from beneath drooping eyelids. "I like that."

She peeled off his deck shoes and closed her hands over his toes. "You're cold as ice."

"Warm me."

"You need a warm bath," she said.

"I want to make love to you."

"Later…after you've regained your strength, your good senses, if you still want me…"

"And in return, I will give you the baby you want," he said.

Her hands stilled on his feet. "We'll talk about that later."

"Given Eric, with only third generation genetics from my world, produced Mandy, there's an even greater likelihood, with my DNA added, your child would be like Mandy. Is that a problem for you?"

She took the throw from the back of the couch. "Later, we'll talk."

"Mandy is well loved," he said.

She tucked the throw around his shoulders and urged him to his feet. "Mandy has two loving parents and no interfering Lucille. Mandy lives in a little burg sequestered from a world that would not be so kind if they figured out her differences from other children."

"You will raise our child with love. You will protect her from Lucille and the rest of the world."

She steered him toward the doorway. "Let's get you into that warm bath."

"Let me give you Eric's baby."

She ushered him across the hall. "I don't know if I can do it on my own."

"Then I will stay."

She stopped dead at the foot of the stairs and faced him. "You can't. You have a world to save."

"A world I've come to realize is not as perfect as it believes itself to be."

She rubbed her temples. "Perhaps if your world survives, they will learn this on their own. Perhaps the knowledge you bring back to them can teach them there's merit to emotion and instinct."

"Perhaps," he said with a shrug. "But a world based on pure logic will be resistant to being proven wrong. Especially if there are factions who want to advance only their theories; and that faction appears to be in the majority. Their being able to ban one-on-one relationships and private thought suggests a paranoia that closes their minds."

Her brow furrowed. "Paranoia is emotion. I thought your society was without emotion."

"Yes. I thought so, too," he said without hesitation.

She shrugged and prodded him up the steps. "At least that's an argument you can use to help those uncorrupted see the error in their reasoning."

"Provided I return."

She stopped mid-step. "You would condemn a world of beings to extinction for me?"

He paused between the support of her arm and the banister. "I don't have to. I've figured out a way to send the element back without me having to go with it."

"You *can't* stay here. This world is death for you."

"To live and love for a short time or exist for eternity. Which would you choose?"

She shook her head. "But I don't lo—"

He pressed a finger to her lips. "I love you enough for both of us."

"Did Joe love Lucille enough for the both of them?"

A smile wobbled across his lips. "She grew to love him."

"Lucille? Love?" She snorted. "I doubt Lucille ever loved anyone."

"She loved Joe in her own way."

"But not in the way he deserved to be loved," she said, as though she were speaking as much about them as she was Joe and Lucille.

He squeezed her shoulder. "Love me however you can. It will be enough."

She began to shake her head again. He leaned forward and brushed his lips across hers with infinite tenderness.

She pulled back from him, a tear sliding down her cheek; and she pressed her fingertips to his lips. "Loving you any less than I loved Eric won't be enough for either of us."

Perhaps his peers were right to spurn the fervent, flawed motivation of emotion, to have ridiculed him for that weakness. Perhaps the logic of the mind was best served without the garnish of the heart. Perhaps forcing Rebecca to love him might turn her into a bitter woman like Joe's Lucille.

But he'd *felt* her urgency as she'd breathed life into him on Ben Jarvey's boat. He'd heard the concern in her voice when she told him to be careful. He'd seen the fear in her eyes when she'd recognized finality in Mandy's good-byes.

Or maybe the concern flaring from her aura was just what she'd said they were, fear that Eric's DNA would be lost to her. Could one love another without the other loving them back as she'd suggested? There was much to debate.

And he was weary. Warmed from his bath and curled around Rebecca in hers and Eric's honeymoon bed, he could barely keep his eyes open. Perhaps she was right. Perhaps he should settle for his celestial one-night stand and return home…where a man couldn't feel the sunlight on his face…couldn't smell its heat rising off dew soaked grass.

Couldn't see it dance among the copper strands of a woman's hair.

He breathed her name into her curls, savoring the soft trill of his tongue against the roof of his mouth, the pop of his lips, and the quiet expulsion of air from the back of his throat. He would never forget how completely her name utilized his mouth. He would never forget what she felt like pressed naked against him, lending him her heat.

He would never forget how much he wanted her at this moment. But he was spent.

At least he'd had the foresight to have prepared a hiding place for The Capsule ahead of time. Once he was replenished, he could reason out the rest. Though he knew he loved Rebecca enough to give her what she needed…even if what she needed wasn't him.

The sun sank beyond the horizon and nightfall blackened the windows in the balcony door. A premonition of winter rattled the panes of glass against their frames. A draft whispered its own warning across the back of his neck. His love alone would never be enough. She was right.

He hitched the quilt higher around them, closed his eyes, and inhaled the strawberry scent of her freshly washed hair, collecting another memory. If only he could stay awake, use every moment of the time he had left in her world to make the memories that would have to last him an eternity.

She turned her face toward his and brushed her lips along the line of his jaw. Heaven on earth, that gentle mouth pressing softly into the hollow below his ear. So soft, so warm, so easy to surrender to. And he would.

Chapter Seventeen

S he woke curled up in his arms. She didn't want to move, but she'd awakened like this at least a half-dozen times since daybreak. The clock on the nightstand told her that they'd slept nearly round the clock, two exhausted souls. But, where he slept the healing sleep of one exhausted by physical exertion, she had stayed because she didn't want to leave his arms and…because she ached for the man she feared she could love only as a replica of her dead husband.

If only she could sort out the thoughts churning through her. If only her feelings for Eric and his clone would stop colliding and littering the paths of logic with emotional debris. If only she could know if the ache in her chest came from a stronger sentiment for the man now vowing his love to her than guilt.

Rebecca eased out from under his arm. She stopped in the bathroom only long enough to relieve herself, brush her teeth, and comb a little order into her hair. She did the last not so much for the woman she was about to face as herself. Lucille seemed to have lost her power to intimidate her, and that felt good.

She found Eric's grandmother at the kitchen stove stirring the contents of a big pot. A chopping board and knife drip-dried on the drainboard, and carrot heads and potato skins were piled on a newspaper to the far side of the sink.

"Stew?" she asked.

"Yes," Lucille answered.

Rebecca snagged an apple from the fruit bowl on the table. "I've never seen you cook."

"No need to when you have a staff to take care of such mundane things."

Rebecca snorted. "Whatever did you do before you moved away from Copper Ridge to the city and hired yourself a staff?"

"Joe cooked. He loved to cook. He had a fascination with food." She glanced over her shoulder where Rebecca stood chewing her apple. "Hasn't your alien showed an inordinate interest in food?"

Her alien? The bite of apple caught in Rebecca's throat. She swallowed hard. "Is that what you called Joe, *your alien?*"

Lucille lifted the big spoon from the stew, tapped it against the side of the pot and set it quietly in the spoon rest on the stovetop before turning to Rebecca. "You think I'm a cold woman."

"Yes, I do."

"You mistake cold for guarded, my dear, and you had better learn to be guarded if you want to keep him in this world. One slip and some government agency will take him and dissect him."

"Yet another reason for me to let him go back to his own world."

Lucille's lips thinned. "I hope you at least had the sense to make a baby with him before he discards Eric's DNA."

She thought about how he'd nearly discarded Eric's body when he was diving for The Capsule in the lake that never gave up its dead to save a world—while she'd willed him to return for selfish reasons.

"You have made a baby with him, haven't you?" Lucille demanded. "Tell me you have done at least that much during all the hours you spent together in bed."

"Even if we did make love, if I'm not ovulating…"

"Their kind can guarantee results."

Lucille's smug smile, even more than her words, turned Rebecca's stomach. She tossed her half-eaten apple into the garbage, her appetite gone. "It's not your business, Lucille. Not your choice."

"Not my business? Maybe not. But I can make it good business for you." Lucille stepped so close their noses nearly touched. "Produce an heir for Eric and you can have this house. You can stay here until its moldering shingles tumble down around your ears. I'll even pay you an annual stipend."

"And the heir," Rebecca leveled back at her. "What happens to him or her? Does he go with you? Is he raised by you?"

"Produce Eric's heir and you will be taken care of for the rest of your life."

"In exchange for Eric's heir, right?" Rebecca shook her head. "I'd never allow any child of mine to be raised by you."

"Even though I can give the child all the advantages there are to be had in this world?"

"Like you have Eric's daughter?"

Lucille's chin came up and she peered down her nose at Rebecca. "The Jarveys refused a paternity test, no doubt because the child is not Eric's."

"Or, they refused because they didn't want you to get your hooks into her."

Lucille sniffed in that imperial way she had. "And you think your child would be better off living hand to mouth the way the Jarveys do?"

"I think a child raised with love has more advantages than any raised by money alone."

"You think I can't love."

"You made Joe give up immortality so you could pretend he was your Joseph. That's not love. That's obsession. I know because I've been there. I won't do to another being what you did to Joe."

"You mean love him?" lifted a familiar male voice from the steps at the back of the kitchen.

Rebecca wheeled at Eric's clone. "She didn't love him."

He strode toward her. "She did."

She met him mid-kitchen. "Not in the way he deserved to be loved."

He caught her fingers in his, his eyes so much like Eric's, yet not at all like them, locked on hers. *She loved him.*

Had she just heard his words inside his head or had she inferred them from the look in his eyes?

Fear of losing him is what made her possessive.

That she definitely heard inside her head. If not for the grip he had on her hand, she might have dropped into the chair behind her.

"I'm hearing *you* inside my head."

He stroked the side of her hand with his thumb. *Because we have bonded. You care for me.*

Of course I care for you. But I don't want to hurt you. I don't want you to die for me.

You love me enough to care whether I live or die. That is telling.

"What if it's only because you can replace Eric like Joe replaced her Joseph?" Rebecca pointed at Lucille. "What if it's only because I want Eric's DNA?"

He squeezed her hand and reiterated, "She *did* love Joe."

Rebecca began to shake her head.

His gaze slid past her to Lucille. "Tell her how you feared losing Joe so much it made you possessive of him."

"You mean feared losing her *Joseph*," Rebecca contended.

He met her gaze. "No. She feared losing *Joe.*"

"How can you know that?" Lucille demanded in a voice less steady than Rebecca had ever heard it.

He looked at Lucille. "Because I read Joe's journals. All of them." He faced Rebecca. "He knew the truth about her. He knew she loved the man *he* was."

"He became the Joe I loved." Lucille's chin hovered its familiar autocratic angle, but it quivered, and her voice sounded like a thin thread through air thick with tension. "Far more than that insipid boy who'd infatuated me."

She looked Rebecca in the eye. "If I hadn't loved him so much, do you think I would have stayed until his dying day in this God awful isolated corner of the universe he loved?"

Hope telegraphed from Rebecca's fingers into his. Hope pulsed through her aura. Hope shimmered uncertainly in the eyes she lifted at him.

A knock at the door shattered the moment. He already knew who it was and why the man had come to The Bluffs.

"It's Ben," he said, looking Rebecca deep in the eye. "Mandy is missing."

Rebecca didn't question how he could know such a thing. She didn't question, either, the apprehension arcing between them. She accepted there was nothing she could do to stop what was coming. Slipping her fingers from his, she headed for the door.

"Don't let him in," Lucille said, stepping into her path.

She sidestepped Lucille and opened the door. Ben stood on the porch, eyes bloodshot and haunted.

She motioned him into the house. He stepped past her, bringing the bone-chilling cold into the kitchen with him. He'd been out in the weather a long time. Desperation telegraphed from the unsteady thump of his heavy boots across the linoleum.

Agitated, Lucille's heels clacked as she moved to *Eric*'s side.

"Mandy's missing," Ben said, stopping in front of Eric's clone, hat in hand, his voice ragged. "I put her down after lunch for a nap. When I went to check on her, she was gone from her bed." He shook his head. "She's never wandered off like this before. But she's curious. She likes to explore."

Like her biological father and biological great-grandfather, so Joe's journals had revealed.

The door closed beneath Rebecca's sagging weight. A woman who'd lost the love of her life could understand the anguish of a father who'd lost his child.

She moved to *Eric*'s side opposite where Lucille flanked him. Ben was focused on the man between them, the man he thought to be Eric Tierney, his eyes dark as the overcast closing on The Bluffs. "I seen what you did out on the boat."

The breath hissed out of Lucille.

Ben held up a silencing hand. "I don't care how it was done and I ain't said nothin' to nobody about it. Won't if that's the way you want it. I just want my Mandy back…" Ben's voice broke.

Rebecca reached for her alien's hand and found his reaching for hers. They laced their fingers together.

"Exactly what do you think you saw?" Lucille demanded.

Ben turned his cap around and around in his hands as he answered Lucille. "He went off the sonar screen and the next thing I know, he's popping out of the water from a dive nobody shoulda' survived. Then his heart stops. Then it starts up again, and he's cold as death and he won't see no doctor. I don't know how he survived."

Lucille pursed her lips.

Rebecca's fingers tightened within her alien's grip.

Ben's fingers fidgeted along the edge of his Brewers baseball cap, the embodiment of the abject servant on the master's doorstep with hat in hand. Rebecca knew the pose from the inside out. She'd struck such a pose herself too many times in her short life not to recognize that Ben had come to ask for help. She knew something else at that moment. Whatever help he needed was going to change everything.

"I'm thinking," Ben said, "maybe you got some of them talents your granddaddy had."

"No," Lucille stated firmly.

Ben's pale eyes flicked from Lucille to Eric's clone, pleading. "Joe found Sonny at the bottom of the lake and brought him back. Maybe you can find my Mandy and bring her back."

"No," Lucille repeated, even more forcefully this time, stepping between the clone of her grandson and Ben Jarvey.

"The whole town's been searching all afternoon. We searched the town, the woods around the house, the marina." Ben's voice faltered. "And the rocks below the bluff on our end of the ridge."

He closed his eyes and drew a shuddering breath. "If she went in the water, she won't never come back to us."

Ben's eyelids lifted at the alien and he nodded in the direction of the treacherously deep Superior with her relentless waves and savage undercurrents, his voice rough and tight as a rusted hinge. "Even if she's out there…"

"You'd like to know," *Eric* finished for him.

Lucille turned to Rebecca. "He isn't recovered from the last dive."

"At nightfall," Ben rasped out, "they're gonna call off the search."

"Over-stressing his body could kill him," Lucille argued. "It's what killed Joe."

Tears shimmered in Ben's eyes and the hinges of his jaw popped as he struggled with his pride…and something more.

He looked over Lucille's head into the eyes the same shade and shape as his daughter's. "You gotta find her and you know why. She's your—"

"This is not his problem," Lucille snarled, taking a threatening step towards Ben.

A smattering of rain pelted the kitchen window, and Rebecca thought of Mandy out there in the cold and wet with darkness falling.

Eric's fingers tightened around hers. He had the same thought…or had read hers. She felt it telegraph from his fingers into hers. She saw it in the lines creasing the outer corners of his eyes, heard it inside her head.

And she heard his question. *If this body does not survive the search, I won't be able to clone another. Can you survive what that loss will mean to you?*

Rebecca's heart pounded in her chest. Moments ago, they'd been talking of love and, for an instant, she had dared to hope.

Then, in one shattering moment, everything changed. She could lose him as she had Eric…forever. It was a real possibility.

But a child's life was at stake, and she could never live with the knowledge her selfishness might have cost a child her life…any child…and this one was Eric's. He wouldn't need words to tell him her answer. Eyes locked on Eric's clone, Rebecca raised his hand in hers and kissed his knuckles.

"No," Lucille roared, spreading her hands against the alien's chest. "It killed Joe."

He stood on the edge of the bluff, a cold, wet wind slapping at his face and bare hands. He felt the chill to his bones…except in the center of the hand he held palm out to the lake.

He lowered his hand. "She's not in the lake."

Ben Jarvey's knees buckled with relief. Catching himself against a boulder, he nodded. "Thank you."

"He's done enough," Lucille said, her face shadowed by the hood of the yellow slicker she'd donned. Yet he knew her mouth would be pinched tight. She was a lonely, frightened woman who'd never reconciled her losses. He didn't want that for Rebecca.

He pivoted toward the woman he'd come to love, the stony crest of the bluff behind the house slick beneath the rubber soles of his deck shoes.

Careful, she telepathed. *That's a long step down to the lake.*

He reached through the damp chill for her. She took his hand.

I don't have to do this, he mind-spoke.

We both know you do.

You understand I have a limited energy source here in your world. You understand this body may not survive.

Tears gathered in her eyes and she nodded.

You are stronger than you realize, Rebecca.

I'm learning how to be strong from you.

He tightened his fingers around hers and raised his free hand to the woods, closed his eyes, and scanned for the child. It was hard. The body he wore was weakened, and the woods were full of living creatures.

Then, a heat traveled up his arm from his and Rebecca's joined hands. The woman who had distracted him, who had tested his powers of focus, now lent him her strength. It burned through his chest and into the hand he held toward the towering evergreens.

There.

"I feel it," she said.

"What?" Ben gasped. "What do you feel? Is it Mandy?"

"She's out there," he said. *Along with something else, something that wants me. I sensed its presence the night I prepared the cave to hide The Capsule.*

The night Sonny and Flora were here and I thought…

He squeezed her hand. *I understand.*

"Ben can call the searchers over to our end of the ridge," Lucille said. *"They can search our woods."*

He shook his head. "There's not enough time."

Ben gazed toward where the sun backlit a patch of black clouds as it slid toward the horizon. "Sheriff's pulling his people at dark."

"Leave this to the locals," Lucille pleaded, clutching his arm, her fear chilling. *"His* people, they'll keep looking."

The alien lifted his face into the wind whipping through the trees. "There's danger in the woods."

"What do you mean?" Ben asked, his voice deathly thin.

"Mandy didn't wander away from her bed. She was taken."

"No," the father croaked out. "No," he wailed and turned for the woods. "Just tell me what direction to go and I'll find her."

Eric shook off Lucille's fingers and caught Ben by the shoulder, stopping him. "You can't save her. It wants me. She's just the lure."

Ben gaped at him, confusion pulling at his face.

Lucille Tierney cursed.

And Rebecca…

Rebecca looked up at him with watery eyes. *You were going to send The Capsule back with the other, weren't you?*

He nodded.

"If that's the case, why does he need to ransom Mandy for you?"

It doesn't know I would have given him The Capsule to take back to our world.

Then you'll go out there where Mandy is, give it to him, and everything will be fine.

He looked long into her eyes, his heart heavy.

She grimaced. *He's the one who left the body on the rocks at the foot of our bluff.*

He gave another nod.

"What does he want?"

Apparently, what we determined to be a flaw of my world is being proven. He has his own goals and they are not for the greater good.

Alarm blanched across her face. *Have you the energy to fight him?*

Sadness pulled at the muscles of his face. *He didn't spend much of his energy cloning a new body. He entered one that was already alive here.*

Then he's stronger.

Yes.

Her fingers tightened within his. *You can't fight him, weakened as you are.*

You're right. I can't fight him in this weakened body. But I can fight it in my own form.

She nodded, but he felt her tremble.

If I can't return, there will be no baby for you. Can you live with that?

She looked him in the eye. *I have loved and been loved by two most remarkable men. Eric started the process of showing me I was worth loving. You finished it by teaching me I can sacrifice my happiness for the life of another, that I am a worthy human being worthy of love…even my own. It is a legacy with which I not only can, but must live.*

He took her in his arms, closed his mouth over hers, and kissed her long and deep.

"No," wailed Lucille.

Their lips parted, he stepped back from her, ordering, "Everyone, turn away."

One lightning-bright flash and he dropped to the ground.

With eagle-eyed clarity, he spotted the child in the dusky shadows of the woods. She was in an indentation in the forest floor, a natural bowl perfect for easy watching.

He circled, searching for the Other Visitor. He was there…somewhere.

There, through a hole in the undergrowth on the high side of the bowl, he spotted the tawny coat ripple over sinewy muscle. He rode the wind currents to the treetops silent as a ghost, then dropped like a missile through the tree branches toward that hole.

An instant before impact, yellow eyes lifted at him and the big cat lunged. But the cat was too late. He hit the cougar full force in the back of the neck and sank his talons through its thick fur.

The cat yowled.

Mandy jumped to her feet, her face lifting at the commotion on the hillside above her.

Run, he telepathed to her.

Without hesitation, the child scrambled up the far side of the hollow as he tore at the cat's neck and ears…as the cat spun and tumbled through the brush, trying to dislodge its attacker. Feathers and fur flew.

Near the top of the bowl, Mandy slipped and he lost his concentration for a moment. It was long enough for the cougar to clip him with a paw and send him rolling.

But, an instant later, the child was out of sight. Now he needed only to keep The Other from going after her and get himself back to Eric's body before it died.

He righted himself and hopped beyond pounce range of the cougar. The cat yowled. But what he heard inside his head was laughter.

The child can go. She's served her purpose. She brought you here to me.

He flexed his wings, making sure nothing was broken. *How did you know to use* her *to get to me?*

She could see my aura. She could mind-talk with me. And you were always a soft touch for the weak…like your antiquated Merlin. I knew you'd come to her rescue.

The feathers on his back bristled. The cat rubbed its ripped ear and licked the blood from its paw. *You threw me off at first. I'd been looking for the dual aura of two souls inhabiting one body and Eric Tierney didn't have two souls. I hadn't anticipated you'd expend the energy to clone a new body.*

Dual auras for dual souls. Perhaps Merlin had another reason for privately instructing him to collect Joe's memories from his DNA. Perhaps he'd suspected The Elite would never send one they considered inferior alone to do such an important job. Perhaps the suggestion to clone himself had been in part a defensive maneuver.

The cat circled him, all but purring. *I want The Capsule.*

So you can return the hero?

The yellow eyes narrowed and the glistening lips curled fiendishly back from a lethal set of fangs. *You are the one who wants to play hero. I have better use of the antidote.*

He'd thought he'd recognized the sinister shimmer to The Other's aura. It had been hard to be certain, given the overlying auras of its Earth-bound hosts. How could The Elite not have seen this one was no friend to his own kind?

Because they were not perfect, not all so pure. Because there was a faction among them who coveted control of their world.

He cocked one sharp yellow eye at the cat. *He who holds The Element holds the power.*

Right you are, my man, The Other said, using Sonny's vernacular.

As if he needed any clues about which human body The Other had inhabited. He'd known the moment he'd seen Sonny's dual auras.

Time to give up the location of The Capsule, The Other mind-spoke.

You aren't my friend. You aren't even a friend to the world we come from.

Too late, the eagle saw that the cat had put itself between him and the direction in which Mandy had run off.

Which shall it be? The child or The Capsule?

There was no way he could deliver into the hands of this enemy of his world the key to its survival. He didn't want to sacrifice the child, either. Maybe there was a way around this problem.

He fluffed his feathers, testing the air currents eddying up off the bottom of the hollow in the forest floor. Mandy, though well away from this spot, was still within easy loping distance of a cougar inhabited by a Visitor who wouldn't hesitate to use a child, however it needed to gain its ends. But there was another nearby who could match the cat's stride. He just had to get to that soul and make another switch before the cat caught on and overtook the child.

But, each body exchange took energy and he had little left. What if he hadn't enough remaining to make the leap back into Eric's body? Rebecca had said she'd be okay if Eric's body didn't survive. But, what if he wouldn't be?

Ben blinked from the prone figure to Rebecca. "Is this like what happened on the boat?"

Rebecca stared at the lifeless body crumpled on the rain-slick grass at her feet. From somewhere came the notion that it might be better to leave him lying there this time, to not force oxygenated blood through his system.

"He's looking for Mandy," she said.

Ben dropped to his knees beside Eric's body. "We gotta keep the body alive. That's the way it works, right?"

She nodded without knowing whether or not anything they did could bring him back this time, without knowing if it was the right thing to do. Maybe the fairer thing to do was to let him go. Without Eric's body to return to, he'd have to return to his world.

Rebecca knelt over Eric's body, sending a message into the forest. *Don't come back for me. Don't give up immortality for me.*

In spite of that message she sent into the forest, she took over the CPR when Ben had tired. She still wasn't sure she was doing the right thing. Not for *him*.

But they worked in tandem as they had on Ben's boat. Taking turns breathing air into Eric's body, compressing his heart until…

"Oh my," gasped Lucille.

"Mandy," Ben cried out, jumping to his feet.

In mid-compression, Rebecca looked up. At the edge of the woods stood a black wolf and on the wolf's back sat Mandy.

The child slipped off the wolf and ran to her father, who swept her up in his arms and hugged her close. Rebecca released the body prone at her knees, sat back on her heels and looked into the wolf's pale eyes, a final *good-bye* forming inside her head.

He shook his, and she called out, "Close your eyes."

An instant later, a blinding light flashed from the dark woods. When they opened their eyes, the wolf was gone and the man on the ground whom they'd forced breath into, stirred.

Rebecca grabbed him by the shoulders and hauled him up against her. He was cold, deathly cold. "Why did you come back?"

To give you what you need.

She shook her head, her voice little more than a hoarse whisper. "You fool. Do you even have the energy to stand? Stay in this body and you'll die."

Not with you taking care of me.

She hugged him tighter, her voice failing her. *Don't you think Lucille took care of Joe after he rescued Sonny? Don't you think she did everything to keep him alive?*

You only need to keep this body alive long enough for me to make love to you.

A tear slid down her cheek and she choked out, "No."

He eased back from her, moonlight bathing his face. A weary smile lifted across his lips, a smile that made his eyes shine like two suns. *I can at least leave with you Eric's and my baby.*

"I don't deserve—"

He pressed icy fingertips against her lips. *Yes, you do.*

Her lips parted, another protest on her tongue. Lucille's gasp turned everyone's attention back to the forest where the black wolf had delivered Mandy. In its place crouched a cougar.

Help me to my feet, her alien said, struggling to right himself.

Intent on getting them into the house, she helped him up while Lucille stepped between them and the big cat, flapping her arms and shouting, "Scat."

The cat hissed at her.

Eric's clone growled. "Get in the house, all of you."

"We run and it'll come after us," Ben said, inching his way backwards toward the house, clutching his daughter in his arms.

"It won't go after any of you," the clone said. "It's here for me."

Icy understanding shivered through Rebecca's veins. Still, she questioned, "Why?"

He needs to get inside my head to find out where I hid The Capsule. He wants it for the power it will give him over a world in need.

Lucille pushed the rain hood off her head and looked at Rebecca. "What did he tell you?"

"He said the future of his world depends on him."

Lucille glanced from Rebecca to him. He said nothing, and Lucille's shoulders sagged.

Rebecca nodded toward Ben and Mandy. "Your future is in that little girl,

Lucille. Go take care of her."

The old woman's chin lifted toward Ben and Mandy, the stray light from the house catching the wet shimmer of her eyes. She nodded and strode off, herding Ben and Mandy ahead of herself toward the house.

Rebecca looked into the gold cat-eyes gleaming at them from the shadows of the woods. *You're going to have to fight it, aren't you?*

Yes.

Her arm tightened across her alien's back. *Looks like my having Eric's baby isn't meant to be.*

His hand tightened on her shoulder. *I promise I'll co—*

"You'll do your best," she said, stopping him before he promised the impossible. Then she kissed his cheek and stepped away from him, certain she had touched him for the last time.

The big cat yowled and she almost jumped back into his arms. "He sounds angry."

A slow smile lifted across Eric's clone's lips. *He is. He can't hear what we are saying to each other.*

She soaked in her would-be lover's reassuring smile. She understood the importance of what he told her. She also knew she had energy yet to give him. She moved back toward him, even though it could mean dying with him.

No, he telepathed.

Their gazes locked, she took his hands in hers and gave him her heat—her strength. She'd have given him every ounce of energy she had, if the skidding of tires in the gravel driveway had not distracted. The cat snarled and slunk back into deep shadow.

"Cougar," Ben called toward whoever had driven up, pointing across the yard as Lucille shoved him and Mandy into the house.

Sheriff Wickes advanced from the corner of the garage, fingers unsnapping the holster guard from his hip-mounted gun. As good as it was to see a man with a gun at this moment, that particular man seeing a clone of Eric Tierney wasn't the best option for any of them.

Rebecca advanced on Wickes and caught him by the arm. "We found Mandy. She's in the house with her father."

The sheriff wasn't so easily steered away from the man standing in the shadows at the edge of the yard. "Who's that?"

"Just a passing stranger. Mandy's in the house." She tugged on Wickes' arm. He stood firm, scanning the dark woods behind the man at the edge of the yard.

"Ben said there's a cougar."

"There was. It's gone now."

Wickes barely shook his head as he pulled his gun from its holster in one fluid movement and leveled it in *Eric's* direction.

"He's not the problem," she cried out, reaching for Wickes' gun arm.

Wickes strong-armed her behind him. "No, but the eyes in the woods behind him are."

There was a rustling in the woods. Wickes followed it with his gun. Training a high-powered flashlight down his gun sights, they glimpsed the long, tawny coated form of the cat as it bounded away from the bluff. He watched and listened for another minute before lowering his gun and turning the flashlight on the spot where *Eric* had stood. He was gone.

"What the—" Wickes swept the high beam light back and forth along the woods and across the yard. He strode forward, sweeping it across the deck where it overhung the bluff and into the gazebo at the far corner where the stairs descended the steep stone to the dock to Lake Superior.

Rebecca tripped after him, unsteady in her drained state. She'd known in her heart the importance of her visitor's mission from the moment he'd shared his purpose with her. But she'd been too blinded by her own needs and wants to see what had to be done...until tonight.

A bright light flashed behind her, momentarily casting her shadow across the bluff. She turned. Sonny Lindstrom appeared at the corner of the garage.

"Ma sent me up here to tell Ben the sheriff shut things down for the night."

Wickes gave the woods one more scan with the high beam flashlight, muttering, "I deliver my own messages, Sonny. That's why I came up here."

Wickes looked at her. "But now we got ourselves another mystery." He jabbed a finger at her. "You stay put while I radio down to the search party that Mandy's been found."

The sheriff disappeared around the corner of the garage. Rebecca looked at Sonny, hands shoved in his pockets, rocking back and forth between the balls of his feet and his heels.

"How do you know Mandy's been found?" she asked, suspicious of the bright flash coinciding with Sonny's appearance. "How'd you get here? I didn't hear your truck on the gravel."

He shrugged, but the eyes had changed. They glinted with that keen intelligence she'd glimpsed the day he stood in their kitchen. They shone with all the evil she'd felt when she'd touched Sonny in his computer room.

He's not Sonny, is he? She mind-spoke to her hidden visitor.

No. Get in the house.

She turned toward the house.

Sonny stepped between it and her. She sidestepped him and sprinted up the steps for the back door.

He charged after her, vaulted the railing, and intercepted her again.

She backed away from him, mind on the deck-side door. "I know you're the other one."

He stepped toward her, forcing her across the deck, eyes fixed on her.

She shook her head. "I don't know where The Capsule is hidden. I can't tell you anything."

"You don't have to," he said, his voice low and menacing.

The deck railing cut into her back. Far below, the dark waters of Lake Superior slammed against the base of the bluff and wheeled back on itself, carrying away anything that happened into its path. Before The Other even stated his purpose, she knew his intent.

"You need to be in enough danger that *he'll* come to your rescue."

"I'll jump before I let you take me hostage."

"You can't move that fast."

She fingered the rail behind her just as a darkly clad form blindsided Sonny.

"No," she wailed, knowing Eric's depleted body was no match for the stronger being.

The two men tumbled across the deck, *Eric* was the first back on his feet. He edged along the deck rail toward the point that hung furthest over the bluff, luring Sonny close. She saw—understood what he was doing. She couldn't bear to watch.

Closing her eyes, she recited over and over, "For the greater good."

"Let him go," she heard Sheriff Wickes call behind her and she opened her eyes.

Eric had Sonny by the throat and was trying to force him over the railing.

Sheriff Wickes had his gun trained on Eric's back. *Eric* spun around so Sonny was between him and the sheriff, but her visitor's gaze remained locked on Sonny's eyes.

You want to know where The Capsule is. There's only one way for you to find out. Come into my head.

He glanced at her for one eternal moment as he asked for her help…for his kind, for Sonny, for himself.

She nodded, and closed her eyes against the dazzling flash.

Blindly, she reached for the man collapsing in front of her. When she opened her eyes, she was on the floor of the deck, a stunned Sonny in her arms.

Sheriff Wickes bolted to the railing overhanging the bluff, gun still drawn, blinking against the after-effects of the flash, stammering, "He jumped. The fool jumped."

Chapter Eighteen

Rebecca lay in her honeymoon bed, watching the last patterns of sunlight dance across the ceiling. It was the seventh night. Tonight, *he* would catch the next orbit back to his world with The Capsule…if he'd survived.

She drew a deep breath. Once again, she would be alone. But, for the first time in her life, she didn't feel abandoned in her aloneness.

The townsfolk had rallied around her, persuading the sharp-minded Sheriff Wickes that further investigation into the identity of the stranger who'd jumped from The Bluff's deck was a waste of tax payer money. Sonny was back to being Sonny. Even Lucille had softened in her stance regarding Mandy's paternity.

Though, the Jarveys weren't keen on the opinionated matriarch's renewed interest in their daughter. There would be a lot for the two families to work out. But Mandy's future would be secure. That was enough to put her Eric at rest… as he should be.

As for her alien visitor…

She could only hope he had escaped the body before it died. She'd done what she could—had acted on the last image he'd put in her mind. She'd retrieved The Capsule from *The Amanda Jean's* keel nearest the diving deck and moved it to the spot in Joe's cave he'd carved out for it. She hoped that the people of his world who'd not valued him before would now see the value in his instincts, his passions, and his imperfection. Her only regret was that he would never know that she'd finally realized she loved him.

The curtains covering the long window of the balcony door fluttered, though she'd closed that door tight against the late September chill. But the breeze slipping over her wasn't cold. It was warm as a lover's caress.

I didn't leave without knowing you loved me, lifted the familiar voice through her mind, a soft light cocooning her.

Her mouth popped open. "You're alive."

And with you.

The breeze rippled up her thighs, across her stomach and over her breasts, pressing the thin cotton of her nightgown against the contours of her body. Her nipples tightened, tenting the fabric. His soothing light drifted around her, cradled her.

Make love with me, Rebecca.

She spread her legs and received his light energy as a woman takes a man. It filled her. It flowed through her. It touched her in places only a man who loves a woman knew where to touch.

All at once, he touched every hungry nerve-ending of her body. He lifted her beyond earthly splendor. He waltzed her through a ballroom studded with stars, not foil wrapped imitations, but real novas glinting in an eternal universe. In one shuddering instant, he filled her with his love and her body glowed.

In that moment, she smelled his musk, felt him shudder deep inside her, heard him groan out her name inside her head. She wanted to call him by *his* name but she didn't know it.

Who are you?

You would not be able to pronounce my name. But Merlin called me Rhys. He said it means son in Welsh.

"Rhys." She breathed the name, letting it whisper off her tongue and over her lips.

You understand coupling in this form will not impregnate you, he mind-spoke.

"I'm happy you could give me this final farewell."

I will be back. I'll bring them their Capsule, make sure it gets into the right hands and then, I'll come back renewed, reenergized and in human form. I promise.

"I've stopped holding people to promises," she said. "Sometimes they're impossible to keep."

I'll keep mine.

"I believe you will, if you can. And, if not, know always that you're in my heart forever, my love."

Epilogue

R ebecca hustled through the three-story Victorian house, flinging open windows, as the Lake Superior April winds nipped, chasing out the mustiness of being shut up.

To her surprise, Lucille had not only stopped trying to evict her from The Bluffs, but had signed the place fully over to her. There'd been a bit of a row when Rebecca spread Eric's ashes over Lake Superior. Lucille had railed for a while about good DNA being thrown away, her argument being Eric's DNA should have been kept on hand for future Visitors…or one particular Visitor who might return. Rebecca had made it clear, if *he* ever returned it would not be to become Eric.

In the end, Lucille had conceded. The deed was done. But to be certain such waste wasn't repeated, Lucille had made her promise Joe's ashes would remain in the house for as long as the house stood.

Lucille's as well, which had been Rebecca's decision.

Rebecca strode into the parlor to the fireplace where two urns now sat on the mantel. Joe's and Lucille's, Lucille having died the summer after the mysterious deaths of the town drunk and a stranger who looked like Eric Tierney…which were fast becoming part of the local folklore.

She swiped at the fine, gray dust coating the twin urns. "I'll polish you two up properly once I've got the place aired out and the dust swept away."

Joe looked down at her from his ever-smiling self-portrait.

She smiled back at him. "I hope the two of you are happy together wherever you are."

She brushed the grit from her hands as she stepped from the fireplace. "Goodness, Joe, but you've collected more than your share of dust this past winter. That'll teach me to stay away so long."

Rebecca turned for the windows, but paused, realizing she stood on the very spot where she'd first seen *him* that night nearly three years ago, when he'd cloned himself from Eric's ashes. She'd waited here through the first winter for him to return. When the second had approached, she knew she couldn't spend her life waiting for life to happen to her. She'd already wasted too many years doing that.

She drew open the drapes and peered out at the deck. The weekend after that last Labor Day before she'd left, after the tourists had cleared out, she'd lined the railings with track lights, set patio torches to burning in the yard, filled the gazebo with candles, and invited all her friends from Copper Ridge for a Bon Voyage party…which amounted to the entire population of Copper Ridge.

They drank apple cider and ate smoked white fish. Sonny had bounced about, telling anyone who'd listen about the UFO club emailing him about an autumn sojourn into their area and asking him if he could guide them to "the best spots."

Though Ben still complained about charters of ungrateful kids and over-zealous dads, he didn't complain as vigorously as he once did. He seemed more at peace, now that his daughter's future was secure with the trust fund Lucille had set up for her. Mandy had graduated from coloring on lined notebook paper to art paper, and Flora had rattled on about how well the local-made crafts had sold to the tourists that summer.

Rebecca smiled at that last. During the long first winter alone at The Bluffs, she'd learned how very talented the people of Copper Ridge were…and industrious, filling the idle winter hours with handiwork. She'd organized a guild to sell their wares to the summer tourists. The result, their first summer had been the craft corner in Flora's store, the local diner, and bait shops.

At her post Labor Day farewell party and celebration of the town folk's overwhelming successful craft sales, there was talk of house-front boutiques for the following summer. All had hailed Rebecca as an inspiration. That was a first for her. *Her*, an inspiration.

Still, she'd needed to know she wasn't just waiting out her life for someone else to fulfill her, whether it was the good folk of Copper Ridge who had protected her when she'd needed protecting, nurtured her through her grief, and welcomed her as one of their own…or a lover who had touched her soul. After two winters away from The Bluffs educating herself with schooling and travel, she knew what she wanted in life. And what she wanted was here with the people of Copper Ridge, where family wasn't determined by blood ties, but by shared trials and triumphs.

It didn't matter whether the man who'd taught her that she was worthy of love was physically with her or not. He would reside in her heart forever. No regrets. Not from a woman who'd loved twice the love of her life.

She strode through the hall and opened the deck-side door. The crisp Lake Superior air blew through the house. She laughed, twirled in the breeze, and surveyed the hall, the grand staircase climbing the center of the house, and the old stained glass that lent charm to an otherwise ordinary front door.

Charm, a spectacular lake view, and a little sprucing up and the old place would be a jewel of a Bed and Breakfast…in the summers. In the winters, though, it would be all hers…except when Alice came by to teach her embroidery, or when Mandy visited so the child could learn about the people whose blood ran through her veins. Joe. Eric.

Flora had promised to come and teach her how to make strudel. Heaven help her, she needed to learn to cook if she was going to pull this off. A Bed and Breakfast wasn't a B and B without breakfast.

She leaned a shoulder against the parlor doorframe and gazed up at Joe's portrait. "A fresh coat of paint, new wallpaper, and a few minor repairs and I can put my hotel management courses to use."

A gust of wind wheeled through the still open deck door and past her, stirring the dust bunnies out from under the couch and scattering the thick dust from around the base of the urns and Lucille's locket. She'd removed that piece of jewelry from her neck and placed it around Rebecca's neck before leaving The Bluffs for the last time. She'd said it was in case some terrestrial traveler was in need of some *young, in-his-prime* DNA. Rebecca had left the locket on the mantelpiece when she'd left because the only terrestrial traveler she was interested in would know only to return to The Bluffs.

She moved to the fireplace and fingered the thin gold chain and saw that the locket wasn't snapped tightly shut. Rebecca's heart gave a little lurch as she carefully picked up the locket, daring not to hope…though there was nothing wrong with hope. Hope had made her reach for the sky. Hope had enabled her to touch heaven.

She opened the locket fully and found the lock of Joseph Tierney's hair still there, though who could say if one or two strands were missing. Not that she'd know the difference even if she counted them. She didn't know how many strands there'd been in the first place. Heck, in her world it would take more than a snippet of hair to clone anything. That could be the case in *his* world as well.

She snapped the locket shut and let her gaze slide up to Joe's painted face, over the enigmatic smile that lifted across his mouth and glinted from his soft, hazel eyes. She shrugged. "Ben would have told me if any strangers had shown up around here."

She sighed and set the locket back on the mantel, her intent to gather the bucket and scrub brush and get started with her cleaning. But, when she stepped into the hall, the front door rattled beneath the rapping of knuckles. Through the stained glass, she saw the silhouette of a man, one with broad shoulders, narrow hips, and the stance of a sailor.

Her heart stuttered a beat and she had to remind herself that she hadn't looked for familiar eyes in the body of a stranger in over a year. Yet, as she strode toward the front door, she knew she would look this one last time.

She opened the door. Sunshine glinted around him, blinding her.

"I hear you're looking for a handyman," he said in a gravelly voice that sounded faintly familiar.

She shielded her eyes against the blazing sun and peered up into the face framed by sandy brown hair that was a tad too long. She looked into the soft, hazel eyes looking back at her from beneath heavy lids. She'd seen those eyes before, been watched over by an identical set. A slightly wide mouth angled the cockiest of grins, the contagious kind that made a person smile.

Or maybe she wanted to smile anyway. Maybe she wanted to sing, or howl, or shriek for joy. Instead, she retorted through a widening grin, "What I really need is someone who can cook."

The man's grin stretched. "I love to cook. My name is—"

She grabbed him by the lapels of his pea jacket and hauled him into the entryway. "I know who are."

Then she kissed him, and he kissed her back as only the man who loved her could.

If you enjoyed *The Visitor* by Barbara Raffin, you may enjoy these other books from Written Dreams Publishing…

Freewheel

Book 2 of the Tri-Angles Series

Katharine M. Nohr

Freewheel **takes readers for a spin in Hawaii in the real world of personal injury litigation, where the drama takes place outside the courtroom.**

Olympic gold medalist, Ryan Peterson can't seem to get a break. He was ousted from professional cycling for doping. After he switched sports to triathlon, he was blasted by the tabloid press for allegedly causing an accident that wiped out his competitors. In an effort to redeem himself, Ryan starts the Freewheel Movement to help homeless and isolated people financially and emotionally. Although *Freewheel* is an instant success and Ryan becomes a television talk show regular, his bad luck continues. He's sued for allegedly causing the death of a competitor in a Hawaii triathlon, and no matter what he does, he can't convince the beautiful claims adjuster, Alexia Moore, to go out with him.

Young and ambitious new attorney Zana West is hired to represent Ryan and provide him a defense in the lawsuit, but by doing so, her relationship with Jerry Hirano, T.V. star of "Fighting in Paradise," is threatened. Will Zana be able to help Ryan get his life back, and keep her relationship together?

Death Nosh

Book 3 of the Noshes Up North Culinary Mystery Series

Mary Grace Murphy

Someone is sneaking into houses, committing murders, and escaping without a trace. Can Nell Bailey convince the police to take her seriously?

The police chief thinks it's the normal passing of senior citizens when people start to turn up dead in a small Wisconsin town. But Nell Bailey, food blogger and restaurant reviewer, has a different opinion.

To further complicate her life, Sam, her gentleman friend, isn't acting very gentlemanly. Plus, his plans don't include Nell investigating any more murders.

Can she hold her own against two men, Sam Ryan and Chief Vance, who are so accustomed to doing things their way?

Parts Unknown

An Alaskan Mystery

Toni Niesen

Somewhere over the Alaskan wilderness a plane has disappeared.

As winter approaches Anchorage, flight instructor Beri Quinn races to find a student who took off in one of her planes, and hasn't been seen since. She's convinced he's still alive despite the Civil Air Patrol calling off their search. She strives to locate the missing pilot, save her reputation as a flight instructor and keep her business. But both in the air and on land, she must overcome gathering forces conspiring against her.

A single mother, Quinn fears losing custody of her son. She draws on her knowledge of aviation and musters the emotional strength necessary to overcome unseen adversaries and protect her family. With missing gold, sabotaged aircraft and unsolved murder, the stakes are high for Quinn and for her enemies.

To resolve her dilemma, Beri must answer one underlying question: did her student misjudge the weather and make a fatal mistake, or was he the victim of an elaborate murder plot? In her quest for an answer, she discovers unexpected betrayal and a massive criminal conspiracy.

Told with suspense, humor, and a fighting spirit, this is a mystery for anyone who has ever dreamed of adventure in Alaska.

Acknowledgments

My thanks to Brittiany Koren,
for her support and
for always inspiring me to be better.

About the Author

A ward-winning author Barbara Raffin lives in the Upper Peninsula of Michigan which is all but surrounded by the glacially carved *Great Lakes*, the biggest and deepest of which is Lake Superior. A country girl, she loves to visit the big city and live the hurried pace now and then. Blessed with a vivid imagination, she's created stories and adventures in one form or another for as long as she can remember. She wrote her first book at age twelve in retaliation to the lack of female leads in the adventure stories she loved reading. But it is a love of playing with words, exploring the human psyche, telling stories, and making her readers laugh and cry that keeps her writing. Whether a romantic romp or gothic-flavored paranormal, her books have one common denominator: characters who are wounded, passionate, and searching for love.

When Barbara's not writing, reading, or daydreaming, she hangs out with her Keeshonden (dogs) Katie and Slippers (as in Cinderella's glass slippers). A favorite activity for the trio is training for agility competition. See what a Keeshond looks like and learn about Barbara's other books at www.BarbaraRaffin.com or find her on Facebook https://www.facebook.com/BarbaraRaffinAuthor/. Chat with her on her blog: http://barbararaffin.com/blog/, or sign up for her newsletter on her website and get a free read and insider news.

www.ingramcontent.com/pod-product-compliance
Lightning Source LLC
Chambersburg PA
CBHW020613120726
47905CB00003B/776